Music of the Twentieth Century

CW00821212

Music of the Twentieth Century

A Study of Its Elements and Structure

TON DE LEEUW

Foreword by ROKUS DE GROOT

Amsterdam University Press

Originally published as: Ton de Leeuw, *Muziek van de twintigste eeuw*
(Utrecht: Oosthoek, 1964; 3rd edition: Bohn, Scheltema & Holkema, 1977)
Translated into Swedish as: *Nittoohundratalets musik* (Stockholm, Bonnuers,
1967 (Aldussereien))
Translated into German as: *Die Sprache der Musik im 20 Jahrhundert*
(Stuttgart, Frei Geistesleben, 1995)

Translated into English by Stephen Taylor

Cover illustration: Arlette de Leeuw
Cover design: Studio Jan de Boer bno, Amsterdam
Layout: PROgrafici, Goes

ISBN 90 5356 765 8
NUR 664/665

© Amsterdam University Press, Amsterdam, 2005

Table of Contents

Foreword

Ton de Leeuw basically wrote *Music of the Twentieth Century* in the period 1961 to 1962, a time of considerable change, both in contemporary music and in the author's own life. The strong post-1945 emphasis on concerted radical structural innovation of music had however largely passed. New music was opening up in many new ways to many worlds of music, both past and present.

In 1961, De Leeuw travelled to India with a commission from the Dutch Ministry of Education, Arts and Sciences to explore the possibilities of cross-cultural artistic interaction. He shared a positive outlook on this type of interaction with other composers and 'culture makers' in a time of de-colonialisation. The trip to India reinforced De Leeuw's awareness of the polarity that had once been associated with 'East' and 'West'. De Leeuw at that time considered this to be one of the major defining issues of contemporary Western art. On the one hand, he pointed to the exaggerated cult of personality, and on the other, to a way of life which he characterised as a liberation from subjective individualism, and as a 'return to original being'. He illustrates this notion in chapter 6, in an account of Zen archery in Japan. Although he does not explicitly advocate either attitude in this book – which he does, for example, in many of his other texts – it is clear from his wording that his sympathy rests with the latter.

Parallel to this polarity, he also compares the musical practices which directly relate to romantic aesthetics, the central notion of which he describes as a 'servitude to oneself', with those that preceded and followed it. One of his motives for writing this book was to wean his readers away from romantic aesthetics, which had already lost much of its vitality and relevance, and toward the opening of their ears to unheard worlds of music, such as the work of Debussy and Webern, which is sometimes described as where 'silence becomes audible'. De Leeuw focuses on both of these interrelated polarities. Musically, the polarities consist of, for example, harmonic tonality on the one hand, and melodic and rhythmic modality on the other, not only in relation to music structure, but also as an expression of general attitudes toward life.

Although a positive Western attitude toward Eastern sources and cultural practices, however biased, can be traced back to at least the end of the eighteenth century, it was still a relatively rare viewpoint in the study of music at the time De Leeuw was writing his book. A breakthrough had yet to occur. This finally happened at the end of the 1960s, during which time De Leeuw's compositions, his work for radio, and for the print media – including the present book – played a role in this development, at least in the Netherlands. During his apprenticeship with the ethnomusicologist Jaap Kunst from 1950 to 1954, De Leeuw studied both written and sound sources of what was then still called 'non-Western' music cultures. Ton de Leeuw wrote his book from the viewpoint of a composer, with an eye to cultural criticism, especially in the final chapter. Therefore, his book is neither a history of music or a proposal for a new musical theory, nor a scientific study of musical structure. All of these aspects, however, do play a role. The reader is offered a general historical framework in chapter 1, while the last three chapters also offer a diachronic dimension. The author's treatment of notation and terminology, meanwhile, contributes to the transmission and development of music theory. He also makes references to insights from scientific fields such as (psycho-)acoustics.

The author's two perspectives – as composer and as critic – will certainly serve as an incentive for readers to develop their own thoughts about music in a creative way. De Leeuw sets a good example in his various moments of wonderment, such as his awe for Debussy's discovery of 'listening', and his discussion of the surprising parallels that Hidekazu Yoshida observed between Webern's world of sound and Japan's traditional art forms.

De Leeuw's book is presented as a study of the 'elements and structure' of twentieth-century music. This is most evident in the extensive discussion of rhythm, melody, simultaneity and timbre, each of which is covered in its own chapter. The issue of terminology also plays a significant role here; it was important at the time of writing, and remains relevant to this day. New musical practices call for the development of a new language.

The music that De Leeuw focuses on is a continuation of – and reaction to – the classical-romantic Western traditions that cover the period from Debussy until the mid-1960s. The final chapter offers an additional assessment of musical developments and attitudes during the period from the later 1960s to the mid-1990s. The author, in a separate chapter, also expresses a marked interest in the approaches of Western composers to the various practices of folk music, of classical music traditions outside Europe and North America, and of jazz. The emphasis is on those aspects of twentieth-century music that were new during the time they were emerging. De Leeuw therefore focuses on a relatively small group of composers whom he considered as principal innovators: Debussy, Schönberg, Stravinsky, Webern, Bartók, Hindemith, Messiaen and Boulez. Varèse, Milhaud, Stockhausen and Ligeti also receive ample attention, as does the Dutch composer Willem Pijper, with whom De Leeuw had wanted to study in 1947, but who passed away that very year. Ravel is mentioned only in passing, although the author was a fan of his work.

Ton de Leeuw's concise analyses are rare gems of musical acuteness. They represent a distinct invitation to readers to engage in their own research, and are inspired by De Leeuw's promise of an ever-increasing sensitivity to both structure and sound.

Rokus de Groot

Preface

It is remarkable how poorly informed those active in musical life generally are about even the most elementary technical matters concerning contemporary music. Such a lack of knowledge would probably not be tolerated in any other profession. Since even specialised literature hardly offers solace, the present book aims to underline certain technical aspects of contemporary musical language. It has been written from the point of view of the composer rather than that of the theoretician, an approach which has its advantages and disadvantages, as one can easily imagine.

This book is intended for various categories of readers. First and foremost it is addressed to the music student of today, for whom some knowledge of contemporary music may now be considered normal. Subsequently, it is written for all musicians engaged in one way or another in new music: performers, teachers and others who in practice often face certain problems that can be solved through a deeper investigation of the structure of the musical language. But the well-informed musical amateur too may consult many chapters to his advantage.

To make matters as concrete as possible, much use is made of easily accessible scores; thus compositions are discussed that may regularly be heard in the concert hall or through recordings. Electronic music has been left out of consideration. Not only are scores scarce, but a technical approach to the subject is hardly meaningful unless the reader is at home in the world of the electronic studio.

The above-mentioned paucity of technical literature has obliged the writer to organise the content in his own way. It proved necessary, even with regard to terminology, to devise names and definitions for certain concepts. This, together with the hitherto unknown diversity of individual styles and techniques, will safeguard the reader from generalising about what is discussed, a path that would merely lead to new academicism. The specific purpose of this book is to encourage everyone to become better acquainted with living music.

Preface to the Second Edition

A period of more than seven years lies between the preparation of the first edition and this second one, a considerable length of time in view of the rapidly changing contemporary music scene. Beside a few corrections this new edition therefore contains a number of additions that cast light on the developments of recent years.

After the many – fortunately favourable – reactions to the first edition, one critical remark persisted: the names of a number of important contemporary composers are hardly mentioned or have been omitted altogether. This is indeed the case, and the reason lies in the aim that I have pursued. For what I have written has no documentary pretension at all, but is based on the study of those aspects of twentieth-century music that are new in respect to classical traditions. I chose the period around 1910 as my starting point, with the works of composers then in their thirties, since it was then that these new phenomena first occurred with some frequency, and in a manner essentially integrated into musical thought.

Preface to the Third Edition

New names and new trends continue to emerge, and each new impression of this book would perhaps justify the addition of a new chapter.

I have nevertheless decided not to tamper with the essence of the book, which is a survey of the most important technical aspects of twentieth-century music up to the 1960s. It would appear that the half century thus covered contains in its essence all those elements that characterise the music of today. New developments hardly occur in terms of the technical aspects of music.

An exception is formed by electronic music, which in the past few years in particular has developed rapidly. But this same period has seen the publication of so much literature on the subject that it would not seem useful to incorporate it again in the present book.

Amendments in this third edition are therefore limited to a few additions, slight alterations and corrections which owe their origin to comments made by many alert music students and other readers.

Introduction

The musical world of the twentieth century is a divided world. None of the dreams and expectations of enthusiastic minds at the beginning of the twentieth century has been fulfilled. In our new society an old nucleus has persisted, with its own customs and imagination stemming directly from concepts rooted in the nineteenth century.

Worldwide social revolutions, a series of unbelievable and radical scientific discoveries, entirely new views concerning almost every field of life, and different generations of composers and performers, scholars and technicians have not succeeded in preventing the official music world from revolving, and continuing to revolve, around a very definite period of the past with a span of scarcely two hundred years.

This historical heritage is in itself a strange amalgam of a number of brilliant masterpieces alongside musical follies as numerous as they are popular, of – broadly speaking – an exceptionally high level of performance, and of related musical theory developed to a similar degree. This is coupled, on the other hand, to a most rudimentary musical aesthetic, characterised by entirely bourgeois, romantic concepts which continue to rule our democratised musical life as a mere imitation of what was once – in the nineteenth century – a living and authentic intellectual movement.

The contemporary creative artist can hardly function in such a musical practice. The public at large that fills our concert halls has become both anonymous and amorphous. It has no need of nor does it make demands upon creative contemporaries.[1] The small and select social groups that determined European artistic life until far into the eighteenth century are no longer; the so essential interaction between creator and receiver has therefore disappeared. Through the lack of any collective stimulus, only the most vital of individuals are able to maintain contact with contemporary art. The enjoyment of music has become a strictly individual matter, just like composition. The disinclination to regard oneself as a revolutionary is typical of many modern composers. Stravinsky, in his conversations with Robert Craft, claimed that he could not imagine that his music could sound strange to the public.[2] Equally characteristic is the attitude of Anton Webern, who spoke of his most radical pieces as if they were classical sonatas.

Yet here is precisely the dichotomy: modern music is not the result of wanting to be 'different', but is indeed *normal* in the imagination of the creator. The fact that this 'normality' sounds so abnormal to so many people indicates the full extent of present-day individualism.

2

When individualism increases, signs indicate that subjectivism decreases. Debussy, an individualist *par excellence*, maintained close contact with nature, though in a different way from the romantics. The romantic mind projected itself in nature, while Debussy in the first place listened. Webern listened too. Silence became audible. A new world was revealed. Those who had ears, heard the new sound: the sound of an overpowering universe in which humanity had lost its central position. The gardens of Versailles and the idyllic Viennese Forest made way for the mysteries of microcosm and macrocosm.

Unprecedented elementary forces came to the fore in mankind too, leading – especially at the beginning of the twentieth century – to volcanic eruptions. The dynamic world of technique released new and vital energy. On the other hand, the importance of craftsmanship, the general preference for lucid, neo-classical contours, and a religious trait in various creative contemporaries which should not be underestimated, bore witness to a new mentality in which the romantic desire to be expressive seemed to have lost all meaning.

This is probably where the problem lies for many people. Is not expressivity the purpose of music making? The desire to be expressive has even become second nature to many performers. The inclination to 'interpret', to create an expressive sound, is revealed in even the tiniest details of performance. The average listener and critic expect nothing more. A musician either is expressive or has no feeling. There is hardly room for gradations within such a restricted musical antithesis. The fact is ignored that by far the most music ever produced by mortal man never had expressivity as its purpose. Music has been made to exorcise spirits, to symbolise the order of the universe, to bring man into harmony with his surroundings, for the pure joy evoked by the movement of dance, to sing the praises of God, to pray, to work better, to calm animals and children, and to honour kings. The making of music to convey one's own personal emotions arose only at a time when the artist could feel that he was the centre of the world, in which there was only one form of servitude, namely to himself. This enslavement to oneself has given rise to immoderate overestimation of the self and to pathological conditions. It is not surprising that the romantic period was so successful in producing the type of artist who had been shaken out of balance, and who could therefore create enormous mental tension in his work.

A rapid expansion of all musical resources was to increase the transmission of this tension, particularly from the time of Beethoven onwards. The artist freed himself conclusively from any social servitude and delivered a soliloquy. A tendency arose to overwhelm the listener, to make him defenceless. Not only the fascinating monologues of Wagner, but also the loudspeakers of Stockhausen thundering from all corners of the auditorium were the result of a sometimes barely hidden effort to shock, which was very far removed from the balance and perfection of the classical masters. The ideals of both classicism and romanticism are known in our time, indeed in an acute form. Among various present-day creative artists, however, the view that expressivity is not the purpose but rather the result of the action of music making is gaining ground once more. For the genuinely musical, music making is a completely autonomous activity that can bring a satisfaction and deep joy incomparable to any definable emotion.

3

The contrasts mentioned above hardly constitute a problem for those who are truly sensitive to music, unless milieu or training have debased the capacity to feel. This applies likewise to a related misunderstanding which is very widespread in present-day musical life, namely an underestimation of the element of craftsmanship. It is astonishing to discover how even musicians accept as a matter of course the highest demands made on them in instrumental or vocal proficiency, but adopt a most negative attitude as soon as there is any mention of craftsmanship in the creative process. This is seen at best as a necessary evil; it is the familiar problem of form and content viewed as two separate entities, with the emphasis on content – the artist's emotions. For a genuine artist this problem is meaningless, and the splitting of form and content inconceivable. What he puts on paper, in sudden visions or through long and persistent work, is one and indivisible. What he brings to the surface is a living organism, with innumerable internal relationships. Where is the form and what is the content? Any intervention disturbs and falsifies this fabric. The theoretically minded deform it into a scheme, the hunters after expression hold up a colourful soap bubble in their hands. Naturally, emotions may play a large part in the creative process. They can stimulate or accelerate, they can slow down and extinguish. There is a close interaction which escapes our perception. It is certain, however, that the value of the result is subject to totally different criteria, the essence of which we cannot describe, but only experience. Provided we are receptive... to music.

The element of craftsmanship therefore comes to stand in quite a different light. Like the directly emotional, it can accelerate or slow down, stimulate or extinguish the creative process. It is really as unavoidable as it is unreal for the ultimate essence of the musical work of art. It is entirely unimportant whether a composer 'calculates' little or much, whether he allows himself to be carried along by his emotions, or controls himself. The sources of the phenomenon of music are just as unknown to him as they are to the listener. Our only concern is to reveal this mysterious human utterance as accurately as possible. It is the composer's own affair what means he uses, what attitude he adopts, whether it be one of nervous tension or complete mental balance. What we are really trying to say is that the element of craftsmanship embraces immeasurably more than the mere technical aspect. To the real creator each act and thought are a function of his creative work. His emotions, experiences, daily contacts, consciousness, in short his whole personality, are attuned to it. The most brilliant of ideas can be disturbed by a blemish on the wallpaper.

Conscious control of the material, or technique, therefore plays a part too in this complicated and somewhat impenetrable process of creation, in which not the partial man – the emotional man – but the whole personality is involved. We are now going to extricate this control from the whole, because it is the most easily approachable and, at the same time, the most neglected aspect of contemporary music.

Where weak figures are involved, conscious technical intervention may result in sterility. In the work of great creative artists, the opposite is often seen: the more inner charge, the more need for rigorous mastery of the material. Great romantic composers form no exception.

In another manner this also applies to us. Any analysis is worthless if we do not have the required musical fantasy. Those who regard technique and analysis as necessary evils not infrequently do so precisely because of their own lack of fantasy.

4

The romantic composer had a different attitude from his classical predecessors. He believed that music had to express something from his subjective world of experience. Although he adhered essentially to the forms of the classical period, his increasing need for expression resulted in their becoming hollowed out; yet also enriched, since the slow disintegration of the classical structure into its elements was coupled with an unprecedented differentiation, particularly in harmony, which is the expressive resource *par excellence*. From about 1850 *floating tonality* made its appearance. The bonds of classical balance had become too narrow, and the desire for expression sought an escape by avoiding an all too emphatic effect of key. The means to this end included the following:
– frequent modulation
– absence of (or indistinct) chord resolution
– resolution otherwise than suggested
– increasingly ambiguous harmonic functions
– chords inclining towards harmonic ambiguity
– enharmonic devices
– relations based on the mediant instead of the fifth
– increasingly intensive chromatic leading-note function (thwarting the vertical-functional relationship)

As a result the music 'floats' between keys, and, in extreme cases, the tonic is avoided completely until the end. The influence of the tonic, however, is always present. It is precisely the friction between the centrifugal forces of the music and this latent basis that constitutes the typically expressive element in much romantic music. Here lies a basic difference from Debussy, for example, who gave independence to harmony, releasing it from its functional bond. When Schumann declined to resolve a dominant seventh, he evoked mental tension: we expect something that does not occur. In the case of Debussy, the intrinsic value of the chord is restored. It is not 'unresolved' and therefore not 'vague', as many listeners consider who interpret in a romantic manner. Many young modern composers, particularly those who have had German models, began with floating tonality (Schönberg, works written before 1908; Bartók, *First String Quartet*, *Two Portraits*, etc.). The increasing exaltation of late-romantic floating tonality led, in Schönberg, to the dissolution of the classical tonal basis. The era of *free atonality* and later that of *bound atonality* (12-note technique) was ushered in. (Further information on this is found in chapter 7.) In the case of Bartók and Stravinsky we find rather the phenomenon of *extended tonality*, which likewise already had its origins in the nineteenth century. In extended tonality a central, centripetal effect persists and is indeed so strong that even relatively complex harmonic structures cannot undermine it. Elementary harmonic functions still occur, but the forces active at the centre are often of a horizontal nature. Extended tonality may be manifest in numerous variants: from the simple addition of modal elements, parallel harmony, intermixture of major and minor, added notes etc., to polytonality with various simultaneous centres. For the rest, the actual concept of extended tonality is very closely related to our aural capacities. What perhaps sounds chaotic and 'atonal' to an untrained listener may be perfectly cohesive to the insider. What was considered polytonal in 1920 is today monotonal, if we are but able to relate all the parts to one centre.

5

Concepts of form in classical tonality have their limitations too. Once again, it was the increasing demand for harmonic expression which, for example, began to disturb the classical balance of sonata form. This balance is very closely related to the tonal balance of the sections. In strong contrast to the firm planes of sound of the exposition, with its central points of tonic and dominant, there is the harmonic quicksand of the development, based on a well-considered plan of modulation. The transition from the unstable harmony of the development to the original tonal basis of the recapitulation is in many works, particularly those of Mozart, a breathtaking musical occurrence. An absolutely superior game is played here, as the very structure becomes expression, while the consciousness of form is perfectly classical.

The romantics' gain in terms of harmonic wealth went hand in hand with the loss of this classical awareness of form. In the second half of the nineteenth century, the first subject of a sonata sometimes contained so many modulations that the development lost its contrasting function. The same applied to so-called thematic assimilation. Tonal forces contributing to form were levelled out, and larger tension relationships lost their function in favour of differentiation of detail. Naturally, this did not apply solely to harmony. *Disintegration into elements* was general, but this tendency itself became independent at the same time. Harmony, tone colour and dynamics underwent this process, to which the early modern composers also added rhythm. This process of disintegration and independence came to a temporary end in recent serial music, but in the meantime something had happened. The early moderns were becoming aware of this independence, and the elements began to lead an autonomous life: rhythm in Stravinsky, sound in Varèse, atonal chromaticism in Schönberg, etc.

What has been said here briefly could easily fill a whole chapter. The imaginative reader, however, will realise that one of the turning points lies here. The generation that tried to take a different path on the basis of these emancipated elements marked the beginning of a new music. Other concepts of form arose, but traditional ones were to continue until the present day. All sorts of transitional phases occurred, depending on the composer in question. Let us look at just one example from the work of Debussy, but from a broad angle, since it is impracticable to discuss all important details here.

From a classical point of view, the first movement of *La Mer* is an insoluble problem. It comprises four sections, the first and last of which have the character of a prologue and epilogue. The symmetrical enclosure of classical form is absent here; what is more, the sections have no unity of key, tempo or theme. The whole nonetheless forms a unity. How does this arise, and to what extent is it expressed in the musical technique? In chapter 3 we will find the surprising solution: a unity of interval in all the melodic material. This unity lies on a material level, as it were, before the material is shaped into higher categories of form. The contrasts are therefore not as large as they appear (on paper): all the melodies are different crystallisations of the same basic intervals.

In *Nuages* (from *Trois Nocturnes*) we encounter exactly the opposite: with a few exceptions towards the end, this piece consists of a continual alternation of two most rudimentary melodic motifs. There is no question of classical thematic development in this continual repetition. Ostensibly, Debussy does nothing at all, and there is a lack of contrast. The more one delves into the score, however, the more the master appears to exploit an extremely subtle and highly developed art of variation, particularly in terms of tone colour. With regard to form, this element became an absolutely indispensable factor, without which we miss something essential. The emancipated element of timbre acquired an autonomous formal function, replacing earlier means of contrast.

In both works we speak of free form, i.e., the causal relationship between the sections has been reduced to a minimum. One section does not necessarily lead to another as in enclosed classical forms: rather than emanating from one another, they exist in free juxtaposition. The themes are not classical themes, they have no thematic function; they can at best be repeated a few times in succession before definitively making way for others.

To classical ears such themes never 'finish', but the reader knows that the classical causal relationship between antecedent and consequent has disappeared. Each element of this music has a superior freedom in the form as a whole, moulded by a composer with an astounding intuition for correct proportions.

6

The absence or reduction of causality and symmetry may also be perceived in the harmony (abandonment of harmonic functions) and rhythm (abandonment of the metrical context). The resulting open, asymmetrical chain structures occur in many modern works but are in fact as old as the history of music itself. Exceptional is the *enclosed, symmetrical development form*, the very type that flourished during the era of classical tonality. It is remarkable that the romantics among the moderns, Schönberg and Bartók, did their best to adhere to this type, as is expressed particularly in their pursuance of a strongly developed motivic development technique, a procedure not found in composers such as Stravinsky, Debussy and Varèse. This genetic manner of writing gave rise to a method that can be referred to as germ-cell technique. Yet in a figure such as the Dutch composer Pijper, for instance, theory and practice diverged considerably: his germ-cell technique was far from genetic and consisted rather of an additive juxtaposition of the same or related individual motifs.

Aesthetic views revolving around the question of *what is or is not foreseeable* do not make the situation any clearer. Certain composers were nothing less than allergic to anything foreseeable. They were found most easily in circles influenced by the Viennese school which, from the very beginning, primarily stressed the principle of variation in every aspect of music. This tendency obviously moved towards atonality and all that goes with it, and it has continued until the present day. But here again this all too simple view was clouded by Anton Webern, who from about 1928 in particular increasingly incorporated the element of symmetry in his structures, even reinstating repeat signs.

After all that has been said, the reader will realise that it is impracticable to put down on paper even an approximation of the whole subject of form in modern music. So many factors are involved that insight into this new, confusing and so individual world of form can be gained only through an exhaustive study of relevant compositions.

Tonality is in some respects very old and very general. Its traditional interpretation, however, is a historical phenomenon with the limited range of approximately two centuries. As soon as music outside these two centuries is discussed, a surprisingly large number of musicians sometimes have difficulty in escaping from it. They neither see nor feel that the linear polyphony of the Renaissance, for instance, is quite a different matter; they give a vertical interpretation to originally horizontal phenomena and are supported in this by apparent similarities. Something similar also occurs in contemporary music. A different view can result in a distorted interpretation and a lopsided picture of what is actually taking place. Anything falling outside traditional modes of interpretation is easily experienced as arbitrariness. It need hardly be said that the norms that protect artistic freedom from arbitrariness cannot be linked to a world of ideas that was valid only for a certain period.

CHAPTER ONE

Panorama

I

The nineteenth century was not only the age of romanticism but also the period of great scientific discoveries and the tremendous rise of industry. Science and industry brought unsuspected change to society: on the one hand they stimulated an élan and optimism, in the hope of a better world, while on the other hand industrial development in particular caused great upheaval and disquiet, expressed in increasing criticism of the society of the time. Both of these forces were active in the early years of the twentieth century. The triumphant march of discovery proceeded, but at the same time more and more nationalist tendencies and political tensions developed, leading in 1914, from central Europe, to World War I. This disaster brought Europe to ruin, and despite attempts at repair, political and economic crises have been rife ever since. Many lands introduced a form of controlled economy, and in some countries, dictatorial rule was established: Russia in 1917, Italy in 1922, Germany in 1933 and Spain in 1936. The democratic countries of the West were weak and divided. The world picture changed slowly but surely. America, Japan and other non-European countries developed considerably, partly through the destitution of Europe after World War I. Tension increased in Europe, and inner conflicts led to World War II some twenty years after World War I. Spengler's pessimistic prophecy of 1918, *Untergang des Abendlandes*, seemed to approach fulfillment. The decolonisation of almost all African and Asian countries was completed at a furious speed. Meanwhile America, Russia and China became world powers, and in between them the 'Asian peninsula' of Europe was threatened with suffocation. However, the opposite occurred: the first steps toward European unity were taken, and an unexpected upsurge was felt in all fields, bearing witness to the vitality of this ancient but torn part of the world.

2

Among the first to announce the new era in spectacular fashion were the *futurists*. The past was over and done: 'destroy it, only then can a new world arise', as Marinetti cried in 1909. With Milan as the focal point, artists of various backgrounds gathered around Marinetti, idealists dreaming of a new world. Their ideas were revolutionary in every field, but the movement did not advance beyond its visions, perhaps because time was not yet ripe for their many proclamations. Russolo was the key figure in the music world. He glorified the new sounds of motors and technique: the modern, creative use of the machine was fertile, unlike the romantic fear of it. He advocated new instruments producing noise, and discovered unsuspected life forces in rhythm. But none of this developed: atonality, microtones, free rhythm, primitivism, objectivity, noise, the discovery of the machine – only later, generally speaking, did other composers translate all of this into creative achievement. World War I brought an abrupt end to such futuristic dreams. Other members of the group included the painter Severini and, briefly, the poet Guillaume Apollinaire.

Expressionism found fertile ground in the heavily afflicted German regions. Poets including Stephan George, Rilke, Werfel, Trakl and others had already set their mark on the culture of these lands before World War I. Pechstein, Nolde, Kirchner and Kokoschka were among the expressionist painters, while Schönberg and his pupils must be mentioned as expressionist musicians.

Schönberg stemmed directly from the late-romantic tradition. Expressionism in music may therefore be considered as a continuation of late romanticism. One could attempt to define expressionism as subjectivism taken to the furthest boundary. The world of the artist's personal feelings is expressed through the most extreme of means. A characteristic of this expansion was the release from old bonds (tonality).

The concepts of subjectivism and expansion were hardly strange to late-German romanticism. The breach, however, lay in expansion. Where the romantic expressed himself in general forms as handed down by history, the expressionist seized means that were strictly individual, breaking radically with tradition. The expressionist exhibited ecstatic and absolutist leanings, he was the true interpreter of current threats. Like the futurist he hated the romantic flight into dreams – the mask was cast off. His tragedy was that he was and still is misunderstood, not through a lack but rather an excess of subjective expression. His superabundance of inner tension, and the extreme resources which he employed to express them, led him towards an isolation that has not essentially been broken until this day.

3

The diversity of movements that arose before and during World War I may be illustrated in another manner by juxtaposing two extremes that both became concrete around 1917: *surrealism*, a movement particularly evident in literature, and *neo-plasticism*, born of the activities of the painter Mondriaan. The precursor of surrealism was dadaism, which can be viewed as a revolt against the utter senselessness of war. Here again we encounter the name of Apollinaire, the French poet who during his short life (1880-1918) did so much for the futurists, for cubist painters such as Braque, Picasso, Juan Gris and Fernand Léger, finally introducing the new concept of surrealism in 1917. The greatest theoretician, however, was the poet André Breton, who wrote the first surrealist manifesto in 1924. 'Le surréalisme se propose d'exprimer par l'automatisme psychique le fonctionnement réel de la pensée', he wrote (surrealism intends to express the true functioning of thought through psychic automatism). And this without any control by reason, and free of all aesthetic or moral prejudice. It was a reaction against the intellectualisation of the Western world. The unconscious, the state of dreaming or hallucination, rather than logical thinking, brought the true reality of man to the fore. Nonconformism was the slogan. A familiar surrealistic element, for instance, was *l'écriture automatique* or automatic writing, brought about without any control by consciousness or the intellect.

The strange, unreal world evoked for us by the surrealists stemmed from a time when the study of psychology thrust forward into unknown areas. Carl Gustav Jung defended the theory of innate collective unconsciousness, enabling man to comprehend general human symbols of unknown cultures.

The surrealists sought after this lost, irrational world of myths and symbols. The ambitions of painters such as Ernst, Delvaux, Miro, Tanguy and Dali, their kindred spirits Chagall and Chirico, and poets such as Breton, Aragon, Eluard and Artaud, went beyond the ambitions of painters and poets alone. They proclaimed a way of life, a revolt against the existing world and against one-sided rationalism, an impatience with faded standards of beauty, in search of a better world, in search of the *whole* man and his freedom. And although surrealism developed mainly in France, many of its traits have become characteristic of the whole field of modern art.

Another extreme is to be found in the neo-plasticism of Piet Mondriaan. Abstract art can be lyrical – as proved by Paul Klee – but Mondriaan's art pursued a most strict and reserved concept of form characterised primarily by simplicity and functional regularity. Nothing of the nonconformism of surrealism here, nor of the eruptions of expressionists. In so far as his work was a logical continuation of cubism (1909-14) it had a completely different attitude: not an abstraction of basic forms found in nature, but a personal, logical world free from nature and any figurative imagery, in which pure geometrical forms in their own right were elevated to a new order. Mondriaan, together with Van Doesburg, exercised enormous influence on the development of European painting. Their mouthpiece was *De Stijl*, a magazine established as early as 1917 and discontinued only in about 1930. But their ideas lived on, and since their time modern visual arts display every shade from their strict, consciously controlled formal language to the indeterminate, chaotic signals from the deepest layers of the subconscious.

The world has become larger, and with it the whole range of experience of modern art. Mondriaan discovered the frozen beauty of geometrical figures and elementary colours, Miro descended into the darkness of time and gained his inspiration from drawings in prehistoric caves, Kandinsky evoked the secretive world opened up for us by the microscope, while the surrealists groped in the mysteries of the subconscious. In so far as man played a role here, it was 'the unknown man'. Here was the beginning of the great mental adventure of the twentieth century. If one realises this, one also understands something of the visionary, the enthusiastic, but also of the chaotic, of the fear and uncertainty that went hand in hand with the discovery of this new world.

4

The great centres of the day were Paris and Vienna. Paris in particular was a hive of artistic activity. Even before Stravinsky settled there, Claude Debussy had created a new art. In a hardly revolutionary tonal language he reacted against the expansive subjectivity of the Wagnerians and the academicism of other contemporaries. The further we fathom the works of Debussy, the more wide-ranging his innovations appear to have been. In succeeding chapters his name will therefore be mentioned frequently.

The impresario Sergey Diaghilev's Russian ballet company made its first appearance in Paris in 1909. Despite an interruption during the war, Diaghilev's activities were to set an enduring stamp on the artistic climate of the time. He pursued an independent ballet style in which musicians and painters were also involved, and unusually, he understood well the importance of decors and music, and sensed exactly which artists were of importance. French cultural life knew more such versatile figures, including Breton, Cocteau and Apollinaire. Of the most important composers associated with these annual Russian ballets, mention should be made of Stravinsky, Debussy, Satie, Milhaud, Poulenc, Prokofiev, De Falla, Hindemith and Auric. Painters included Picasso, Derain, Matisse, Braque, Gris, Utrillo, Miro and Chirico.

Of the musicians, Stravinsky (1882-1971) was to dominate the scene.[1] This versatile composer reached a first peak at the age of thirty with his ballets *The Firebird*, *Petrushka* and *The Rite of Spring*. We speak of his 'Russian period': the ties with his fatherland were indeed not yet broken; this was expressed in his music through the use of Russian material and in the influence of his teacher Rimsky-Korsakov, particularly in instrumental aspects. Not until after the Russian Revolution of 1917 was Stravinsky to break the ties completely and assimilate Western – particularly Latin – culture astonishingly quickly. In the year of the revolution he wrote *The Wedding*, perhaps the most 'Russian' work from his hand. Although the rhythmic-syllabic structure and instrumentation for four pianos and percussion accompanying choir and soloists deviate from *The Rite*, yet the similarities are greater. We would draw attention to such matters as the form, the interlacing of short formulas without development, and similar melodic characteristics. Folkloric elements are used as material, while the story interests the composer less than the musical potential that it conceals. Here we encounter one of Stravinsky's essential characteristics: his strongly speculative sense. The solution to a given problem is the basis of his inspiration. For the rest, the folkloric element in *The Wedding* is much more stylised than in earlier compositions, and the work displays the first signs of a more sober approach. This was to be confirmed by *The Soldier's Tale*, especially in its small-scale, lucid and heterogeneous orchestration. Distorted chorales announce neo-classicism, while echoes of jazz are indicative of an increasingly Western orientation.

Although it is customary to view the ballet *Pulcinella* as the beginning of Stravinsky's neo-classical period, this can hardly be maintained. There is rather mention of the 'free adaptation of material by Pergolesi' upon the request of Diaghilev. The instrumentation in particular (in so far as this corresponds to the suite that was compiled later) is far from characteristic of Stravinsky's early neo-classicism; in comparison, instruments such as the oboe, horn and strings are much too prominent.

This is a different matter in the *Symphonies of Wind Instruments*. The use of wind characterises a number of Stravinsky's next works. This symphony is one of the most important compositions by the master, since its sacral aspect focuses on one of his most essential traits. This is music reflecting a higher order of being, beyond the reach of direct, subjective emotions. No intoxication, no bewilderment, but severe and clear sound as an action of the whole person, and in Stravinsky's case a person strongly preoccupied with ritual. The inflammatory mood of *The Rite* is of the past: here the writing is block-like and static, stripped of any tendency to shock, but great and almost liturgical in its command and tranquility. Through this attitude towards life, Stravinsky became the first great and genuine anti-romantic. His neo-classicism too can only be explained in the light of his pursuance of clarity and balance, characteristics which he so admired in pre-romantic masters.

The second centre, Vienna, formed quite a different picture. Here conservative influence was much stronger, and instead of the vital optimism of many Parisian artists' circles we find the loaded tension of central European expressionism. Moreover, Vienna had had no Debussy to prepare the way. The great generation of late romantics was therefore suddenly succeeded by that of Schönberg (1874-1951) and his most prominent pupils Berg and Webern. Their expressionist art was just as volcanic and certainly more charged than that of Stravinsky, but the spark did not ignite. The Schönberg group remained isolated in the big city; little became of it except for a few minor scandals, and not until forty years later did its music gain widespread attention. The list of works in section 5 includes a single but prominent exception: the opera *Wozzeck* by Alban Berg. (Further information on the Viennese composers is to be found in chapter 7, section 3.)

Béla Bartók (1881-1945) grew up in Hungary, far from the musical centres of Vienna or Paris. His influence at the time was therefore negligible; generally speaking, this also goes for figures who lived on the periphery such as Ives, Janáček and even Varèse (New York).

For Bartók too, late-romantic German composers constituted the most important example (the official Hungarian music world was under strong German influence). A visit to Paris in 1905, however, brought him into contact with music by Debussy and Ravel. In the same period (from 1903) he was occupied with the folklore of his country. Although late romanticism still predominated in his *First String Quartet* (1908), Debussy and folklore were to become the two great determining forces in his development. As far as Debussy was concerned, this was a question of his stimulating influence rather than concrete and lasting adoption of stylistic elements. Where folklore was concerned, Bartók assimilated more and more elements in his work. Though the resulting style is not outwardly similar to folk music, melodic and rhythmic elements betray a clear relationship. Bartók remained a romantic, and his innovations can be viewed as an extension of the romantic means of expression. Although he did not by any means go as far as Schönberg, expressionism was nevertheless to leave its mark on his work. This is illustrated by his choice of libretti (*Bluebeard's Castle* and *The Miraculous Mandarin*), and particularly in hard and pithy chords which reach their climax in the granite-like *Fourth String Quartet* (first movement). In such works chromaticism temporarily dominates the fundamentally diatonic structure of his music. But the same quartet features another element, counterpoint, which had already been present in his work for some years and was about to gain greater significance. Imitation technique in particular is employed in many ways, and hardly a new motif appears without imitation in the other parts. Canon and fugue occur much less frequently, probably because Bartók's style at the time was strongly motivic. Contrapuntal technique is therefore closely merged with the development of motifs as we know it in Beethoven. Only now do we understand the meaning of Bartók's pronouncement: 'Debussy has re-established the sense of using chords. He was just as important as Beethoven who revealed the genetic form of development to us, and just as important as Bach who initiated us in counterpoint in the highest sense.' 'Can we', he followed, 'combine these three elements and make them live for the moderns?' At this time a process of austerity and stabilisation began that was to bring Bartók to the great works written between 1930 and 1940 (see section 8).

In broad outline we have seen how the music of the three great figures Bartók, Schönberg and Stravinsky developed in the first quarter of the twentieth century. Beside the many differences there was a striking similarity in the earlier-mentioned breadth of experience of the modern artist. Stravinsky, the man who brought elementary, primitive forces into European art music for the first time in human memory, reached out later in his severe and uplifted views on music to a highly developed spiritual ideal, beyond the grasp of most mortals. Schönberg, the tormented expressionist with an excess of tensions, attempted to capture them later in the strictest technique that our century has produced. Bartók, the type of the modern artist: city dweller, rational, nervous and restless, nurtured a lifelong nostalgia for the sources of music, which he hoped to rediscover in folklore.

5

The following panoramic survey includes the most important works by the three composers discussed above, as well as those of later figures.[2] Despite all individual differences, considerable parallel undercurrents are evident, which we have attempted to present by distinguishing between three major periods. The list of works for each period is followed by a discussion of particular details and tendencies, in so far as these have not been mentioned above.[3]

The First Period (ca. 1908-ca. 1925)

(a) ca. 1908-ca. 1914. A volcanic and definitive eruption of new ideas in various places. Prior to 1910, something similar in America through Charles Ives. The period of ca. 1880: an extremely vital, optimistic, largely antagonistic generation. This contrasts with the Viennese expressionists, who despite many innovations placed more emphasis on ties with tradition. In all cases: accent on intuitive exploration of new possibilities. In 1913: Russolo's *Futuristic manifest*. In the same year Bartók's first academic publication: *Chansons populaires roumaines du département Bihar*.

1908	Schönberg, *Three Piano Pieces op. 11, Five Orchestral Pieces op. 16*
1909	Schönberg, *Erwartung*
	Webern, *Five Movements for String Quartet op. 5*
1910	Berg, *String Quartet op. 3*
	Bartók, *Allegro barbaro*
1911	Stravinsky, *Petrushka*
	Schönberg, *Herzgewächse*
	Bartók, *Bluebeard's Castle*
1912	Schönberg, *Pierrot lunaire*
	Stravinsky, *The Rite of Spring*
1913	Webern, *Six Bagatelles for string quartet op. 9, Five Orchestral Pieces op. 10*

(b) ca. 1918-ca. 1925. Same vitality and innovative drive as before World War I. But strong tendency towards austerity as consolidation of the attained (Stravinsky, Schönberg, Bartók), as reaction against excess (Satie, Les Six), or as reaction to expressionism (Hindemith). Disillusionment of World War I quickened these tendencies. Expressionist peaks in Vienna (*Wozzeck*), consolidation in 1923 in 12-note technique of Schönberg. Return to Baroque counterpoint in Hindemith, shortly after in Bartók too. In Latin countries neo-classicism and aesthetics of Les Six (1919, *Le Coq et l'Arlequin*). From ca. 1918 first jazz in Europe. Protest continued to sound, but now as social commentary in work of Kurt Weill and Bertold Brecht. At same time, *Gebrauchsmusik* as attempt to reach wider community (Hindemith). New sense of reality also evident in influence of industrial technique on music (*Pacific 231* and *The Steel Step*). Related, but more prophetic and radical: Edgard Varèse.

1916	Satie, *Parade*
1917	Prokofiev, *'Classical' Symphony*
	Stravinsky, *The Wedding*
1918	Stravinsky, *The Soldier's Tale*
1919	Stravinsky, *Pulcinella*
	Milhaud, *Le Boeuf sur le Toit*
	Poulenc, *Le Bestiaire*
	Bartók, *The Miraculous Mandarin*
1920	Stravinsky, *Symphonies of Wind Instruments*
1921	Berg, *Wozzeck*
	Honegger, *Le Roi David*
1922	Hindemith, *Suite 1922*
	De Falla, *El Retablo de Maese Pedro*
1923	Schönberg, *Five Piano Pieces op. 23*
	Hindemith, *Das Marienleben*
	Milhaud, *La Création du Monde*
	Honegger, *Pacific 231*
	Varèse, *Octandre*
1924	Milhaud, *L'Orestie*
1925	Prokofiev, ballet *The Steel Step*
1926	Pijper, *Third Symphony*
1928	Bartók, *Fourth String Quartet*
	Weill, *Die Dreigroschenoper*

6

'Frei ist die Tonkunst geboren, und frei zu werden ihre Bestimmung' (music was born free, and free will be its destination). These words of Busoni would be a fitting motto at the cradle of new music.

Schönberg's *op. 11*[4] announced the period of free atonality based on intuition. The expressionist urge to discover new resources explains many hitherto unknown phenomena such as *Klangfarbenmelodik* (Schönberg *op. 16*, Webern *op. 10*), athematicism (*Erwartung*, beside other works), aphorisms (*Six Bagatelles* by Webern, lasting three-and-a-half minutes), *Sprechgesang* in *Pierrot lunaire*, etc. Schönberg and Webern began to part company, and Berg went his own way too – his *String Quartet* betrays his attachment to the romantic tradition. The same applies to Bartók's *First String Quartet*; his musical language was fundamentally simpler than that of the Viennese composers. The *Allegro barbaro* was a first expression of a spontaneous rhythmic impulse, stimulated by Balkan folk music. The rhythm of *The Rite* was more complex and self-willed. In *The Rite* and *Petrushka* Stravinsky created two startling and eruptive ballets which perfectly captured the spirit of the period.

After World War I a tendency towards austerity and consolidation became evident, although other elements continued to emerge that were to complete the picture of new music. Satie had already launched a new sound in 1916. Although he was of little importance as a composer, his ideas exercised great influence. To this extraordinary figure any form of excess was like a red rag to a bull, and he reacted (and was often the first to raise his voice) successively against Wagner, Debussy, and later in 1916, against the excesses of the pre-war Russian ballets. The decors for Satie's clownesque ballet *Parade* were by Picasso, and the text by Jean Cocteau, who in the same year announced a new ideal: classical clarity of form, coupled with inner emotion. Remarkably, it was before his departure for the West that Prokofiev wrote his *'Classical' Symphony*, which also harks back to classical examples. We have seen how Stravinsky pursued the same course (section 4), and around 1920 two related and clearly defined tendencies emerged: neo-classicism and the (temporary) aesthetic of Les Six. The latter group arose by coincidence, and its members Auric, Poulenc, Honegger, Milhaud, Tailleferre and Durey were to quickly go their own ways. But Cocteau's tumultuous manifesto *Le Coq et l'Arlequin* – 'Assez de nuages... il nous faut une musique sur la terre' (enough of clouds... what we need is music on earth) – revealed the spirit of the time: against Beethoven, Wagner, Debussy and Mussorgsky, and for the naked simplicity of Satie, the vehemence of Stravinsky and the linearity of Bach. Precision and clarity, but also music from the street, fairground, circus and music hall; but certainly no problems or pretensions, no 'musique sérieuse'. Though Parisian artists were fond of forming groups, they remained individualists. The ballet *Le Boeuf sur le Toit*, with music by Milhaud, was entirely in keeping with Cocteau's programme; but the powerful trilogy *L'Orestie* (Aeschylus-Claudel), written between 1913 and 1924, already revealed the versatility of this composer. In *Le Bestiaire* Poulenc set poems by Apollinaire, creating refined aristocratic songs very far removed from 'music of the street'. And Honegger's fame rests precisely on his 'musique sérieuse': *Le Roi David*, a music drama in which baroque traditions were revived even before Hindemith.

Neo-classicism is the appropriate term when this reversion to early examples went hand in hand with the pursuance of a lucid and really rather Latin balance. Thus, neo-classicism took root mainly in France and southern Europe. Preferably, *pre*-classical composers provided the model, not so much by reason of their material but because of the mental balance which it reveals. This preference for a clear and temperate style is also expressed in small-scale instrumentations, often of heterogeneous timbre; melodic writing usually predominates, and of other musical elements the harmony in particular bears a modern stamp, though it is moderate enough to be adapted to the melodic style.

Beside the above-mentioned works by Stravinsky our list includes one of

De Falla's best compositions: *El Retablo de Maese Pedro*. After his better known, impressionist works, De Falla revealed an inclination for the austere. Employing neo-classical resources (dances from the sixteenth and seventeenth centuries, the harpsichord), but also medieval liturgical chant, the composer penetrated the austere, ascetic spirit of ancient Castile. Here, inspired by folk traditions, De Falla is the great counterpart of Bartók, indeed more so than in his earlier works with their Andalusian flavour.

La Création de Monde, Milhaud's Negro ballet, opens with a neo-classical introduction inspired directly by Bach. More important, the work was one of the few successful examples of the assimilation of jazz influences. We hear echoes of the linear improvisation of the New Orleans style, and passages already announcing the world of Gershwin (his *Rhapsody in Blue* dates from 1924). Naturally, the heterogeneous sound of jazz ensembles greatly appealed to the neo-classicists.

Technique was to the vital and dynamic young generation as nature to the romantics. Honegger glorified the steam locomotive in *Pacific 231*, and was also inspired by sport (*Rugby*, 1928); Prokofiev, who lived in the West from 1918, wrote the ballet *The Steel Step*, celebrating industry and the machine even before his return to Russia in 1934. In this respect, however, the work of Edgard Varèse was of much greater significance. The music of *Pacific 231* was still traditionally conceived, with or without the train; *Octandre*, on the other hand, presented an entirely new and comprehensive musical world. Sound became a tangible and acoustic reality, separate from any technical analogy, separate too from harmonic and contrapuntal associations. Varèse evoked sound in its rough and elementary natural state, and was thus further removed from the European tradition than any of his contemporaries.

Hindemith likewise pursued austerity, finding inspiration in baroque music. His first period (ca. 1920) was in fact characterised by influence from his own surroundings rather than any personal characteristic. An example from these wild years is the *Suite 1922*, with its carefree sound and American dances: Boston, Shimmy and Ragtime, the latter with the recommendation: 'Play this piece really wildly but in strict rhythm like a machine; treat the keyboard as an interesting sort of percussion.' Bartók's percussion style, the machine, jazz, the aesthetics of Les Six, indeed the entire mood of the time was captured in this piece. Hindemith's own ideal was revealed as early as 1923 in the song cycle *Das Marienleben* to texts by Rilke. He became the great German anti-romantic, characterised by objectivity, linearity and the strict application of form, and he developed to become more embedded in tradition than any other composer of our time. For the moment, however, the carefree composer was active on all fronts: music for mechanical instruments (1926), *Gebrauchsmusik* and *Zeitopern* at about the same time, and strongly simplified music for amateurs around 1930, including *Plöner Musiktag* (1932) for students. His activities coincided briefly with those of Kurt Weill, who in his *Dreigroschenoper* succeeded in creating popular, sometimes banal and sometimes gripping, satirical music as a late-German and somewhat morbid parallel to Cocteau's frivolous oration.

Expressionism achieved great heights in this second half of the first period, but was to disappear, or become much more mature, at the same time. For highlights we naturally turn to Austria: *Wozzeck*, which Berg worked on from 1914 to 1921. This opera too was written in the free atonal style, with occasional but clear traces of late-romantic floating tonality. The music was not only freed from cadential bonds and period structure but also exploited all the refinement of the modern orchestra. The work was thus a most supple and direct reflection of the content of Büchner's drama. In this respect too it was therefore a continuation of Wagner, but with considerably more differentiated resources. The orchestra had become a large, breathing organism, transmitting fear and oppression in a suggestive manner. A typical trait of the Viennese school persisted as Berg attempted to confine atonal freedom by utilising strict classical forms.

But the great period of expressionism was over. In his *Five Piano Pieces* Schönberg was to introduce the 12-note technique: a technical and at the same time mental process of consolidation with which the tumult of his expressionist period came to an end. Like Berg, however, he remained a romantic, in contrast to Webern who developed a new and strictly circumscribed formal world. While expressionist tendencies can be detected in the eight books of songs composed by Webern between 1915 and 1926, they are outnumbered by aspects of the consolidation process, which reached a first culmination in his *Symphony op. 21*.

In 1928 Bartók composed his *Fourth String Quartet*. We have already seen how the counterpoint in this work formed a definitive indication of the synthesis and balance that he was to attain particularly after 1930. The *Third Symphony* by Pijper occupies a similar position. Holland was only vaguely stirred by expressionist storms (the composer Pijper, the writer Marsman), probably partly due to French influence in the country. After the tumult of the *Third Symphony* Pijper's style too matured considerably, especially after 1930, and reached a peak in the *Sonata for Two Pianos* (1935).

7

The Second Period (ca. 1925-ca. 1950)

Initially still dominated by the great figures of the first period, most of whom died around 1950. No new currents. Neo-classicism, modernism (International Style), *Gebrauchsmusik* and humanism with a religious tinge determined the picture. Experiments (Varèse, Cage, Hába) remained incidental. Dictatorships in several great Western countries deeply affected artistic life. Many composers took refuge in America (Bartók, Schönberg, Stravinsky, Milhaud and Hindemith).

1926	Stravinsky, *Oedipus rex*
1928	Schönberg, *Variations for Orchestra op. 31*
	Webern, *Symphony op. 21*
1930	Stravinsky, *Symphony of Psalms*
1931	Varèse, *Ionisation*
1934	Hindemith, *Mathis der Maler*
1935	Berg, *Violin Concerto*
	Messiaen, *La Nativité du Seigneur*
	Honegger, *Jeanne d'Arc au bûcher*
1936	Bartók, *Music for Strings, Percussion and Celesta*
	Webern, *Piano Variations op. 27*
	Orff, *Carmina burana*
1939	Bartók, *Sixth String Quartet*
1940	Webern, *Orchestra Variations op. 30*
1942	Schönberg, *Ode to Napoleon*
1944	Messiaen, *Trois petites Liturgies*
1945	Stravinsky, *Symphony in Three Movements*
1948	Stravinsky, *Mass*
1949	Orff, *Antigone*
1951	Hindemith, *Die Harmonie der Welt*
	Stravinsky, *The Rake's Progress*

8

The first period determined the gamut of new music, while the second built on these foundations. The older generation sought consolidation, while the younger one – even the greatest individuals such as Messiaen and Orff – summoned sufficient strength from the potential already created. The only figure to cause a brief stir belonged to the older generation: Edgard Varèse, who maintained his initial élan in *Ionisation*. Stravinsky's neo-classicism was confirmed only too clearly in *Oedipus rex*: his pursuance of a superpersonal monumentality became an impersonal, conventional language in which even rhythm lost its force. He employed Latin for the text, since the fossilised monumentality of this dead language excluded any romantic subjectivity. It is surprising that he did not turn to Greek, since ancient Greek vocabulary rules out any personal element, both in length and accent. The ancient Greek language is a substantial eminence in itself, beyond human influence; it reaches into the world of the original unity between subject and object, which most languages thereafter lost. It is a language of the mask, as ancient Greek drama is a drama of the mask. What we do understand is that Stravinsky was fascinated by Greek culture for a long time. But the sacral-ritual tendency also made itself felt, and strongly so, in the *Symphony of Psalms*. Nearly twenty years later his increasing profoundness found utterance in the ascetic *Mass*, a work already anticipating the most austere pieces written after the opera *The*

Rake's Progress, the last purely neo-classical work from his hand. Sometimes a Dionysian element broke through, as in the *Symphony in Three Movements*.

Schönberg's *Variations for Orchestra* was the first large-scale work in which the 12-note technique was developed in a well-controlled and versatile manner. Many later compositions were less flawless due to the inner discrepancy between technique and mental condition which the artist Schönberg proved unable to resolve. The *Ode to Napoleon* is an example of his later tonal preoccupations within the boundaries of dodecaphony. The opera *Moses und Aron* is among the works in which Schönberg's religiosity found expression, strongly Jewish and Old Testament orientated. The late-romantic spirit of Berg is heard right up to his last composition, the *Violin Concerto*. Meanwhile his friend Webern climbed the steep path to a highly concentrated ascetic language (*Piano Variations op. 27*), after which he achieved a classical balance in his later works, such as the *Variations for Orchestra op. 30*. The definitive turning point in this new development was the *Symphony op. 21*.

In the meantime Bartók too achieved true mastership in the classicalness of many works written after 1930, including the *Music for Strings, Percussion and Celesta*. His *Sixth* and last *String Quartet* marked a turning point. Thereafter – in America – he wrote a few more pieces, such as the *Concerto for Orchestra*, in which the line of classicalness was prolonged, perhaps occasionally at the expense of the power and dynamism that gave the pre-1940 compositions such imposing élan.

Hindemith reached a culminating point in the opera *Mathis der Maler*. A few years later he expounded his ideas on composition in the theoretical work *Unterweisung im Tonsatz*. Unfortunately, his craftsmanship did not escape a certain academicism, while the full-blooded musicianship of his earlier years also became tempered by mystical tendencies. His symphony *Die Harmonie der Welt* looked back to Johannes Kepler's vision of the world, and attempted to create a musical-symbolic representation of the mathematical order thought to lie at the basis of the universe.

Of the old *Groupe des Six*, Honegger in particular received an unusually strong response to his oratorio *Jeanne d'Arc au bûcher*, written in collaboration with Paul Claudel. In view of the global tendencies of the time, one wonders what the new group *La Jeune France* was actually reacting against in 1936. Messiaen, Jolivet, Lesur and Baudrier desired a return to lyricism and a new humanism which was long present among the older generation. Their reaction against every form of extremism also seems somewhat strange at a time when extremism was absent. Moreover, the most important composer of the group, Olivier Messiaen, was soon to occupy a most extreme position in French musical life. He had already written a number of pieces, including his organ cycle *La Nativité du Seigneur*. Musical symbolism gained a religious slant, though of a strongly sensual nature in contrast to parallel works by Schönberg or Stravinsky. Technically speaking, Messiaen developed a refined system of modality and a complex rhythmical style. In this baroque accumulation of sound, harmony was simply a source of colour. In his instrumentation too the sound pursued, for instance in the *Trois petites Liturgies*, is like a sensual caress.

Carl Orff wrote his first characteristic work, *Carmina burana*, in 1936. He had something in common with Stravinsky: a preference for Latin, for additive forms, ostinato effects, elementary melodic lines, rhythm, etc. But the essence of his style lay elsewhere. His entire development moved toward a concept in which drama was primary; music, dance, text and action were merely different aspects of it and had a subservient function. Stravinsky was a composer, and he differentiated his material. Orff tended to the contrary, simplifying music more and more until, in his later dramas such as *Antigone*, it served at best only to lend rhythm to the text. In purely musical terms the significance of Orff was limited, though the musical world probably underestimated the value of his spiritual conception.

Naturally, beside the above-mentioned composers there were others who contributed to this period. Most did not advance beyond a somewhat pale neo-classicism, stripped of its original stimuli. But there were exceptions, including Blacher, Britten, Dallapiccola, Egk, Hartmann, Kodály, Martin, Petrassi and others, all of whom wrote important works. Our concern here is to present a characteristic picture of the period rather than to be historically comprehensive. In order to avoid arbitrariness we have limited our list to the essentials.

9

The Third Period (ca. 1945-the present)

World War II brought an end to two Western dictatorships. The avant-garde flourished once more. Its centre moved from Austria and France to Germany and Italy. The first period included many east European artists such as Stravinsky, Bartók, Prokofiev, Diaghilev, Chagall and Kandinsky. The Iron Curtain turned the recent avant-garde into a mainly Western affair: perhaps it therefore became more rational, and its currents less variegated, than in the first period. From ca. 1960, however, a broader picture emerged. Eastern Europe thawed: 1956, first 'Warsaw spring'; 1961, first Zagreb Biennial. Polish, Czech, Yugoslavian and even Russian composers became increasingly active. All these contacts, in addition to those with Japan and the USA, led to new currents and insights. It was no longer possible to speak of *the* avant-garde.

1946	Boulez, *Sonatine for flute and piano*
1948	Schaeffer, *Étude pathétique*
1949	Messiaen, *Mode de valeurs et d'intensités*
1951	Cage, *Music of Changes*
	Feldman, *Projections*
	Nono, *Polifonica, monodia, ritmica*
1952	Boulez, *Structures I*
	Brown, *Music for Violin, Cello and Piano*

1953	Stockhausen, *Kontra-punkte*
1954	Xenakis, *Metastasis*
	Varèse, *Déserts*
1956	Stockhausen, *Gesang der Jünglinge*
	Nono, *Il canto sospeso*
	Xenakis, *Pithoprakta*
1957	Stockhausen, *Klavierstück XI*
	Stockhausen, *Gruppen*
	Boulez, *Third Piano Sonata, Improvisations sur Mallarmé*
	Berio, *Omaggio a Joyce*
1958	Cage, *Piano Concerto*
	Stravinsky, *Threni*
1959	Berio, *Différences*
1960	Penderecki, *Threnody for the victims of Hiroshima*
	Messiaen, *Chronochromie*
1961	Ligeti, *Atmosphères*
	Brown, *Available Forms*
1962	Xenakis, *Stratégie*
1963	Berio, *Sequenza II*
1964	Stockhausen, *Mikrophonie I*
	La Monte Young, *The Tortoise, His Dreams and Journeys*
1965	Ligeti, *Nouvelles aventures*
1966	Xenakis, *Terretektorh*
1968	Kagel, *Der Schall*

10

A new generation, born between 1920 and 1930, emerged after 1945. Dictatorship, loyal to itself, opposed any utterance of modern art and created a sort of vacuum in Europe. The thirsty younger generation pounced upon all music that had previously been banned. Central figures and places arose spontaneously, with followers thronging around to study the forbidden art. Messiaen, teaching in Paris, had a broad interest in everything related to music: the cries of primitive peoples, the art of Asian cultures, birdsong, Greek music, it all had his unremitting interest. The horizon of his pupils, including Boulez at the time, was consequently widened; the world of music became more spacious and greater than it had ever been before. At work in the same city was René Leibowitz, whose books, supplying the first extensive information on Schönberg and his pupils, were of enormous influence in the years prior to 1950. Many students came to him to run the high school course of classical dodecaphony. In Germany, an international centre formed in Darmstadt within just a few years. Concerts and courses met the generally felt demand to 'catch up'.

The first, decisive turn of events occurred around 1950. Of all music, it was Webern's pure world of sound that was to make more and more impression. Webern had never had much influence: the tranquility of his life was not interrupted by great successes or scandals; even his tragic death in 1945 had something unintentional, and at that moment hardly anyone in the musical world felt his death to be an important fact. The development of Webern, not as 'the pupil of Schönberg' but as the creator of an entirely new sound world, was to fundamentally influence the music of succeeding years.

A new and scientific approach to many musical phenomena grew in the same period: acoustics, information theory and experiments with the electronic generation of music, leading to the establishment of the first electronic studio in Cologne in 1953. In Paris Pierre Schaeffer had already commenced with his concrete music in 1948, and his *Étude pathétique* became a classic in this direction, which ran aground, however, in a repetition of futuristic clamour.

The manner in which Messiaen produced the first concrete example of a multidimensional composition in his *Mode de valeurs et d'intensités* is discussed in the final chapter. Four musical elements – pitch, duration, dynamics and colour (attack) – are made autonomous and ordered according to modal-serial qualifications. For the younger generation this was more than a technical stunt, it was the proclamation of a new ideal, which they had also undergone when listening to Webern. From this point things moved quickly. The first and exuberant works by Boulez, such as his *Sonatine for flute and piano*, were already written. Formative for this composer, beside Messiaen and Leibowitz, were Stravinsky in particular and, later, Debussy. Consequently, elements such as rhythm already played a major role in his youth works. A swift development led to the 'punctual' style of *Structures*. *Le Marteau sans Maître* brought relaxation and can be viewed as a transition to the *Improvisations sur Mallarmé*, one of the first outstanding works of the new music. Stockhausen made his debut with *Kreuzspiel*. A somewhat rigid way of thinking, combined with brilliant giftedness, was to guide him in 1956 to the first masterpiece of electronic music: *Gesang der Jünglinge*. Many elements of this work were governed by serial determinacy, even including the human voice.

Meanwhile two Italians, Nono and Berio, appeared on the stage. Like his compatriot Dallapiccola, Nono expressed his lyrical sympathy with the suffering of humanity. His many vocal works include *Il Canto sospeso*, the 'interrupted song' of resistance fighters who had been condemned to death. Berio was more virtuosic and jocular, though no less lyrical. His *Omaggio a Joyce* employs a text by this writer (from *Ulysses*) in three languages, the point of departure for electronic manipulation aimed to gradually transform the text into completely autonomous music. Not only Joyce but Mallarmé too proved to be a stimulating example, in the first place for Boulez in his *Third Piano Sonata*. Together with the slightly earlier *Klavierstück XI* by Stockhausen, this work formed the basis of a new development through which the performer was given more freedom to intervene. This was made possible through changing concepts of form, which have now become conscious but which can really be traced back to Debussy, the younger contemporary of Mallarmé.

The significance of composers such as Boulez and Nono diminished after 1960, while Berio became one of the most fertile composers of his time. His compositions entitled *Sequenza* (from *II* to *VI*) were as many attempts to achieve a more direct and physical expression. The instrument became an extension of the human body. *Différences* reveals a similar association between instruments and electronic resources, as the latter became an extension of the former. The same occurred with Stockhausen, though in an entirely different manner. In *Mikrophonie I* the vibrations of the tam-tam – the only instrument – are explored, transformed and reproduced during performance. Stockhausen underwent a remarkable change, probably to some extent through the increasing influence of Cage. Of all 'liberated' Europeans, however, it was the German-Argentine Kagel who demonstrated the most jocular approach to the new material.

The serial aesthetic was also rejected in *Atmosphères* by Ligeti. *Nouvelles Aventures*, also a form of music theatre, is the most important work by this Hungarian composer. But the most serious attack on serial concepts came from the Greek composer Xenakis. As early as 1954 he introduced mathematical composition methods in *Metastasis*, and after 1960 his concepts led to the breakthrough of musical constructivism, contrasting strongly with increasingly neo-romantic tendencies among many Polish composers and also in the later works of Ligeti.

Finally, the Americans. From the early 1950s we see not only the development of a striking parallel with contemporary serial composers (Brown, Schillinger, *Method of Composition*), but also attempts to renew music notation and to create music theatre, aleatory music etc. Cage, Feldman and Brown proved to have a freer relation to musical traditions than most progressive Europeans. Cage was the spokesman, and particularly after 1958 his concepts gained influence in the Old World. Instead of totally determined music he pursued the opposite: complete indeterminacy of the musical product. Indeterminable elements of chance in both the creative process and performance went to avoid any human purposiveness. A certain relationship was therefore created with the surrealistic cleanup of forty years earlier. For the first time in music we can speak of surrealism, even though it was mixed with a pinch of Zen Buddhism. Surrealism in painting, indeed, was not yet dead. Tachisme, as it was called, a cross between surrealism (automatisms, chance) and an abstract expressionism, emerged around 1950. But here most painters, like the musicians, lapsed into a sort of decorative curtain of colour or sound which at best could be described as neo-impressionist. Cage's concepts were followed up by younger Americans including La Monte Young and Terry Riley, forming a second generation of composers born around 1935. Particularly characteristic was the abandonment of music as an autonomous entity: it was used increasingly as a sound environment, free of traditional ideas on form and concert performance.

This takes us back to the beginning of the century. Two familiar names remain: Stravinsky and Varèse. *Threni* was Stravinsky's first entirely dodecaphonic work. After Webern stripped the 12-note technique of its original expressionist basis, Stravinsky was able to embrace the technique without scruple. But he remained himself. *Threni*, the lamentations of Jeremiah, confirmed his strongly religious character, as did the *Mass, Canticum sacrum* and other later compositions. Moreover, the strong simplicity of his final period had already been announced by songs written after the war, including the wonderful *In Memoriam Dylan Thomas*.

Varèse could at last employ electronic resources to realise his pre-1925 ideals. *Déserts*, for an ensemble of wind, percussion and electronically prepared sounds, was a late echo of that eruptive *époque*, an *époque* in which the entire picture of the new art was determined if not by technical means, then through mental and spiritual processes.

CHAPTER TWO

Rhythm

I

The twentieth century brought great development in the field of rhythm, in the following two ways:

1. The structure and development of rhythm in general became richer and more diversified;

2. Interest in percussion increased, while other instrumental groups were also assigned important rhythmic functions.

In Stravinsky's *The Soldier's Tale* melodic and percussive instruments are on an equal footing. Works featuring extensive percussion parts include Stravinsky's *The Wedding*, Bartók's *Sonata for two pianos and percussion*, Edgard Varèse's *Ionisation*, fragments from Milhaud's *Les Choéphores*, and Carl Orff's *Antigone*. External influences may also be noted: not only the rhythms of Eastern music, but also those of indigenous folk music (Bartók) and jazz (Milhaud's *La Création du Monde*, Stravinsky's *Ebony Concerto* and *Ragtime*, Krenek's *Johnny spielt auf*, and Ravel's *Sonata for violin and piano*) made their mark on contemporary composition. A preference for irregular rhythmic structures emerged, whether spontaneously invented or rationally developed. In the latter case in particular, it is generally true to say that rhythm gained independence. Important structural principles, applied in the past particularly to melody and harmony, were now transplanted to rhythm (rhythmic canons, for example). On the other hand, melodic-harmonic structures were sometimes determined by rhythmic factors. An old and familiar example of this is *The Rite of Spring*, in which 'percussive chords' serve to highlight rhythmic figures, to which end they are complexly constructed:

EXAMPLE 1

This brings us to a matter of importance. Not without reason, indeed, did Stravinsky choose strong and complex chords. If we try to render the same rhythm with major triads, the effect proves much weaker; by placing the triads in a higher register, the result already improves. It appears, therefore, that rhythm is determined by other musical elements than duration and dynamics alone. Another example: if we play a melody in a tempo dictated exactly by the metronome, but first very high with short and strong staccato notes, and then low, soft and legato, the first version will seem slower than the second. Again, the duration of the notes is influenced by several elements: not only the notated, metronomic length, but the musical length too, that which is organically incorporated into the whole and to which we react. In a piece of music, innumerable subtle forces react to one another. How we ourselves react to all this is a question for the music psychologist. For the moment it is sufficient to realise the great danger of approaching rhythm abstractly, isolated from the whole. And if we do so, in the course of further analysis, then we must be aware of the danger of drawing all too formalistic conclusions which may lead us onto the wrong track.

2

Before commencing a discussion of the rhythmic phenomena of new music, we have to deal with another difficulty, namely the great confusion concerning terminology. To this end, several short observations on the theory of rhythm are given here.

In musical movement three time categories can be distinguished, three layers which may occur simultaneously:

1. The actual *rhythm* is the highest and most autonomous expression of time-consciousness. It can occur entirely independently, or it may be grafted upon a lower time category, that of the:

2. *Rhythmic modes.* These are certain rhythmic proportions that occur frequently and can, as it were, become species of a certain rhythmic perception. In literature these modes are called metrical feet. The Dutch poet Albert Verwey (1865-1937) wrote of them: 'I view the measures within which human art is made as principles of humanity.'

3. The most elementary time category is that indicated by the *pulse unit.* In the movement of sound, one perceives equidistant nuclear points. One could speak here of periodic rhythm, and in this sense periodicity is a musical reality, the living heartbeat of musical movement. Physiological rhythm too is characterised by periodicity. We also speak of metre, but the pulse unit and the notated metre may not always coincide. In very many cases the pulse unit is smaller than the notated metre, coinciding with the beat. In the slow 3/4 bar of Example 78, the notated metre is not perceptible, unlike the crotchet unit which works as the real periodic rhythm. This is probably related to the time span between two pulse units, which must be neither too large nor too small to remain perceptible. The Belgian musicologist Paul Collaer maintains that the periodicity of elementary bodily rhythms lies between forty and

one hundred and twenty per minute; anything in between is felt to be normal, while periodic movements slower than forty or faster than one hundred and twenty disturb the balance. The extremely slow striking of the gong at Buddhist rituals creates unbearable tension. Many statements from the past draw attention to the narrow relationship that was assumed to exist between musical and physiological rhythm, and the heartbeat often formed the standard for normal tempo. Only from the romantic period onwards was there a tendency to move away from these average values, undoubtedly with the aim of achieving greater expression.

Since rhythm is the highest and most autonomous expression of time-consciousness, as such it is not necessarily bound to lower categories. But it is often woven into the fibre of modal patterns, which in turn may be incorporated into the elementary periodic movement of the pulse unit. These three layers do not differ in essence, but only in function and complexity.[1]

A very simple example of the three layers is found in the second movement of Hindemith's *Third Piano Sonata* (Example 2). Here we have a periodic pulse unit, the iambic mode and an autonomous rhythm above it. The lower part appears to fulfill not only a harmonic function but a rhythmic one too, rendering the mode upon which the rhythm is based.

EXAMPLE 2

Notation is not problematic as long as the rhythm is periodic and the music can be metrically notated. After all, the barline conforms to the natural periodic movement of the music, and indicates the pulse unit or a group of the same. But matters change when non-periodic rhythm makes its appearance, or when it no longer proves possible to bundle equal groups of pulse units, as is increasingly the case in music written after about 1900. The barline followed the now irregular movement and thus lost its original purpose; the era of multiple bar changes had begun. And this was not the only difficulty either. The barline and the dynamic accent were frequently coupled together to become inseparable quantities. Elsewhere, schematisation of the notation prompted a choice for a ticking metronome rather than the living heartbeat of music. All this brought a reaction, one that can be summarised in the often quoted and, in its compactness, so suggestive maxim: 'Metre is nothing, rhythm is everything.'[2] As old bonds were shaken off, free rhythm became popular. And the baby was thrown out with the bath water.

3

NOTATION PROBLEMS. In the meantime our composers continued to struggle with the barline. Could it be avoided? Almost impossible. By now the sign – on paper – had come to serve other purposes than its original one (avoidance of too many accidentals, legibility of scores).

1. As long as there was mention of periodic movement with only incidental interruption, the barline could be easily adapted.

2. Non-periodic music offered various possibilities. In Pijper's *Piano Sonata* (Example 3) the barline largely followed the main points of the musical discourse. It is not always entirely clear, however: in this fragment the rhythmic module ♪ ♪ plays a dominant role; it occurs both in trochaic and iambic forms, but it is notated in no less than seven different ways (after and across the barline, with different sorts of accents, etc.).

EXAMPLE 3

3. Related to this was the use of the barline as a so-called colotomic sign to indicate structural boundaries such as phrases, motifs, etc. (see Example 16). Colotomic signs are used in gamelan music, for instance, where they are made audible on percussion instruments.

4. Other composers joined Honegger in wishing that 'la mesure doit jouer le rôle de borne kilométrique sur une route' (the bar must play the role of the milestone along a road).[3] However, in Honegger's scores, too, some kilometres are longer than others. In the pursuance of clarity such inconsistencies were apparently not entirely avoidable. The logical solution to this view would be the introduction of music paper printed with fine, vertical lattice-

work, enabling durations to be indicated in terms of spatial proportions. Though hardly ideal, such a system could have its advantages for applied music (radio, film, television). See also chapter 8, section 12.

4

DIVISIVE AND ADDITIVE RHYTHM. Instead of making a distinction between periodic and non-periodic rhythms, the terms divisive and additive rhythms are also employed. However, the pairs of terms are not synonymous. One could say that the first division tells us *what* form of rhythm is meant, while the second is more indicative of the *psychic focus* that has induced its creation. Although we are on thin ice here, it is worth throwing some light on this matter, since an investigation of rhythm in this sense may help us to understand it better.

Divisive rhythm. A comparison: one walks with an easy, springing pace. At some point this pace prompts one to whistle a random tune which fits the walking rhythm in a natural, periodic way: the tune is bundled in regular groups of two or more paces. Music-while-you-work is created in this way, as regular bodily movement and corresponding music stimulate one another. The same goes for marches and indeed much dance music: common to it all is this correspondence between music and bodily movement. The music automatically becomes organised in larger and equivalent groups of pulse units. Countless other melodies betray the same tendency towards regularity without having been conceived in relation to dancing, marching or working movements. For the basis of this divisive rhythm is a psychic focus. The music is made spontaneously in larger musical units that are subdivisible in an equal number of pulses – thus the word divisive. In the music of the Viennese classical composers, this divisive rhythm is carried exceptionally far. What goes for the perception of all periodicity probably applies here, too: the larger components of this time pattern must lie within reasonable limits. If they are too large we are no longer conscious of them as musical units. In Indian *tala* patterns, regular blocks of twenty or more pulse units are sometimes formed. However, these are too large to be perceptible as a whole; they are in fact accumulations of smaller units.

Additive rhythm. It would now be only too simplistic to consider additive rhythm as something unnatural. Music is the resultant of many and mysterious forces active in the human being. An additive concept of music proves to be current among very many peoples, while in west European art music of the nineteenth century it also gained ground. In additive rhythm we do not find a regularly subdivisible time pattern that exists *a priori* in the mind. The material is built up from a small beginning, and the notes accumulate as it were, depending on the technique in question. In most cases the result differs considerably from divisive regularity, although this is *not* necessarily true. Much additive music has an elementary periodic layer of subdivisible pulse units. The pulse unit itself, however, can no longer be viewed as part of a higher unit that can be divided equally, even if the movement, when counted up, could be put to paper in 4/4 time for instance.

Conclusion. Additive rhythm is a loose accumulation of concrete independent quantities. In divisive rhythm, values are less independent: they are always heard in relation to a higher coordinative unit.

Examples of divisive rhythm are hardly required. The fact that the heyday of this rhythmic concept occurred in the Viennese classical period has already been mentioned. Tonal cadence formulas lend themselves well to this rhythm;

EXAMPLE 4

MUSIC OF THE TWENTIETH CENTURY

see further section 5 in the present chapter. However, two examples of modern divisive rhythm are given here.

In the Scherzo from Bartók's *Fifth String Quartet* (Example 4), we see an east European counterpart of our 4/4 time in which the fourth beat is slightly lengthened. Here, our concept ♩♩♩ becomes ♩♩♩.

The music is typically divisive: larger two-bar groups are directly audible, and these in turn can be equally subdivided. Players schooled in the West tend to struggle with this rhythm; they are not readily able to make a clear distinction between the units ♩ and ♩., and have to grasp the latter via an 'additive approach'. In other words, in their minds they divide these units into two and three quavers, respectively. The result is usually laborious, while a divisive interpretation (as an irregular 4/4 bar) is lighter and springier. See also the analysis of Example 8, and chapter 6, section 3.

Example 5 (Jolivet, *Trois Temps*) illustrates how divisive rhythm as it is now applied is often enlivened by syncopation. This is indeed only possible thanks to divisive rhythm, since syncopation does not occur in additive rhythm.

EXAMPLE 5

In the fragment from Hauer (*Hölderlingesänge*, Example 6), the rhythm is additive. The text helps to determine a simple principle: important syllables are set to double durations. Thus, small groups of both three and four quavers are created. In a divisive concept the C on 'müd', for instance, would be dotted because the next nuclear point must be equidistant to the previous one.

EXAMPLE 6

und das Herz   ist   mir   müd   vom Wei - nen.

Another example of additive rhythm is found in Pijper's *Piano Sonata* (Example 3). Here the rhythm is determined by a free juxtaposition of rhythmic cells. The pulse unit (the quaver) is not a component of higher equivalent units, but can again be subdivided into equal semiquavers.

Additive rhythm often lies at the basis of polyphonic music and of con-

temporary music in which rhythm fulfills a role as an autonomous constructive element. In higher categories of form, too, we find an analogous distinction between the chain structures and development structures of the classical
masters. Sometimes it is just as difficult to make a definitive division between
additive and divisive rhythms as it is between the traditional terms
homophony and polyphony, and in both cases insight into general stylistic
features is required. Only then can one perceive the agents working in the
background of the music, an awareness that can be of great significance
towards a convincing interpretation.

5

Let us now discuss several rhythmic phenomena that may occur in the music
of today, limiting ourselves to matters that are new in respect to the preceding period.

Floating rhythm. In Western music periodic rhythm has always been of
great importance. The movement of the music – without being too tightly
bound – usually flows in a bedding of periodic pulse units (within the range
of the 'tempo giusto'). This was the situation in the era of the figured bass and
melodic continuation technique, for instance. A particular feature appeared
after about 1750: in the music of the Viennese classical composers, the metri-
cal-rhythmic framework was determined not only by the periodicity of the
pulse units but also by a strong tendency towards symmetry; in other words,
pulse units were bundled into groups of 2, 4 or 8, and answered in principle
by a group of equal length. This was made possible by the strong function of
the cadence in classical harmony, to which not only rhythmic patterns were
subordinate but melodic lines too, changing from the Baroque continuation
type to the period structure of the classical masters. For the sake of conven-
ience let us now leave all exceptions (including early dance music) and transitional phases aside and have a look at the general picture sketched above, in
all its extreme contrasts:

FIGURE I

Baroque period

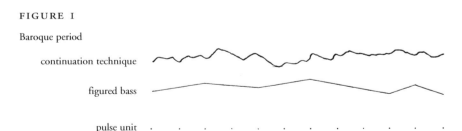

continuation technique

figured bass

pulse unit

Classical period

period structure			
harmonic cadence	T	S	D
pulse unit	. . . .

From the moment that the classical harmonic basis slackened, and particularly during the period of floating tonality (the second half of the nineteenth century), it was to be expected that classical period form would disintegrate. And disintegrate it did, in two directions: composers either reverted to the pre-1750 situation (the Baroque motorial rhythm of the line Reger-Hindemith), or found a different solution in so-called floating rhythm.

'Floating rhythm', of which we are particularly fond of speaking in relation to some of Debussy's works, is really nothing other than a mitigation of the elementary metrical layer. The latter is still present, but the higher rhythmical layer traverses it freely, and is so much more important that one is inclined to forget the metre. This explains why syncopation, which one would expect from such friction, hardly occurs. The same situation was already increasingly manifest in late-romantic music. Classical tonality, however, did not lend itself to an entirely floating rhythm because of the purposiveness of the cadence functions. It could only be realised in the free modality of Debussy, and indeed in free atonality, which is related in terms of rhythm. The composer indicated this in Example 7 (*Voiles*) with the words: 'Dans un rythme sans rigueur et caressant' (in a rhythm without strictness, caressingly). The first two motifs could just as well come on the first beat of the bar, for instance, which indeed happens when they are repeated further on (bar 10 ff). There the motif marked ⸺ (bar 2) is omitted, so that the distance between the first and second motifs is shortened, likewise with few consequences. (If a classical composer shortened material in this way, it often created a hasty impression because the metrical proportions were impaired and harmonic progressions accelerated.) The semiquavers at the end of bar 4 slow the movement down in respect to the preceding demisemiquavers; thus the second motif is lengthened and asymmetry created. The entry of the next melodic idea (*pp expressivo*) is similarly characteristic: the first melodic climax, the note C, does not coincide with a metrical nuclear point. Nevertheless, there is no effect of syncopation due to the extremely weak perceptibility of the metre.

EXAMPLE 7

In Example 78 (Webern, *op. 5*) the mitigation of the metre is caused by the following:

1. many entries of important material do not occur on the first beat. None of the groups A-D begins or ends on the first beat. Where repeats occur (e.g., first violin bar 5, second violin bar 11), literal repetition in respect to the bar-line is avoided;

2. the parts shift polyphonically in relation to one another; this also goes for the crescendo and decrescendo effects;

3. anti-metrical figures (triplets and quintuplets);

4. very frequent changes of tempo.

Like *Voiles*, Webern's *opus 5* is a typical example of floating rhythm: an elementary layer of periodic rhythm remains present – not in the form of the 3/4 metre notated here, but as crotchet units in an extremely slow tempo (29 crotchets per minute!).

In general it may be said that in floating rhythm there is a tendency to mitigate or disrupt the periodicity of the metre *without abolishing it*. It is the rhythmic pendant of the phenomenon of floating tonality. This aim is pursued through the use of complicated anti-metric figures, shifting, pauses, important material beginning on other beats than the first, and particularly changes of tempo. Many compositions, therefore, do not end on the first beat of the bar.

In Bartók and Stravinsky floating rhythm is less common. Even Bartók's rubato melodic technique has quite a different structure in which the metrical layer is indeed often strongly emphasised. This is logical, since in respect to tonality too, it was these very composers, Bartók and Stravinsky, who remained on much firmer ground. In section 6, 7 and 8 the specific aspects of their rhythm will be investigated.

EXAMPLE 8

6

Béla Bartók also continued in the classical tradition with respect to rhythm, although he employed new rhythmic elements which gave his music particular enrichment. One such element originates from a practice current in the Balkans but quite unknown to us, namely that of *aksak* or limping rhythm: two different units are combined in a single rhythmic mode, in the proportion 1 : 1 1/2 (see further chapter 6, section 3).

In the fourth movement of the *Music for Strings, Percussion and Celesta*, these elements are mixed in a striking manner (Example 8). The 2/2 notation is correct for the first four bars, in which the movement speeds up to arrive at bar 5 where, however, a new situation occurs. Here, in triple time, we see two forms of limping modes, one on top of the other:

EXAMPLE 9

The lower mode (violins 3 and 4 plus violas 2) is subdivided, likewise entirely in correspondence with folk music practice in the southern Balkans. It takes the *tupan* (drum) players years to master this non-symmetrical long-short proportion, and it is therefore hardly surprising that performances by Western musicians are rarely satisfying. A correct notation would be: (1 1/2 + 1 1/2 + 1)/4 for the upper part and (1 + 1 1/2 + 1 1/2)/4 for the lower one. It is an east European and Turkish counterpart of our triple bar. The rhythm is divisive. See also Examples 4 and 72.

In the previous movement of the same work, we find a typical example of Bartók's rubato style, with strongly differing note lengths (contrast) and frequent use of the rhythmic mode ♫. (Example 28).

7

In *The Rite* rhythm occupies a primary place – it is the driving force of the music. We have already noted the use of the percussive chord and indeed the larger role of percussion instruments in the orchestra. Let us now investigate an important principle of Stravinsky's rhythm: the continual alternation of constant and inconstant units. In this case the units concerned are rhythmic cells. In the simplest case a single cell appears repeatedly, but interposed by variants to form a *variable ostinato* (Example 10). Here the variant of the cell is nothing other than its shortening to 3/4 and sometimes 4/4: one or two crotchets, respectively, are taken off the end. This example comes from a sec-

MUSIC OF THE TWENTIETH CENTURY

tion of the *Danse sacrale*; the same technique is applied in movements such as *Glorification de l'Elue* and *Evocation des Ancêtres* (see Example 25).

EXAMPLE 10

At the beginning of the *Danse sacrale* we find the same technique, but now using more cells. With the exception of the first bar, which amounts to an introduction, this fragment can be divided into three equivalent parts of 12, 12 and 11 semiquavers, respectively: A-A-B. A comprises two rhythmic cells, (a) and (b); B introduces a third cell (c). Of these three cells, (a) and (c) are inconstant. With respect to (a) this is well illustrated in Example 11: there are three values, namely ♪,♪ and ♪.. Only (b) remains constant: ♫ .

EXAMPLE 11

Note that the cells may borrow material from one another. Thus, (c) is a fusion of (a) and (b). Here again we see a typically Stravinskian combination of constant and inconstant quantities. The same recurs in the polyrhythm of *The Soldier's Tale* (see section 9), but then one on top of the other. The cells are juxtaposed in free order, and the rhythm is therefore additive.

8

Naturally, one could devote an entire chapter on rhythm to Stravinsky. In *The Wedding* yet another procedure is applied, one that is determined by the syllables of the text. Curt Sachs called this 'numerical rhythm'.[4] It is a form of additive rhythm, because the text syllables are linked by means of equivalent note values regardless of the total number of syllables per line. Accents follow the rhythm of the words consistently.

We find a contrasting, very clear divisive rhythm in the fugue subject from *La Création du Monde* by Darius Milhaud (Example 12). The rhythm is strongly syncopated, and the work is also an example of the early influence of jazz (discussed further in chapter 6, section 4).

A much simpler form of rhythm is found in the music of Carl Orff. Although rhythm plays an essential role in his work, he returns to the most elementary musical resources in his pursuit of primary dramatic force and direct, almost magical effects. In his rhythm this results in a frequent use of ostinato, among other things. The monotony of this can create more physio-logical-psychological tensions than musical ones, as is the case in primitive music. Stravinsky's variable ostinato was an essential step forward.

We have already noted other ways of returning to elementary resources in Bartók and Stravinsky. *The Rite* also contains extensive ostinato passages. The cell technique in this work, however, illustrates that quite a different devel-opment of rhythm is possible, namely one in which it comes to play an inde-pendent-constructive role in the musical structure. We will go into this in the following examples, but not before discussing several forms of polyrhythm.

9

POLYRHYTHM. In the light of our observations on time categories (section 2), polymetre is nothing other than a form of polyrhythm. We can even say that in certain cases polyrhythm is suggested without being written down (as a single part can be written to suggest two). If we compare Examples 2 and 5, it appears that in the first case the three rhythmic layers form one and the same movement, while in Jolivet the metrical layer (= periodic rhythm) func-tions as a basis of tension for the rhythmic layer. Syncopation is created. Such musical elements, not (completely) realised but nonetheless perceptible, are of great significance. As the author of a novel may sometimes achieve more through the suggestion of a few words than a lengthy description, the com-poser too has many and subtle resources of creating musical relationships and tensions. What we normally refer to as polyrhythm is indeed realised; in other words, two or more parts lead their own rhythmic lives. Let us look more closely at some characteristic forms of this.

In the fugue from *La Création du monde* (Example 12), there are two layers: (1) the fugal entries and (2) the percussion and piano. The fugal entries are organised in a five-bar pattern. The piano chords come once every three crotchets and therefore suggest a 3/4 metre. After the fifth chord, however, the distance is lengthened by a crotchet, and the game starts again from the very

EXAMPLE 12

beginning. The pattern therefore embraces four bars (5 times 3 + 1). The same goes for the percussion part, which consists of three rhythmic cells separated by a crotchet rest, repeated every four bars in a certain order (A, B, A, B, C). The structure of the piano and percussion parts, while forming a single whole, is nevertheless differentiated. Both layers together, with their 4-bar pattern, clash constantly with the 5-bar fugal pattern. This shifting causes each fugue entry to come at a different moment in relation to the percussion. The rhythm of both layers is very metrically conceived, so that the entirety, partly as a result of tight repetition, is more schematic than the polyrhythm of Stravinsky. The continual metrical shifting reinforces the impression of linearity. This is indeed necessary since, unlike for instance the fugue from Bartók's *Music for Strings, Percussion and Celesta*, the melodic life of this fugue is secondary. Primary is the whole arrangement of metrical patterns; the melodic lines are grafted onto them, as it were.

More developed in terms of rhythm is Stravinsky's earlier work *The Soldier's Tale* (1918). The composer has a predilection for the combination of constant and inconstant rhythms, so that the 'shifting variant' of the various parts is greater than in Milhaud's technique. In Example 13 there are three layers: the bass and violin (layer A) repeat a direct-constant rhythmic figure; the percussion (layer B) has an indirect-constant figure: the group ♫♩♩♩ alternates with ♫♩♩♩♪ (interpolated quaver rest). Above this, finally, is the variable rhythm of layer C, consisting of a melody with additive rhythm. The combination of constant and variable rhythms occurs frequently in this work, but always in different proportions.

EXAMPLE 13

In Example 14, from Pijper's *Sonata for two Pianos*, the upper stave could in itself be a 3/4 metre (♩♩♩♩♩♩). But it is a 6/8 with syncopation, as illustrated, because the 6/8 metre of the middle stave predominates (through the harmonic progressions and the tritone leaps in the bass part). The lower stave has a neutral series of semiquavers and could therefore have been in 6/8 (♫♫♫♫♫♫). The melodic profile, however, suggests groups of four semiquavers. The question of why it is not written in 3/4 (♫♫♫♫♫♫), which would simplify the score, is answered by the fact that a 4/8 metre occurs directly before and after the fragment in the example. Four-eights is therefore correct: this weak duple secondary metre functions as a link between the preceding and succeeding material. Once again it is evident that an analysis of rhythm must be determined by many factors, such as the harmonic and melodic development, and nuances of dynamics, colour, register, etc.

EXAMPLE 14

10

The first composer of the twentieth century to *consciously* assign a primary structural role to rhythm was Olivier Messiaen, who liked to call himself a *rythmicien.* He built on the foundation laid by Stravinsky, but enriched his technique with new elements mainly derived from the ancient Hindus and the isorhythm of the Middle Ages. The lesson of *The Soldier's Tale* (polyrhythm and ostinato technique) was worked out as follows in *L'Ange aux Parfums:*

EXAMPLE 15

The bass has an ostinato motif, called *pédale rythmique*. Above it is a rhythmic canon in retrograde: the rhythm of the right hand is adopted in retrograde by the left hand. This canon is continually repeated, but each time the middle part shifts up a quaver in relation to the upper part. Since the length of the bass ostinato differs, the three parts continually shift in relation to one another.

Also common in Messiaen's music is the so-called *rythme non-rétrogradable*, referring to a rhythmic formula that remains the same when retrograded. The first three notes in the bass feature such a rhythm (♩ ♩.♩); it is immediately followed by the diminution (♫.♪) and then the original version again. This entire bass pattern too, which is repeated, is therefore *non-rétrogradable!*

EXAMPLE 16

Fourteen years later, in 1953, the *Livre d'Orgue* was published. Though Messiaen's style had changed considerably, he remained true to himself in his treatment of rhythm. The cell technique of *The Rite*, with its constant and inconstant quantities, is further developed in the preceding fragment (Example 16).

The first three bars comprise an exposition of three cells. Messiaen liked to speak of *personnages rythmiques*, and gave rhythmic formulas their own individual character. The rhythms used here, for example, come from an ancient Hindu manuscript; the first (♩. ♫) is the so-called *pratâpaçekhara*, which means 'the power that radiates from the forehead' (see also chapter 6, section 6). The technique is quite simple: the cells A, B and C occur in every conceivable combination in six different sequences; cell C is constant, while A gradually becomes longer through the addition of a demisemiquaver, and B becomes shorter through subtraction of the same value.

This process of addition and subtraction brings us to another of Messiaen's innovations, the *valeur ajoutée*, a term referring to the addition of half of the smallest rhythmic value. In practice this is usually a short duration added to a rhythmic pattern of, on average, much longer values. In the first cell the smallest duration is the semiquaver, and the *valeur ajoutée* is therefore a demisemiquaver. Although in our example each note is augmented by this value, this is not always the case. The *valeur ajoutée* lent Messiaen's rhythm a hitherto unknown litheness: instead of traditional regular augmentation and diminution (in which original durations were doubled or halved), an element of irregularity was created which may lend great charm to the music. Melodic material may thus subtly slow down or speed up, canon technique may employ irregular augmentations and diminutions, etc. The asymmetric forms that thus arose are not only known and cherished in India but in other regions, too.

The piano work *Cantéyodjayâ* is a veritable reference work of rhythmic procedures. Below is an example of rhythmic breathing (*anacrouse, accent, muette*), with an inexact augmentation by means of the *valeur ajoutée*.

EXAMPLE 17

Two slightly older contemporaries of Messiaen, Hermann Heiss and Boris Blacher, must not go unmentioned. Heiss wrote a *Tonbewegungslehre* in which he too attempted to apply existing contrapuntal principles to the purely rhythmic element (*Schlagsätze*). Blacher introduced the principle of *variable Metren* which, when treated with levity and imagination, gave rise to fascinating rhythmic structures despite the fact that it avoided the real rhythmic problem. In short his principle amounted to the following: the size and sequence of the bars is determined by a given series; the simplest arithmetic series produces, for instance, the sequence 2/8, 3/8, 4/8, 5/8, 6/8, 7/8,..., but retrograde and other permutations may also be employed. The continually changing bars are not marked by accents but by the melodic and harmonic structure of the music (*Second Piano Concerto*):

EXAMPLE 18

Needless to say, in the first instance the variable metre created formal problems, prompting the question: how can such rhythm be integrated into the whole while avoiding juxtaposition of totally different principles of structure? Notable, incidentally, is that works by Blacher without variable metre possess the same rhythmic sparkle.

Less striking, but no less important was Webern's treatment of rhythm, especially in his later works. Although he retained a simple metrical notation, his rhythm, in contrast to that of Schönberg and Berg, gained a great degree of structural independence. By means of register changes, interval relations, dynamics, tempo changes, phrasing and shifting accents, Webern created a subtle spectacle of rhythmic nuance. In Example 93 contrapuntal variants are also applied, such as diminution and retrograde. The beginning of *op. 24* demonstrates how Webern achieved a fascinating rhythmic interplay with simple but efficient means, by juxtaposing four small rhythmic cells which are subsequently retrograded (Example 19).

EXAMPLE 19

Rhythmically speaking, Pierre Boulez's first works rested on the foundations laid by Messiaen and Stravinsky. However, he reproached Messiaen for a lack of compositional unity between his highly developed rhythm and an all too simple harmonic style. Inspired particularly by Webern's example, Boulez attempted to integrate this rhythmic enrichment in the musical whole by adopting a rigorously polyphonic style in terms of both rhythm and melody. Through frequent application of irrational proportions and the pursuit of continual variation, his music became more complex than ever.

The opening of the third movement of the *Second Piano Sonata* (1948) presents a simple example of the use of rhythmic cells (Example 20). The material is threefold: A ♪♪♩ ; B ♪♪♪ ♩. = A with *valeur ajoutée*; C a sforzando chord at the end of bar 2. Structure:

1a. exposition (bar 1-2): cells A, B and C;
1b. faster movement (bar 3-4): cell A compressed;
1c. slower movement (bar 5): cell B shortened;

EXAMPLE 20

2a. new element (bar 6): irrational proportion (2/3) in respect to ♪;

2b. faster movement (bar 7-8): cells A and C overlapped;

2c. slower movement (bar 9-10): cell A with interpolated quaver rest.

The three quavers of cell A are heard in 2/3 proportion (♪♪♪), but the succeeding fragment (not included here) introduces the proportions 3/2 (♫♩) and 4/3 (♩♩♩), presenting refined possibilities for creating rhythmic structures. Meanwhile, traditional relations to other musical elements are evident: the rhythmic curve of faster and slower movement, for example, is related to crescendo and decrescendo, respectively.

The examples by Stravinsky, Messiaen and Webern have been fruitful. The loose, additive juxtaposition of increasingly varied cells lends this music great suppleness. This is reinforced by the many changes of tempo fondly prescribed by Boulez. Despite all differences, it is tempting to draw a comparison with Debussy!

But the very next year, 1949, saw the appearance of Messiaen's *Études rythmiques*, in which the composer systematically treated the various musical elements entirely autonomously. A new stage had been reached. The problems presented by this dissociation of the elements of music will be dealt with in the discussion of serial music in chapter 8.

CHAPTER THREE

Melody

I

How many attempts have been made to define the concept of melody? It is not our intention here to add another new and undoubtedly limited one to those already current. For we can assume that any definition of melody is related to our general musical attitude. How very different must the concept of melody be, or must have been, among peoples living beyond or before Western polyphony, in comparison for instance to the ideas of our nineteenth-century forefathers! Jean-Jacques Rousseau anticipated that century when he wrote: 'Melody arises from harmony.' And however much those same forefathers focused their expressive urge on the melodic, the indispensable basis for melody was nonetheless formed by harmony.

The disintegration of this harmonic system, however, brought one consequence: the melodic element began to collapse and was thus in need of revision. Classical period form, for example, was replaced immediately by melody moving more freely in relation to metrical nuclear points, harmonic cadences and symmetrical structures.

A far more important outcome was that the melodic element slowly but surely became primary, a development which was often misunderstood. This is not to say that musical expression became even more concentrated on the melodic than it had been before, but that the melodic, or more generally the *melic* element, began to play the same structural role as that previously assigned to harmony. For many composers it became a constructive factor of great significance.

Once more, it was the dodecaphonic world which applied this most thoroughly. The structural principle that emerged was exactly the opposite of its predecessor: the melic element – a succession of notes – came to determine much of the construction and sequence of the vertical sound.

But elsewhere too, the constructional role of the melic element came to the fore in many shapes. We must bear in mind, however, that the disintegration into elements that typified all developments of the past one hundred and fifty years also applied to the strictly melodic. Melodies became motifs, motifs in turn could be reduced to intervals (or incidentally even to single notes), and from these small units larger structures were determined.

2

Before examining several examples from the work of modern composers we should give some thought to general differences of melodic treatment among the 'great three': Schönberg, Stravinsky and Bartók.

Schönberg continued along the path that had led from Beethoven via Wagner to the late romantics, employing strongly concentrated expressive units in which chromaticism and wide intervals served to push expressivity to the extreme. It was hardly a coincidence that Schönberg himself was to model his later melodic style increasingly on traditional procedures. Here again the conflict of this most complicated of personalities emerges strikingly. Yet the 12-note technique was to become an important stimulus for many composers to revitalise the melodic element in their own individual ways.

Bartók's use of melody, like that of Schönberg, was inconceivable without the historical background. We should bear in mind what has been said about him in chapter 1, section 4. However, in order to revitalise the somewhat worn melodic style of late romanticism, he also turned to other resources: folk music. Fresh blood from the Balkans, from Spain, and from jazz and early polyphony was to play a significant role in the hands of many composers.

Stravinsky also ventured into folklore, but his attitude was quite different. In his music, melody was never a means towards intimate, subjective expression. As far as he made use of folkloric elements, he did so precisely in pursuit of the non-subjective, the extra-personal. Once more we see the astounding genius of a man who literally transformed all that he assimiliated to serve that single, great concept behind his work. In his melodic style too, whether folkloric or not, Stravinsky was the great antithesis of Schönberg and Bartók; his example had far-reaching consequences.

3

In exploring new melodic paths it was again Debussy who had taken the lead. Of great influence on his approach to melody was one particular aspect of his work, that of floating rhythm (see chapter 2, section 5). His lines, almost weightless, originated without a strong relation to metrical-harmonic stress. This 'quasi-weightlessness' had another side to it too: in Debussy's works such melodic writing had become completely detached from classical thematic functions, in accordance with his attitude to musical form in general (see introduction, section 5). His melody had therefore also been liberated from the emphatic-expressive load that continued to play such a prominent role in German developments, acquiring an almost ornamental significance, to use a dangerous word. The traditional thematic function meant that the main themes of a work were directly related to one another, either as variants or by means of contrast, lending a great degree of unity to all thematic material. Since Debussy abandoned this generative, thematic concept, the question arises of how the master created the required unity in large-scale works.

Many roads lead to Rome, and we can look at one of them in *La Mer*:

EXAMPLE 21

Above are the four main large melodic forms of the first movement. One is struck by the widely divergent structure, a divergence accentuated moreover by the fact that each of the four melodies has a different tempo. There is no symmetrical recapitulation of an opening theme to end the work in the classical manner. Neither is there mention of a development!

Four different melodies, four tempos, and yet unity. Upon closer examination all this material proves to be very similar in terms of interval structure. The major 2nd and minor 3rd predominate by far, and are often joined to make a 4th, whether or not filled in to produce a tetrachord:

EXAMPLE 22

The many little separate motifs in the work also prove to possess largely the same interval structure. Indeed, the interval as such acquires constructive significance. It ensures, as it were, that the material of these most divergent melodic lines remains consistent. Just one example by Beethoven is sufficient to illustrate the very different structure of classical themes:

EXAMPLE 23

Of importance in this theme are the opening motif ♪♫♫♩|♩ and the melod-ic curve ⌒, two elements which are extended to create a larger, strongly cohesive unit. The fact that the 4th in bar 1 becomes a 6th in bar 2 and an octave in bar 3 is of only secondary importance: in principle the theme is recognisable by means of the above two elements.

Quite the contrary applied to Debussy: here the interval was primary, and the rhythm and curve of the motif were therefore much freer. This was a first step on the road to athematic music.

4

La Mer is instructive in other respects too. The intervals of the major 2nd and minor 3rd, together amounting to a perfect 4th, form an ancient melodic nucleus in the history of music. Some ethnomusicologists assume that it was the basis of later pentatonism, in which two such nuclei are combined at a rather obvious distance from the two centres:

EXAMPLE 24

But this was already familiar among peoples with a much higher level of musical development. Pentatonism therefore formed the recognisable begin-ning of an endless modal development in which the division of the octave into seven parts was to become predominant. The ancient melodic nucleus, however, crops up again and again: we find it in Gregorian chant, in children's and folk songs, and now... in *La Mer*, the work of one of the most sophisti-cated composers of our time.

Thereafter this nucleus became a familiar sight, beginning with *The Rite* (1912). And what entered the stage in Debussy became quite clear in Stravinsky. For one of the first reactions to the disintegration of classical tonality was the search for other cohesive means. This had already begun in the nineteenth century, and was manifest for the time being in increasing interest in medieval modal elements. But this remained superficial, grafted onto the classical diatonic basis. Debussy was the first to go much further, by... going much further back beyond early modality (see chapter 6, section 2).

The increasing significance of that elementary building block, the interval, as a basis for melodic structure indicates that in this field too modern composers were reverting to elementary matters. A category of *pre-modal melody* emerged, essentially monophonic and often comprising intervals arising from one central note. The pendulum movement around a central note in three of the four themes quoted from *La Mer* also points in this direction. Naturally, the vertical sound environment of such melodies did nothing to alter the primary melic focus or the role of the interval in the same.

5

We have already discussed *The Rite*, and elsewhere the variable ostinato that the work employed (see chapter 2, section 7). Here is an example of melodic structure by means of this technique:

EXAMPLE 25

Stravinsky's melodic writing is always an additive juxtaposition of short motifs to create a larger, hardly cohesive whole. As in this case, he frequently embarked from a single motif which appears in varying rhythmic shapes. In contrast to this extreme sobriety is another type of melody which is much richer, and which can be found in each of the composer's periods. It is characterised by an abundance of ornamentation, whether written out or not, and, particularly in the neo-classical works, by the pursuit of greater coherence. This is illustrated by a passage from the *Violin Concerto* in D major (1931):

EXAMPLE 26

This passage also reveals two other features. Firstly, it forms a good example of the composer's polyvalent technique: although the piece is clearly in F ♯ minor, each part goes its own way within this mean, functionally independent of the other parts. Secondly, we should note that this type of melody, despite its baroque model, is quite different from the baroque melody of Hindemith. The reason lies in the whimsical and far more differentiated rhythm of Stravinsky. Hindemith preferred regular rhythms with continual repetitions of typical rhythmic modes such as ♫ which were so common in the baroque era.

The implied polyphony (end of bar 3 to bar 5) and the *Sekundgang*[1] are typical of their baroque origins. This again is frequently encountered in Hindemith, as is the baroque melodic structure comprising head – elaboration – cadence.

6

Another common phenomenon was *declamatory melody*, which had become increasingly popular from the sixteenth century onwards and was therefore hardly new. With the (spoken) text as point of departure, the melody attempted to translate its inflexions, accents and length proportions more or less exactly into pitches. This became easier as the notes became less dependent on harmonic-metrical laws, and it is therefore obvious that declamatory melody was used increasingly in our period. In German-speaking countries in particular, it was also transferred to instrumental melody, and as a parallel to Debussy's floating rhythm something was created that could be described as 'melody with free articulation'. Common features of this type of instrumental melody were rhythmic and dynamic contrast, wide leaps, and an attempt to escape from an all too clear sense of the bar (by means of syncopation, anti-metrical figures, etc.). The most conspicuous difference in respect to Debussy's free melody was the evident will to create melodic expression. In this respect the German aesthetic, in comparison to that of Debussy, was essentially more bound to the romantic tradition until far into the twentieth century. Thus, this desire to push melodic *Ausdruck* to the extreme by employing the model of human speech.

An example of normal declamatory melody to text is not included here, since the vocal works of Schönberg and Alban Berg are full of it, and there is no essential difference in respect to Wagner. What we do include is a special case: the *Sprechgesang* from Schönberg's *Pierrot lunaire* (1912):

EXAMPLE 27

Here we see a new attempt to create an idiosyncratic, autonomous speech melody that is neither speech nor song. The given durations and pitches follow the inflexion of the text in a free approximation of normal declamation. While the notes marked **x** are to be performed with rhythmic precision, the given pitches are free, in so far that after the initial attack they are to be departed from immediately in rising or falling portamenti. While the normal intonation of speech is certainly not imitated, we do come much closer to the great wealth of inflexion of spoken language, in what is a typical example of the expressionist pursuit of *Affektsteigerung* through extreme means. A good impression of an instrumental melody with a declamatory character is offered by the flute part. Such melodies occurred frequently in free atonality and later music. The pitch and rhythm of *Sprechgesang* (Schönberg used the terms *Sprechmelodie* and *Sprechstimme*) was notated much more strictly than most speech melody. Of interest in this context is the opinion of Erwin Stein, one of Schönberg's first pupils: in his book *Orpheus in New Guises* (Rockliff, London 1953) he claimed that the performer, despite the absolute pitches given in the score, had a certain degree of freedom, and that it was of importance to observe only the given curve and the mutual relationships of the intervals. But in most performances even this has proved to be unattainable as yet.

There was therefore mention of a mutual permeation of instrumental and vocal music. On the one hand, many vocal melodies of the new era were instrumentally conceived, while on the other hand instrumental melody proved to bear characteristics of vocal-declamatory origin.

7

All this goes to show that freer melodic development was pursued along many paths; Debussy's freely floating melody, Stravinsky's ornamentation, and the declamatory melody of the Viennese School were the first fruits of this endeavour. Not yet mentioned is the so-called *rubato melody*, a type found frequently in Bartók, but also in Hindemith. There are, incidentally, various remarkable stylistic similarities between these two so divergent composers. Despite the indication 'rubato' (in Hindemith: 'frei im Zeitmaß'), the technique of rubato melody is essentially different from the free melody of Debussy, since remarkably enough it is strongly related to the metrical bedding. Example 28 from Bartók's *Music for Strings, Percussion and Celesta* makes this clear:

EXAMPLE 28

Characteristic here are the emphases on the metrical layer, strongly divergent and contrasting durations, thetic motifs and dynamic accents. The rhythmic mode ♩♫. appears very frequently in Bartók's music. His thetic motif structure is probably related to the inflexion of the Hungarian language, with the accent on the first syllable. (See also Example 30, the rubato melody from *Mathis der Maler*.)

Bartók's rubato melody was the antithesis of 'tempo giusto' melody, of strictly metrical organisation; in Hindemith it contrasted to the similarly strict, motorial melodic writing of the Baroque, a style so familiar that no example is required.

In section 1 we already noted the disintegration of melody in the twentieth century. Lengthy and cohesive melodic lines were rarely pursued; on the one hand, a clear harmonic-metrical basis for this was lacking, and on the other the relationship between melody and accompaniment had in many cases changed. Both could be derived from one and the same series in the music of the dodecaphonists in particular; they were therefore much more closely related in terms of structure, while the two elements continually interacted. This in turn stimulated a strongly motivic and at the same time instrumental manner of writing (in the case of songs). Yet there were sufficient exceptions to this rule, and in the remainder of this chapter some examples of more extensive and largely monophonic melodies will be discussed, enabling us to deal with certain hitherto unmentioned aspects at the same time.

The melody forming the main thread of Béla Bartók's *Sixth String Quartet* is introduced in a monophonic exposition by the viola (Example 29). It is a typical example of 'the other side' of Bartók, in which the rhythmic impulse withdrew to the background and expressiveness lay mainly in a strongly chromatic idiom. Of the four segments of the melody, A and B are marked by strongly condensed chromaticism, while C and D bring contrast through wider leaps. Characteristic chromatic features also found among the Viennese composers are:

1. A structural element by means of which the most important note of each of the four segments (G♯, C♯, D, A♭, respectively) does not occur in the preceding segment.

2. The melodic formula that is so very typical of Bartók: the crosswise relationship in 2nds (——), avoiding direct repetition of a preceding pitch. Both (1) and (2) are characteristic of chromatic expansion, the pursuit of *completion* of a chromatic field.

3. The above-mentioned *Sekundgang*, which is largely chromatic. Note the falling and rising chromatic line beginning in bar 6!

EXAMPLE 29

Despite this chromaticism, and in contrast to Viennese atonality, the whole remains in an extended tonal environment due to the 5th relationship of three of the four main notes, the final cadence with a characteristic descending 4th, small leaps and the function of the leading note.

In other respects too the melody is bound up with tradition: its symmetrical structure, the melodic climax coinciding with the dynamic and rhythmic climax, the ensuing slow relaxation in the melodic sequence of segment C and dynamic and rhythmic decline, and finally, generally speaking, the inversion tendency of the second half in respect to the first, giving rise to an antecedent-consequent phrase relationship. The resulting highly coherent effect is underlined by the similar nature of the melodic cells (see ——— and ------). Note too the enlarged intervals in segment D, coupled to a broader rhythmic movement, something really already suggested when the two chromatic *Sekundgänge* part company in bar 6.

The celebrated melody from Paul Hindemith's *Mathis der Maler* belongs to the rubato group, the general characteristics of which have already been discussed. The orchestra plays in unison, reinforced by the wind from the end of bar 3. The type of structure is familiar:

EXAMPLE 30

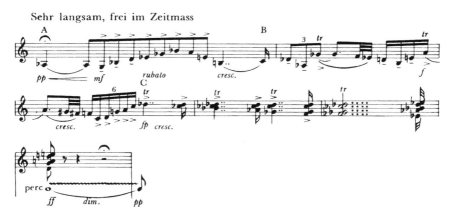

A. In an initial impulse in bar 1 a first definition of curve, intervals, rhythm and tempo is presented. Ascending 3rds in minor triads contrast with the larger descending 4ths.

B. This material is developed in the main body of the melody. The initial curve (rising-falling) is repeated in three smaller waves and indeed in the melody as a whole. The top of each wave goes to make up the minor triad again (G♭-A-D♭); the 4ths are now used to create rising lines, each of which also has an accelerated rhythmic movement.

C. The end has the effect of a cadence. A *Sekundgang* makes its first appearance, descending against a repeated D♭. The dotted rhythm already announced in (B) now predominates.

Rhythmically speaking, the accelerated movement in (B) is retarded in (C). Tension generated by the thrust is not released by the dotted rhythm but rather by the rustling of the percussion, which therefore fulfills a most essential role in the melodic proceedings! As in Bartók we see strongly developed chromaticism (the twelve chromatic notes are introduced at the very beginning) which, however, is embedded in the tonal framework A♭-D♭. Again there is mention of the same type of climax, though more accentuated.

In Messiaen's *Les Corps glorieux* for organ, an extensive monophonic melody presents a modern interpretation of a Gregorian chant (*Salve Regina*):

EXAMPLE 31

EXAMPLE 32

The given fragment is based on two modes (see chapter 4, section 3): A and A1 are in mode 2, and B and B1 in mode 7. The contrast between A and B is mainly determined by this modal difference, since B is actually a variant of A. In comparison with the preceding examples the type of melody is quite different. There is no attempt to create a cohesive curve of tension and relaxation. The rhythm and the juxtaposition of small melodic cells are additive, and a remarkable feature of this is the frequent recurrence of the same cells, such as the cadence of A and its variant in B (Example 32), thus forming a continuation of Stravinsky's variable ostinato technique.

The descending tritone, particularly A♭-D, is the most important of the intervals that continually recur (——), being employed no less than 22 times in our fragment! Note also the correspondence between the two descending tritones at the end of each phrase (----) . Despite the fact that this is a purely instrumental melody, its compass remains limited to a 9th. The modal framework also imposes a very limited action radius, which is why the rhythm of this melody is so important. The free and highly supple rhythmic structure erases the last traces of metrical organisation; the barlines serve only to separate segments of the structure.

Although Pijper's *Sonatine II* for piano employs one of Messiaen's modes (no. 2), the work is based on quite different premises. Here we encounter Pijper's germ-cell technique:

EXAMPLE 33

EXAMPLE 34

Bar 1 introduces this cell, a four-note motif that — according to the composer's intentions at least — is to determine the melodic-harmonic and rhythmic development. We can imagine the germ cell as a seed from which the whole plant grows organically. One is therefore to assume an absence of *a priori* existing form schemes: each form is entirely defined by the properties already present in the germ cell. Let us examine what happens.

In terms of rhythm the germ cell is a mode, while melodically it consists of two descending 4ths at a distance of a minor 3rd from one another. The entire proceedings quickly prove to revolve around triads that are interrelated by this minor 3rd (A in Example 34). When amalgamated, an octatonic scale arises, equivalent to Messiaen's second mode. Bar 4 (Example 33) brings the first peak: a composite chord (see chapter 4, section 7) and the triad on D are heard for the first time. The ensuing relaxation coincides with a lengthened bar (4/8 instead of 3/8). From bar 6 a new ascending line reaches a peak in bar 8 with another composite chord and a new triad based on F. A kind of modulation follows, brought about quite traditionally by a pivot chord, and indeed the octatonic scale is subsequently transposed up a semitone. Figure B in Example 34 belongs to both scales and therefore functions as the pivot. The episode in bars 8-12 contrasts strongly with the preceding: the mode is transposed and we hear neither chordal density nor the rhythm of the germ cell. Instead, a rapid semiquaver movement is hurried along by a shortened bar (5/16 instead of 3/8). This linear movement resolves in a long A (bar 12) which again has a pivot function, and the accumulated tension is released in a brilliantly spread composite chord in the initial mode. Only the (opening) triad on Ab would be required to close the circle of relationships based on the minor 3rd.

This passage is a wonderful example of primary melic-rhythmic organisation, in which the vertical sound, incorporated in this static-modal environment, has no constructive role. The melodic framework moves (in broken chords, for instance) through a bedding of vertical sounds that is modally determined and that does not allow any development.[2]

Webern is more difficult than any other composer when it comes to analysing a single aspect of his music – in this case his melodic technique. The analysis of Example 93 demonstrates that all musical elements are incorporated in the entire structure in a highly developed and autonomous manner. We must therefore ask the reader to supplement the following remarks on the composer's *op. 30* with what is said at that point. In terms of melody several striking differences in respect to the preceding examples may be noted: (1) extreme economy and sobriety; (2) far-reaching motivic disintegration: though found elsewhere, it is reinforced here by changes of register and tone colour, and rapid dynamic contrasts:

1. Economy was of course a slogan in the dodecaphonic camp; it was one of the main *raisons d'être* of the 12-note series. But Webern went further, splitting his series into three motifs of four notes that determine the entire work both horizontally and vertically. Moreover, the third motif is closely related to the first (both have two minor 2nds and one minor 3rd). Finally, the second

motif proves to possess the same intervals, namely two minor 3rds and one minor 2nd! We therefore encounter an extreme degree of unity in respect to intervals, motivic structure and vertical sound. Is composition possible with fewer resources?

2. This sobriety is compensated by differentiation arising through tone colour, register, tempo, dynamics and other musical elements; the characteristic use of basis intervals in wide leaps may also be included here. If we try to approach Webern without sensitivity to the shades of his tonal palette, then the door will close on us. As in Messiaen's melody we cannot expect to find any classical melodic development. This 'theme' is constructed in perfect symmetry and forms a cohesive musical area in which the movement of motifs is characterised by a balance of power. The fact that a cohesive whole is created despite this differentiation and disintegration is probably due to the strongly unified material and the symmetrical, blocklike manner in which the four phrase segments are juxtaposed.

Finally, the solo for bass flute that ends Boulez's *Le Marteau sans Maître* (Example 35). We are again far from classical 12-note technique, and the strict serial form of the earlier *Structures* for two pianos is also replaced here by a greater freedom, without sacrificing the general principles of the new idiom. Differentiation is taken to the extreme:

1. The motivic-rhythmic structure of traditional themes is obviously completely abandoned. In the example by Webern it was still discernible, but Boulez followed Debussy in this respect and departed completely from classical motivic structures. Instead, the work is built up from melodic cells that continually appear in different rhythmic guises.

2. Although a certain preference for the major 7th, minor 9th and the tritone is noticeable, there is great diversity of intervals. This again is a striking contrast to Webern, though both have wide leaps of atonal melodic writing in common.

3. The entire compass of the instrument is exploited: three octaves, from G to G^3.

4. Rhythmically and dynamically this music is highly variegated, although the dynamics are not independent but usually geared to the melodic curve. Beside Debussy, Stravinsky was the guiding light, as is demonstrated by such matters as the rich ornamentation.

Variegation, therefore, was rife. Where it was 'written out', as in the present case, the score inevitably became complicated, indeed too complicated. The notation of rhythm, for instance, suggested a precision that could no longer be achieved in practice. Yet Boulez pursued suppleness and a fluctuating tempo: elsewhere in the work he speaks of 'mouvements respiratoires'. Here, more than ever, the notation is inhibiting. Several years later he attempted to achieve his aim by introducing a new element: greater freedom for the performer.

Though at first acquaintance it may seem difficult to make heads or tails of this variegation, further investigation does bring recognisable structural elements to light.

In the first place certain combinations of intervals continually recur, as the first eight notes go to illustrate. Between the second and eighth notes are the perfect 4th, major 7th, minor 7th, major 2nd, major 7th and perfect 5th. This amounts to interval reversion, therefore, in which the second half (except the major 7th) also employs interval inversion: the perfect 4th becomes a perfect 5th, etc. This passage includes many such cell structures. This same nonetuplet has eight different notes, a chromatic 8-note field, which determines as it were the subsequent situation. And although this is not 12-note music, *chromatic completion* is nonetheless pursued in other ways: the notes B♭, F♯, G♯ and A, not included in the eight-note field, thereafter become the main melodic notes.

EXAMPLE 35

While common intervals thus lend cohesion to the elementary material, three segments (A, B and C) are evident in a higher structural layer:

A is typified by a very wide compass, very different durations, and the recurring melodic peak on G with a fall to B♭ (bars 1-2 and 5-6). These descending leaps are characteristic: G-B♭ in bar 2 becomes G-F♯ in bar 3;

bar 5 enlarges G-B♭ by an octave, and bar 7 introduces a descending tenth to reach the lowest note of the passage, played in the high register of the bass flute.

B contrasts strongly with A, employing the middle register, a narrower compass, less extreme contrasts of duration, and a much lower dynamic level. The exuberant melodic exclamation of the beginning has now flowed back into a static pendulous movement within a field of 3rds (Example 36). This section ends on G, the lowest note on the bass flute.

EXAMPLE 36

C restores the wide contrasts of dynamics and duration. The climax on G♯, however, does not attain the original heights. A new (10-note) field at the beginning determines the position of the notes that follow, which create a sort of echo of the field. This does not change until bar 15, and in bar 16 the note A comes to the fore. The rising 7th in bar 16 corresponds to that in bars 14-15 (C-B) and bar 19 (E-E♭). And so we detect a mirror, which we can place in the middle of bar 16. At first the intervals are precisely in retrograde, although this gradually becomes freer. The extremes are marked by the notes G and G♯ (bars 12 and 21, respectively).

The position of the climax in segment C, just before the end and followed by a release of tension, is a traditional trait. This also goes for the repetition of the descending major 6th (G♯-B) which is already prepared for in the preceding bars (G-B♭). Another familiar feature is the melodic 'gradualness': for instance the transition from A to B (with E♭ as pivot note) and from B to C (with the low G as pivot note, only disappearing in bar 15). Finally, note the remarkable preference for the notes G-D and the interval of a 5th:

EXAMPLE 37

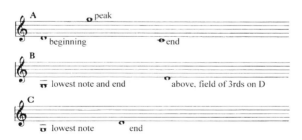

CHAPTER FOUR

Simultaneity

I

For some ten centuries the European tradition has been particularly distinguished from other music cultures by the phenomenon of simultaneity. The eighteenth century in particular saw the erection of a magnificent edifice in which harmony undisputedly ruled over all other musical elements. The great romantics wielded harmony as an expressive means of the very finest sort. Even theoreticians were content, for here lay an open field allowing systematic excavation. Music could now be 'explained', and functions and cadences, modulations and alterations obediently joined ranks in a well-ordered and logical whole. Ever since, generations of musicians have been and indeed continue to be trained in what we call 'the theory of harmony'. While new discoveries in this field would hardly seem likely, the reverse side of the medal is twofold:

1. The theory of harmony as it is understood today covers only a few centuries of the entire development of 'simultaneity' in the broad sense of the word;

2. Even more fatal to unimpeded rhythmic and/or melodic development than this restriction is the fact that simultaneity plays such a primary role in our experience. Here, music reacts like any other living organism: one-sided development of a single aspect can work to the detriment of other ones.

Only now are we able to view these matters more clearly. A deeper study of some Eastern cultures has made us aware of our inferiority in terms of melody and rhythm. But these are indeed cultures in which simultaneity is of only secondary significance! While it cannot be ruled out that we Westerners have a natural disposition for harmony, it is at the same time true that thoughtful musical training can protect us from one-sidedness and atrophy.

Once there was a time when we took care with our dosage of dissonances, and now we do likewise with our consonances. However the case may be, as long as we remain oversensitive to such phenomena, simultaneity will continue to form one of the main problems of Western music.

What did the twentieth century achieve in this field? By now we realise that there is no simple answer to this question, having experienced every aspect ranging from uncompromising counterpoint (Hindemith in the 1920s), in which simultaneity was an entirely random result of horizontal textures, to the most cautious, subtle expressiveness of Webern's chromaticism.

In general we can say of the initial period that one tendency was widespread from Debussy to Schönberg, namely the abandonment of the concept of harmonic functions. The chord was considered not as a function, as a link in a cadence progression, but purely as a sound in itself: sometimes for the sake of an entirely free music that floated before Debussy's eyes, sometimes for the sake of expressiveness driven to the extreme, as in the free atonal works of Schönberg and Webern. The consequence was an enormous increase in diversity and complexity: structures based on 3rds were abandoned, chromatic elements were incorporated as autonomous colours, chords of five, six or more notes became common, modal elements and parallel movement were introduced, etc.

It was not until after World War I that a general reaction occurred in the form of a more austere approach and renewed attention to linearity. By then the dissonance had been emancipated once and for all. Schönberg said that dissonances are only further removed consonances in the overtone series. Hindemith arrived at practically the same conclusion from a different angle by saying that the difference between consonance and dissonance is only gradual. Just for once these two opposites, and with them most modern composers, agreed with one another.

Theoretically, however, the problem was not so simple. For centuries, physicists, physiologists and psychologists had sought an explanation, usually considering the interval as an autonomous sound removed from its musical context. Classical musical theory did the same and arrived at the following classification:
- perfect consonances: 1, 8, 5, 4;
- imperfect consonances: 3, 6 (major and minor);
- dissonances: the remaining intervals.

Acoustical theory largely maintains that dissonance is the result of physiological reactions to the phenomenon of 'beats', which are determined by the mutual distance between the notes, their loudness, register, overtones and combination tones. It is said that as the beats increase, we experience a higher degree of harshness. Consonances do not produce beats.

In this view too, the concepts of consonance and dissonance are therefore coupled to absolute intervals.

Today more emphasis is placed on the potential for continuation in the musical context, and the following view is generally shared:
- the consonance is static and stable and has a low degree of tension (therefore not requiring continuation);
- the dissonance is dynamic and unstable, and has a high degree of tension (requiring release of tension and therefore continuation).

It is thus clear that the combination of intervals, melody and rhythm in particular will determine the musical continuation of a given vertical sound. This means that it is hardly possible to relate the terms consonance and dissonance – as in classical musical theory – to specific vertical relations. For it may occur that one and the same interval must be considered consonant or dissonant according to the musical context.

Let us investigate this more thoroughly, firstly by putting the above view on the problem of consonance to the test in a song by Debussy, *Le Jet d'Eau*, written in 1890:

EXAMPLE 38

The first five bars are purely modal. The series employed comprises the uneven overtones (1, 3, 5, 7, 9, 11) and therefore has a strongly static character. We call this the *overtone series.*[1] In this modal, static environment the 2nd C-D has the effect of a perfect consonance. But this modal tranquility is interrupted by dynamic, tonal elements (bar 6), while in bars 9-10 we hear a tonal cadence from the dominant to the tonic. In this strongly tonal vertical sound the 2nd C-D suddenly becomes dissonant: it must be resolved, and this indeed happens in bar 10 as the D rises to the 3rd E.

2

There is still much to be learnt from Debussy. A second and generally held view is that, since the abandonment of the concept of harmonic functions, the structure and progress of the vertical sound are largely determined by melic and horizontal forces. This is the case in Debussy too. The simplest example is the chord of the dominant 7th, now neutralised and no longer bound to the cadential resolution from dominant to tonic. Debussy often repeated it in parallel movement according to the melodic line; fine examples of such parallel harmony are to be found in *La Cathédrale engloutie*, a piece which reveals other interesting details too (Example 39):

1. To achieve climaxes, classical principles of motif splitting, acuminated dissonance and suchlike are replaced by general principles such as melic and dynamic growth.
2. The fundamental note of each segment (A, B and C) is determined by the preceding melodic peak (see **x**).
3. Segment A is pentatonic. Segment B becomes hexatonic while retaining the pentatonic framework (the 7th D therefore jumps to the fore: 'marqué'!). Segment C becomes heptatonic, but here again the pentatonic frame is still evident, since the notes B and E are kept in the background as passing notes: see (4). Only from bar 13 does the pentatonic basis disappear to make way for genuine diatonicism. Step by step the musical material therefore becomes increasingly condensed.
4. In segment C the interval of the 3rd makes way for the 4th (G-C) above the bass note. The material thus becomes more dynamic, and here for the first time one senses the function of a dominant (for more on the 4th, see section 8). Here the dissonant 4th is used to avoid the leading note B. Rather significant too is the fact that the note E is kept in the background: in bar 13 its effect as 3rd above the tonic will be so much stronger (elimination principle).
5. Many chords feature so-called added notes. These prove to be determined *not* by the overtone structure but rather by the modal environment in which the chord is located.

EXAMPLE 39

3

Modality is a common phenomenon in Debussy's music; we have already noted Examples 21 (2nd stave), 38 (the overtone series common in his work), and 7 (the whole-tone scale).

But it was Debussy's fellow countryman Olivier Messiaen who particularly enriched this modal aspect. He developed the theory of the *modes à transpositions limitées*, based on the equal temperament of twelve chromatic notes. These modes comprise identical groups and return to the original constellation after a number of chromatic transpositions. In all cases, the last note of each group is at the same time the first note of the following one:

EXAMPLE 40

Mode 1 comprises six groups of two notes which can be transposed once; it embraces the whole-tone scale. Mode 2 comprises four groups of three notes and can be transposed twice; it embraces the frequently used octatonic scale. Mode 3 is divided into three groups of four notes and can be transposed three times. Mode 4 has two groups of five notes and can be transposed five times. The latter also goes for the 5th, 6th and 7th modes. Parallel movement reveals the typical harmonic timbre of these modes:

EXAMPLE 41

The modes evoke a certain atmosphere and contain various possibilities to form centres without actually resulting in polytonality. By means of modulation, polymodality, combination with non-modal elements, etc., it proved possible to wield modal harmony with considerable refinement. Example 15 from *L'Ange aux Parfums* illustrates how the first three modes can be combined (from the top: modes 2, 3 and 1, respectively). See also Examples 31 and 64, and section 5.

4

The next new concept, that of the *tone field*, can again be discussed with reference to Debussy, the great innovator in this area. A tone field is a musical episode that is marked by harmonic tranquility, since the driving forces of harmonic movement are hardly, if at all, active. Technically speaking, many such passages are characterised by frequent ostinato figures, long-held notes, strongly modal note constellations or, rather, considerable chromatic density through which harmonic tension may likewise be smoothed over. Timbre often plays a prominent role. Tone fields may occur alone, but they are often employed as 'counterpoint' to a rhythmic or melodic part in which the energy of movement does make itself felt. Transitional situations from dynamic passages to tone fields and vice versa are common. Beside Debussy, tone fields are employed regularly by composers including Bartók, Stravinsky, Webern and Messiaen.

At the beginning of the second movement of *The Rite*, Stravinsky creates a wonderful and suggestive tone field from which, several bars later, a melodic figure in the violins slowly but surely frees itself (see Example 63). Example 78 (*op. 5, no. 4* by Webern) features a tone field in bars 7-9 in which the choice of notes from the overtone series carries the mood of static tranquility to the extreme. Tone fields are also employed in Webern's *Symphony op. 21*, though in a far more sophisticated manner.

Bartók employed this technique in quite a different way. Sometimes his tone fields are rustling backgrounds full of mysterious nocturnal sounds, and sometimes they are sober blocks formed by just a few parts, as in his *Third String Quartet*:

EXAMPLE 42

The use of tone fields can probably be viewed in many cases in relation to a reaction against subjectivism and expressiveness-in-every-note, and to the pursuit of the sacral and suprapersonal, as for instance in Stravinsky.

5

Another phenomenon common from the beginning is the *note nucleus*. Consisting of one or (usually) more notes, a note nucleus can acquire a leading role through continual repetition. Although such nuclei may be given a certain central significance, this cannot be compared to the function of the tonic in tonal music! This is proved particularly by the fact that note nuclei occur frequently in free atonal music too. We should rather think in terms of a melic phenomenon, a horizontal centre that occupies a position amid the other parts but often entirely independent of them. Two examples follow, one from the extended tonality of Bartók, the other from the free atonality of Schönberg.

Bartók's *Bagatelle 2* employs the note nucleus A♭-B♭ (Example 43). Although it is not harmonically functional, its dependence on the other part is evident, as the latter circles spirally around the note nucleus. A similar but melodic interraction is found in *Bagatel 3*: the note nucleus here is a chromatically filled 3rd, with which the melodic line vies (Example 44). In both cases one could speak of a (figured) pedal point: in classical harmony too this phenomenon is fundamentally independent of harmonic movement.

The second of Schönberg's *Six Little Piano Pieces op. 19* also employs a 3rd as note nucleus (Example 45). It plays an important role in the piece without the least tonal influence on the surrounding notes, for in this free atonal environment, simultaneity is determined by other laws (see section 8 on the role of intervals). The sixth piece from the same opus has a note nucleus consisting of a three-part chord of 4ths. In the second of the *Three Piano Pieces op.*

EXAMPLE 43

EXAMPLE 44

EXAMPLE 45

11 (1908), we find a note nucleus in the bass, again a 3rd, which also fulfills a rhythmic role in a continual pendulous movement.

6

We have already briefly mentioned parallel chords, a phenomenon too evident to devote many words to. We should note in passing that such parallels may be either modal (adapted to the prevailing note series) or 'real', i.e., with unadapted intervals. Parallel chords form the most extreme example of a simultaneity governed by melic principles. The choice of (parallel) chords is in many cases determined by the chordal timbre.

Parallel chords become much more interesting if they approach *heterophony*: the simultaneous rendering of the same melodic material, but varied in each part. Example 46 is a passage from Stravinsky's *The Rite* (number 95 in the score). All three parts feature parallel movement of different intervals. Moreover, the middle part is a variant of the upper one: heterophony. The simultaneity is much more differentiated.

EXAMPLE 46

Schönberg's *Five Piano Pieces op. 23 no. 3* provide another interesting example. The composer had adopted a new technique, and in Example 47 we find a series (of five notes) in three layers one above the other, but each slightly different. This variation technique is therefore exclusively rhythmic.

EXAMPLE 47

The employment of parallel chords is often accompanied by *group polyphony*, in which the different horizontal levels do not consist of single parts but rather groups of parts. Example 46 by Stravinsky is really two-part: both upper staves have only one melodic line, supplemented with parallels and heterophony. The lower stave provides a counterpoint, likewise in parallel movement.

7

Considered theoretically, *polytonality* is the simultaneous occurrence of different keys. This implies that harmonies and/or melodies can be split into groups, each with their own centres to which the notes are functionally related. Since such centres can usually only be determined by means of a succession of chords or melody notes, polytonality cannot be ascertained by means of a single chord. This is a problematic situation, since it is necessary to distinguish clearly between three different forms:

1. Genuine polytonality. In most cases this is not evident, since the influence of the bass note is so predominant that the ear perceives monotonality, be it highly enriched. We have already mentioned the concept of *extended*

tonality, and indeed the more the human ear is able to hear far-removed note relationships in one greater context, the fewer the chances are for genuine polytonality. We could even take this line of argument so far as to conclude that polytonality is a typically time- (and ear-)related phenomenon! Example 48 from Milhaud's *Saudades do Brazil* would undoubtedly have sounded bitonal to the ears of the average listener in 1920, who was not yet able to reduce the G major key of the left hand and the B major key of the melody to a common denominator. A well-trained ear of today, accustomed to the enriched simultaneity of the past fifty years, will experience this same melody as a somewhat coloured part in the key of G.

EXAMPLE 48

Genuine polytonality is only conceivable if the melodic force of the various parts is so great that different and unambiguous melodic centres arise. Polytonality is therefore only conceivable in strongly horizontal music. However, I know of no clear example: most polytonality exists only on paper.

2. A common harmonic technique, likewise hardly polytonal, is based on *composite chords* which are subsequently split up into their components; the latter can then be treated separately, but do not display a clearly defined tonal characteristic of their own. Such compound chords not uncommonly consist of triads related to one another by a minor 3rd. Pijper was particularly fond of such combinations (see Examples 3, 14 and 33); their smelting potential is comparatively great.

3. *Polyvalency* is a third phenomenon which is often confused with polytonality. Polyvalent combinations arise if different tonal functions occur simultaneously, related to *one and the same centre*. In contrast to composite chords, polyvalent chord combinations often cause considerable friction through the telescoping of diverse functions that should really occur *in succession to* one another.

A familiar example is the often-quoted combination of tonic and dominant in Beethoven's *Third Symphony*, where we indeed see the telescoping of different functions related to the same tone centre. This is therefore not a case of polytonality as is sometimes claimed, but of polyvalency:

EXAMPLE 49

In today's music we find examples in Stravinsky in particular. In Example 50 (from the *Mass*) all notes can be functionally related to B♭, but each group does so in an autonomous manner.

EXAMPLE 50

The traditional explanation in terms of unresolved, unharmonic elements (appoggiaturas, passing notes, etc.) is no longer satisfactory, because the creation of autonomy implies that what was once unharmonic is now harmonic. The origin may sooner be found in the added notes of Debussy and others, which came to lead an autonomous life, as chromaticism did in free atonality. A further source may have been Russian folkore; its inspiration was already apparent in the *Four Russian Peasant Songs* (1914-1917) of Stravinsky's first period. Typically, in these little pieces the composer would have avoided the temptation to imitate directly. But the type of part writing employed was not unusual for some east European folk music. It is quite conceivable that the polyvalency of Stravinsky's later works found its origins here (Example 51).

EXAMPLE 51

8

THE CONSTRUCTIVE ROLE OF THE INTERVAL. As the shackles of tonality slackened, the significance of what were once subordinate musical elements increased (this is discussed in chapter 7). One such element is the *interval,* which became an independent building block in melody and simultaneity.

1. Let us begin with the simplest example: since it was no longer standard that chords must be built up of 3rds, many varieties occurred. Chords of 4ths are harder and pithier, and for many composers combinations of the 4th and the tritone had a particularly savoury flavour, while chords comprising several major 2nds produced yet another clearly recognisable characteristic, and so on.

We may indeed speak of *interval characteristics,* which were felt more and more strongly as the interval became less a component of tonal-functional harmony. It was this interval characteristic that largely determined the colour of the various modes.

2. The interval was also utilised to create contrast between sections, where changes of key and suchlike had once been used. Debussy's *Voiles* for piano is dominated at length by the whole-tone scale and the major 3rd. Contrast is created by a passage in which the pentatonic scale and the harder intervals of the 4th, 5th and 2nd prevail.

The 4th occupies indeed a special place among the intervals. Acoustically, it is determined by two characteristics: unlike other intervals it occurs only very late in the overtone series (in respect to the fundamental), and the difference notes of the 4th largely go to reinforce the upper note. The interval is top heavy and unstable, has dynamic tendencies, and tends towards a resolution. Only now do we really understand why Debussy, in *La Cathédrale engloutie* (Example 39), introduced the 4th (G-C) above the bass at a particular point. It throws the modal atmosphere, the dynamic-tonal element gains the upper hand, and a dominant-tonic cadential effect is created for the first time (bar 7).

3. Interval augmentation and diminution also played a constructive role. Bartók, Schönberg, Webern, Messiaen and others made use of this. With regard to Webern we may refer to the analysis of the fourth of his *Five Pieces for String Quartet op. 5* (Example 78). A passage follows here from the beginning of the third movement of Bartók's *Second String Quartet* (Example 52). The second violin begins with an augmented 2nd, which in the other parts, via the major 3rd, perfect 4th, tritone and perfect 5th, becomes a minor 7th (———). Each step in this series of intervals is reacted to in another part, related by a 2nd.[2]

EXAMPLE 52

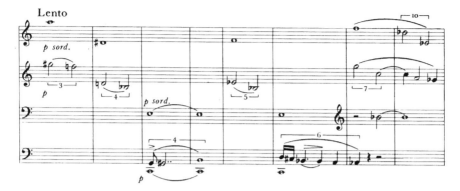

The *Fifth String Quartet* employs interval augmentation in movements 1, 2, 4 and 5, but it is usually purely melodic. Only the final movement (bar 184) features a vertical accumulation of augmented intervals from the minor 2nd to the major 6th.

Interval augmentation and diminution were really just one aspect of a much more comprehensive phenomenon, namely the use of specific intervals for the melodic and/or harmonic *construction*. The most extreme and elaborate examples are found in the Viennese School. We would therefore refer to the chapter on the development of 12-note music, where further analyses of this interval technique will be given.

4. The technique discussed in point (3) tended strongly towards an autonomous role of the interval in which the resulting simultaneity was subordinate in terms of both structure and progression of the chords. Other examples, however, demonstrate that tonal forces were primary and that the interval therefore had the task to create them. Here traditional hierarchical relationships were retained: the interval was not an autonomous building block but a resource within the boundaries of tonal music.

Yet as we know, in our time these boundaries have widened, and the means to realise extended tonality have adapted accordingly. And once more the interval has been assigned an important constructive role. Which interval? In the first place the 5th, of course, that trusty basis of tonal music. Many a chord in modern scores, however 'coloured' it may be, can be reduced to simple tonal proportions thanks to a basic 5th that unambiguously determines its structure. But the *continuation* of simultaneity too can be determined by relationships in 5ths. An example is the fugue from Bartók's *Music for Strings, Percussion and Celesta*, where each new entry of the subject is a 5th higher and lower alternately. Figure 2 presents a scheme of all entries of the subject; a well-knit structure in 5ths serves as a framework for intensely chromatic music. The fugue subject is given in Example 54; the peaks (A-E♭-A) produce the tritone, the chromatic interval *par excellence*. See point (5).

FIGURE 2

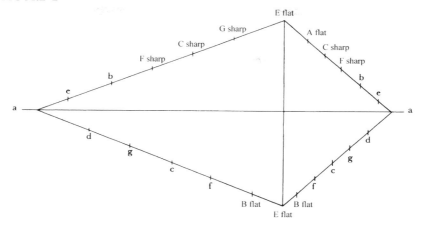

EXAMPLE 53

The Scherzo from Bartók's *Fifth String Quartet* (Example 4) also presents an interesting example of a structure based on 5ths. In the first nine bars the two violins move within a framework of 5ths: C♯-G♯-D♯-(G♯)-A♯. The cello first provides D♯ as bass, but moves up to G♯ at the peak of the melodic line (bar 7, second violin).

Finally, an example from the symphony *Mathis der Maler* by Paul Hindemith (Example 53). The crosses above the notes indicate how the melodic line and thereafter the chord in bar 8 move within a frame of 5ths (G-D-A-E-B-F♯). The trombone D♭ of the cantus firmus ('Es sungen drei Engel') links up with this. The three repetitions of the cantus firmus move up in major 3rds (D♭, F and A respectively). The third rendering ends on C♯, and from this point the frame of 5ths in the above example makes its entry again. Via the notes D♭, A♭, E♭, B♭, F and C (the latter two again combined in a chord) the introduction comes to an end and is followed by an allegro beginning on G. The complete structure therefore incorporates the entire circle of 5ths according to the following scheme:

FIGURE 3

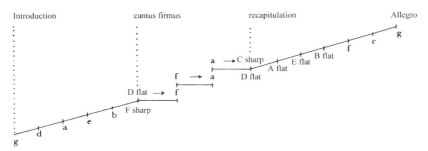

5. If we re-examine the scheme of the fugue from Bartók's *Music* (Figure 2), we notice that at the climax the ascending and descending 5ths meet at the note E♭. The interval A-E♭ is a tritone, one of the most enigmatic intervals known to us. Originating in Western polyphony as the *diabolus in musica*, this interval occupies a key position in contemporary music.

All opposite poles in the circle of 5ths are related by a tritone. Moreover, it is not only the centre of the whole-tone scale but also of all of Messiaen's *modes à transpositions limitées*. The frequently employed composite chords described in section 7 are also based on tritone relationships. In his *Unterweisung im Tonsatz* Hindemith gave a very special place to tritone chords.

The whole-tone and chromatic scales have in common their symmetrical structures and uniform intervals, which make them quite unlike all diatonic scales. The enigma of the influence of the tritone probably lies in this chromatic-symmetrical structure. The tritone is the symmetrical centre, and gains more and more influence as the tonal-hierarchical forces of diatonicism become weaker. Moreover, because it is an interval without an unequivocal fundamental (a fact that the romantics had already turned to their advantage) its two notes form equivalent extremes: they can function as such, far from one another, as in Bartók's fugue, but they can also revert to one another, melting together as we have seen in the composite chord. It is a fact that chromaticism, in comparison with diatonicism, brings quite different structural laws to the fore. The exact nature of these laws is as yet by no means clear, but we can safely assume that the tritone plays an essential role. This is also true of the minor 2nd, an interval discussed at more length in relation to 12-note technique.

Few composers exploited the duality of diatonicism and chromaticism as well as Bartók. Below are just two examples from his *Music*: the chromatic fugue subject from the first movement is *diatonicised* in the fourth (bar 204), only to shrink back into its chromatic form again:

EXAMPLE 54

Conversely, the main theme of the second movement is *chromaticised* in bar 310 of the same movement.

9

Leaving aside our diversion into chromaticism via the tritone, our consideration of simultaneity has as yet made no fundamental distinction between diatonicism and chromaticism. Yet this distinction was gradually to become an important point of difference among composers, and was frequently even related to the question of whether a particular concept was tonal or not.

Let us cast our minds back to the situation in classical romantic music. The basis was and remained diatonic: in other words, the chromatic element played a secondary role, serving particularly to colour and enrich the diatonic foundations. Not until the twentieth century did chromaticism become autonomous in the work of the Viennese School of Schönberg and his disciples. But the classical concept lived on in the form of extended and floating tonality. One of the characteristic differences between the two groups was that the Viennese School developed in a strongly cohesive and conscious manner, while other composers could hardly be considered as a group because each followed and extended traditional paths in his own way. Viennese developments will therefore be discussed in a separate chapter; let us now devote attention to the only figure outside the 12-note composers who developed a clear concept of his own and documented it in writing: Paul Hindemith. In his *Unterweisung im Tonsatz*[3] he assumed the presence of tone centres, and that harmonic progressions give rise to different tensions. Based on calculations from the overtone series he produced an autonomous chromatic series, as distinct from one derived from traditional diatonic scales. A hierarchical order arose in the realm of notes (in their relation to the central note) and intervals (in their harmonic and melodic values). He considered the major and minor triad to be two facets of the same chord, drawing no sharp boundary between the two.[4] This also applied to his concept of consonance and dissonance, as we have already seen.

The triad played a predominant role, but tertiary chord construction, its ambiguity and invertibility, and the concept of alteration underwent thorough revision. Chord construction was now determined by interval value and the influence of the fundamental, the latter being the fundamental of the most important of the component intervals:

EXAMPLE 55

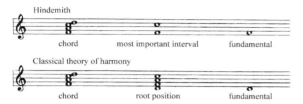

Note: Explanation of the D as sixte ajoutée in relation to the fundamental note F was also known in the classical theory of harmony.

The ordering of chords according to component intervals and position of the fundamental excluded any ambiguity. Each chord had its own inherent tension, not to be confused with the collective harmonic value obtained only through a tonal context. The latter was determined by the course of the fundamental bass, the succession of different chord fundamentals. According to Hindemith, these concepts, together with so-called *übergeordnete Zweistimmigkeit* (the relationship between the bass and the most important melodic part) and the rhythmic and melodic proceedings, offered sufficient basis for the analysis of music of diverse styles and periods.

Hindemith's theory was based on the assumption that note relationships are a natural phenomenon of musical material, which therefore may not be neglected. For this reason he rejected any attempt at atonality or polytonality. See also Examples 30 and 53.

10

Striking differences were to be found in music in which the mutual note relationships were *not* regulated by a tone centre. Here the note relationships distilled from the overtone series were not accepted as an article of law. A development in this direction was made possible by the adoption of equal temperament, not as a compromise but as an autonomous division of the octave into twelve equal chromatic notes.

A first consequence was that the difference in traditional notation between G ♯ and A ♭, for instance, disappeared. The note G ♯/A ♭ gained an autonomous quality of its own. The harmonic and melodic development was now determined by quite different principles. We propose to discuss all phenomena resulting from this concept in the chapters on the development of 12-note music. A side issue is the strongly chromatic style incidentally employed by Bartók.

The reader who has studied this chapter on harmony and the later one on 12-note technique will not have failed to notice that the phenonemon of 'simultaneity' is not only a difficult but indeed a multifaceted subject, in which no single denominator is large enough to reduce all elements to a common factor. This is not easy to accept, especially for those who have a certain predilection, indeed a preoccupation with the music of the classical and romantic periods. But they must realise that this was the only time in the universal history of music when harmony was placed on such a high pedestal. In this light the contemporary tendency to relieve 'King Harmony' of some of his power is really only normal. Thus harmony, or simultaneity, lost much of its constructive significance and became determined far more by other (primarily melic) forces.

To what extent this development went hand-in-hand with generally valid stylistic phenomena, the twenty-first century will be in a better position to judge. Our role is to compile an inventory.

CHAPTER FIVE

Timbre

I

Every period and every style has its own sound; it arises automatically, according to the manner of writing in fashion. Conversely, the composer may consciously seek those instrumental or vocal resources best suited to the realisation of his tonal ideal. In a continuous interaction between these two quantities, the classical orchestra expanded to become its romantic equivalent. A first notable change was a gradual increase in the number of instruments. Each individual group became larger, with three to four players to a part, and new colours were introduced: the piccolo, cor anglais, bass clarinet, double bassoon, saxophone, Wagner tuba, celesta and a certain amount of percussion all made their entry. The clarity of the classical orchestra was replaced by a more flaccid sound, nonetheless accompanied by an unprecedented increase in the range of timbre. The art of orchestration became a study in its own right, and manuals on the theory of instrumentation appeared, the best of which offered refined thought on the handling of this enormous orchestral machine. Precisely because the romantics wished to attach a subjective-emotional value to timbre, great craftsmanship was required to master these new resources, even though the superficial observer may sometimes be inclined to assume the opposite.

And so we approach the years around 1900. The mastery of orchestral colour was passed on to modern composers, but the style changed, and insights into orchestration changed with it. On the one hand a reaction to romantic excess arose, manifest in a renewed preference for lucid, chamber music-like scoring, while on the other hand the expressionists – the direct offspring of German-romantic subjectivism – developed a completely different style of composition. Both groups sought to liberate timbre as a colouristic means and relate it to structure, an aim which can be attained with both large and small orchestras. The result in both groups was that the sound that had previously blended now became divided. For romantic orchestration was entirely based on a tonal concept that automatically produced a high degree of blend. The disintegration of tonality likewise resulted in the division of the sound. Characteristic differences included the following: with or without polyphonic tendencies the romantic-tonal style remained embedded in a homogeneous triadic structure; it was this verticality which brought about the typical system of instrumental doubling that formed the basis of romantic

EXAMPLE 56

orchestration. Both triadic structure and doubling produced a high degree of blend; the new way of writing was essentially more linear, with a preference for sharply drawn lines, and therefore more solo parts and less doubling. Differentiation of timbre became manifest in another way, namely through greater motivic distribution. All this, plus the considerably more complicated simultaneity, gave rise to a new range of sound.

2

Naturally, all sorts of nuances were possible. Since analysis is more effective than words, let us examine essential differences by taking the first few bars of two works for large instrumental forces, both completed in 1910: *Das Lied von der Erde* by Gustav Mahler, and the *Six Pieces op. 6 for orchestra* by Webern. The passages are given at sounding pitch in Examples 57 and 59; Examples 56 and 58 present them in score to facilitate instrumental analysis.

The concept of the two works is comparable: both begin in the middle register, with the lower register introduced several bars later; both are also clearly divided into two groups at the beginning, namely a horizontal (melodic) and a vertical (harmonic) group.

Mahler: the signal-like melodic material is quite unequivocal by reason of its elementary structure (revolving around the notes E and A) and motif repetition. The accompaniment too is simple, being based on the triad of A minor without changes of harmony. The musical structure is therefore both evident and direct:

EXAMPLE 57

Mahler's orchestration reflects this directness only in so far as it concerns melody: the four horns produce a single colour and also adapt their timbre to the signal-like theme. The accompaniment, on the contrary, is treated in a most complicated manner, a complication not issuing from the musical structure but rather from the colouristic instrumentation. Let us examine this bar by bar:

EXAMPLE 58

MUSIC OF THE TWENTIETH CENTURY

Bar 1. A single upbeat is played in quadruple timbres: three flutes, three oboes, E♭ clarinet and violas. The piccolo is an octave higher, and through this septuplet motif runs a quintuplet for two clarinets. Did the composer do this in order to create colouristic opaqueness (upbeat effect), or because the clarinets are to end on C rather than E, and he assumed that this clash would not be audible within the whole?

Bar 2. A single triad A-C-E. The trumpets provide not only pitches but also the basic rhythm, and are therefore used functionally. Trills and tremolos are colouristic additions, as is the combination of violins (double stoppings) and tubular bells. A percussive effect results, reinforced by the artificial 'resounding' (diminuendo) of the cellos; the trumpets are also forced to diminish to allow this resonance effect to remain audible.

Bars 3 and 4. The trumpets are again functional and in fact present all that is actually taking place, in both melodic-harmonic and rhythmic and dynamic terms. 'Flatterzunge' in the flute, auxiliary notes in the oboes, appoggiaturas in the clarinets and repeated notes in the violas once more create a global, colouristic blend.

Bar 5. A contramotif enters in the bass. Clarinets, bass clarinet, bassoons and cellos provide the necessary doubling. How can they otherwise stand up to the sound of the brass? But at the same time the harps create opaqueness by breaking the chord of A minor in short note values moving in the same direction.

What is the result of this complicated instrumentation? In the first place there is a high degree of blend because everything revolves around the A minor triad. Despite, or rather because of these excessive resources, a certain conformation is unavoidable. The total of the resources employed is in no relation to the relatively monochromic nature of the first four bars, for instance, in which the whole picture is determined by the brass. Note too the discrepancy that arises between the sound and the functional use of the instruments. The cellos, for example, have no less than three different functions within these few bars: in bar 2 they contribute to the bell effect, in bar 4 they mark the division in the musical discourse, and in bar 5 they finally lend support to the new motif. It goes without saying that this approach has nothing whatsoever to do with ignorance, as a glance at the musical refinement of the chord structure in bars 2 and 5 goes to show: the 5th E dominates in both bars; in bar 5 the doublebass, for instance, could easily retain the root of the chord, but the 5th in the bass (E in the third trombone) is essential here. For the harmony reflects what is expressed in the melody: the domination of the note E in the entire sound.

Another extreme is found in the first bars of Webern's *Six Pieces for orchestra*. Colour is not an additive here, but a component of the musical concept. As in Mahler, the first three bars (A) present an initial horizontal and vertical exposition, while bar 4 (B) introduces new voices (Examples 58 and 59).

EXAMPLE 59

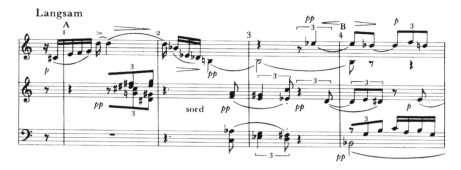

A: the horizontal motif consists of a rising and falling line, both played on the flute. The highest and lowest notes are distinguished from this in both duration and timbre by the trumpet and horn, respectively. The two little groups of chords too each have their own rhythm and timbre: celesta and muted low strings. In terms of form they offer a counterpoint to the high and low notes in the trumpet and horn, respectively. We may therefore refer to them as *colouristic counterpoint*. The whole of A employs the four basic colours of the orchestra: wood, brass, celesta and strings. The end of A is indicated by the ritenuto and the written-out retardation in the second chord group. From a very early stage Webern employed tempo to articulate form.

B (bar 4) restores the tempo and brings four new entries against the held note on the horn. Here again we see an amalgamation of differentiated rhythm and timbre. And again the four basic colours of the orchestra are employed: wood, brass, harp and cello (now solo to contrast with the preceding tutti). Both A and B therefore make use of each orchestral group. Yet the musical structure is simple. A large orchestra is required here to create structural rather than colouristic differentiation. The differentiation of timbre is a logical consequence of this. Since traditional doublings have lost their purpose, the characteristic picture of Webern's orchestral scores emerges, a picture that was to become increasingly clear as years went by: only few and widely spread notes, and many rests. Not a note is superfluous, and neither is a timbre. It is not only difficult for the listener but for the performer too: no longer can anything be concealed.

3

From this one comparison it becomes clear that the essential change of sound was caused by the new style of composition rather than the use of small ensembles. The latter were indeed employed, as a reaction to the large-scale orchestral works of the late romantics, but much less than is sometimes suggested. Both romantic and modern composers were familiar with large and small forces. The number of instruments employed was never of primary importance in determining the sound. To clarify this we need only to compare a somewhat larger chamber work of the nineteenth century (e.g., Brahms' string sextets, piano quintets by Schumann and Franck, or clarinet quintets by Brahms and Reger) with a representative work dating from 1918: Stravinsky's *The Soldier's Tale*. The scoring of the latter is slightly larger – seven instruments – but the sound is determined by two particular factors: (1) the choice and (2) the use of the instruments.

1. The choice made by Stravinsky is the following: clarinet, bassoon, cornet, trombone, violin, double bass and percussion. 'A scoring in which the most representative types, both high and low, from each instrumental group are employed', as the composer wrote.[1] These are quite different considerations, therefore, to those of his predecessors. The fact in particular that Stravinsky excluded the most expressive instruments of all, the horn and cello, is indicative of the different point of view.

2. The manner in which this group of instruments is employed goes to complete our picture. Stravinsky pursued three aims. Firstly, the creation of strong contrasts in order to give clear contours to the polyphonic and polyrhythmic structure. Secondly, an idiosyncratic role for each individual instrument: not only autonomy in melody and rhythm, therefore, but also in instrumental scope; a similar aim is found, *mutatis mutandis*, in the New Orleans style (simultaneous solo improvisation) popular at the time. Finally, an important role for the percussion.

To summarise, Stravinsky pursued a *heterogeneous* sound ideal, in contrast to the above-mentioned romantic chamber music in which instrumentation and composition style contributed to blend colours. In Example 13 we see how the three polyrhythmic layers are also marked by clear contrasts of timbre: three wind instruments juxtaposed to percussion and two strings. The octave doubling here does not blend, due to the high pitch of the clarinet.

4

The term *Klangfarbenmelodik* was coined at a very early stage. Although Webern's instrumentation is really a continuous illustration of this, Schönberg was the first to describe it in his *Harmonielehre* of 1911. Increasing differentiation brought him to consider tone colour as a component of music that was just as essential as pitch. Debussy had preceded him in this. The one-sided approach to musical structure, based on pitch (melody and harmony), was thus abandoned. 'Perhaps it will be possible in the future', he wrote, 'to write real *Klangfarben*-melodies.'[2] The timbre, pitch and loudness of a note are indeed merely different dimensions of the same phenomenon. It would therefore be conceivable to arrange timbre in a determined, musical-logical order, the same logic that now allows us to experience the unity of a pitch-melody.

EXAMPLE 60

* Der Wechsel der Akkorde hat so sacht zu geschehen, dass gar keine Betonung der einsetzenden Instrumente sich bemerkbar macht, so dass er lediglich durch die andere Farbe auffällt.

Here we already encounter one of the first expressions of speculative thought characteristic of the entire Viennese School. Less than half a century later young serial composers were to make a comparable mental leap, in blind trust with regard to the unity of musical material, by taking one and the same series as basis for the structure of all musical elements. It was not the first time, incidentally, that an incorrect point of departure nourished a fruitful artistic development. Moreover, the music of the Far East in particular teaches us that timbre can play a much more substantial role than we have ever known in the West.

In practice the element of timbre, however emancipated it may have become, proved to be strongly linked to pitch structure, as in the case of Webern's *op. 6* (Example 58). *Klangfarbenmelodik* in its pure form – entirely autonomous, with pitch as a secondary element – occurs in the third movement of Schönberg's *Five Orchestral Pieces op. 16*. A 5-part chord, which in all sorts of variants forms the main pitch material, is scored differently every time. Changes of chord are to occur so softly that the listener is aware only of changing timbres and not of instrumental entries. However, since Schönberg aimed to create formal development, he therefore had to make use of timbre to do so. The piece is divided into different phases that contrast with one another through increasing fluctuation of timbre.

In the first phase the chords as a whole change every minim (see Example 60).

Example 61 shows the main component of the second phase. Again the timbre changes every minim, but now differently in each part, as is indicated to the right of the notes.

EXAMPLE 61

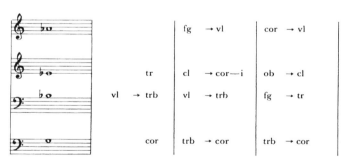

The third phase adds several ornamental motifs, while in the fourth the timbre changes every crotchet or less, and likewise per part. The first bar alone presents the following picture:

EXAMPLE 62

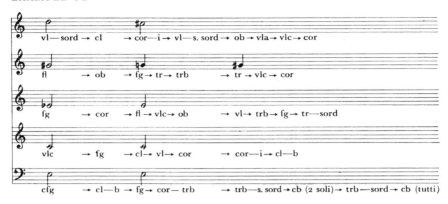

The consequences of this approach can be seen clearly in the given examples. One only has to consider a single chord in isolation, and analyse the distribution of instrumental timbre in each part, in order to measure the huge distance from romantic orchestration. In the meantime this work by Schönberg apparently inspired Webern to write his *op. 6* (Example 58). Comparison of the two examples reveals how Webern directly applied *Klangfarben*-orchestration in his own particular way.

5

We have now considered two reactions to late-romantic composition technique. Besides the tendency of atonal composers to capture tone colour structurally, scores such as *The Soldier's Tale*, but also Milhaud's *La Création du Monde* and the young Hindemith's chamber music, reveal a clear preference for small and heterogeneous ensembles. But there was also a third possibility: the grandiose orchestration of Debussy and Ravel, which made such a deep impression. The beginning of the second movement of *The Rite* (Example 63) illustrates the mark they left.

There are two musical layers: the chord of D minor in the horns and oboes, and the undulating movement in the flutes and clarinets on the minor triads of C ♯ and D ♯ alternately. The chord of D minor is relatively stable in timbre: four low and widely spread horns *pp* plus an upper partial instrumentation, the 5th of the chord, *ppp* in the oboes. The second layer, in contrast, has undergone strong colouristic expansion. Mahlerian doubling, therefore, but now serving to create a subtle blend of timbre: trumpets and strings run through the same chords as the flutes, but always in deviating positions; the regularly advancing flute parallels are, as it were, illuminated in subtle shades. Everything serves to achieve complete fusion of timbre; the techniques –

EXAMPLE 63

EXAMPLE 64

sordino, piano, flageolet, flautando and divisi – contribute to this, as does the juxtaposition of the triad on D and that on C ♯ /D ♯ . Harmonically too, this friction has a highly diffuse effect, evoking the nocturnal mood with which the second half of the ballet commences.

The tranquil, unreal atmosphere of this movement is preceded by one of the eruptive outbursts of sound for which *The Rite* became famous, and which exercised great influence on later music. Presentation and discussion of an example would seem superfluous, since in purely instrumental terms this represented a continuation of the lineage Rimsky-Korsakov – Debussy. It constitutes yet another reason to admire the astonishing inventive power of the then thirty-year-old composer.

6

Bartók occupies only a modest place in this chapter. He is one of those great masters whose work was rooted in tradition. His instrumental style built on the attainments of the romantics and Debussy. Considered historically, more-over, his influence could be but limited, since initially he lived too much on the periphery. But although the element of timbre never played such a role as in Debussy or Webern, within the framework of classical orchestration he cre-ated the most rich and varied nuances. Three characteristic features must be mentioned: (a) his treatment of the piano as a percussion instrument, dis-cussed sufficiently elsewhere; (b) his 'nocturnal sounds' – mysterious sound amalgams which suddenly appear to lend a new dimension to his work; (c) his quartet sound. Hardly surprisingly, it was again in their tonal palette that Bartók's string quartets were most innovative. The last three in particular grew far beyond the intimate chamber style so typical of this genre in tradi-tional terms. Bartók's monumental structures went hand in hand with high-ly virtuosic treatment of the strings. Let us examine a page from the fascinat-ing Prestissimo from his *Fourth String Quartet* (Example 64).

We are in the middle of a series of tone fields, from which glissando arrows suddenly dart upwards. In so far as individual notes are perceptible in the first six bars (A), we mainly hear rising tetrachords leading to bars 3 to 6, where a glissando motif between C and B is imitated at a quaver distance in all parts. Bars 6 to 12 (B) bring new imitations, interrupted by percussive pizzicato chords. Thereafter follows C, again with imitations but now moving upwards.

The timbre is largely determined by playing techniques. Everything is muted; A brings glissandi, B is 'sul ponticello', C 'in modo ordinario'. But two other aspects are also crucial. Firstly, the *colour parallels*: the motifs B and C are written in parallel 2nds, which produce a timbre rather than sounding as an interval or line; everything is very soft and extremely fast (prestissimo!). There is also a *modal* trait which goes to determine the overall colour. A and B are written in the mode C-D-E-F ♯ -G ♯ -A ♯ -B-C, while C is in the Ionic mode (one of the few examples of non-tonal use of this scale in Western music!). The timbre parallels are therefore modal, with alternating major and minor 2nds according to the mode employed. The extent of the influence of this modal timbre is apparent from the transition from one mode to the other.

In addition, there are percussive pizzicato sounds. A percussive chord has a highly complex frequency spectrum due to its compact dissonance. It can therefore be heard as an impenetrable sound, in between fixed pitch and the noise-like sound of percussion instruments. The first percussive chord comprises a concentration of major 2nds, while the second one is in minor 2nds. Here Bartók anticipated later *tone clusters* (see section 8).

7

These examples by Bartók, Stravinsky and the Viennese School present in a nutshell the innovative breakthrough in the field of sound. Here yet again we see that the first period (see chapter 1) was of essential importance. But there was much more: bear in mind the 'piano orchestra' of *Petrushka* (which emerged from an original sketch for a concert piece for piano and orchestra), the sound of *The Wedding* (see chapter 6, section 3), Bartók's ballets *The Wooden Prince* and *The Miraculous Mandarin*, the introduction of the harpsichord by De Falla (*El Retablo* and the *Harpsichord Concerto*), the preference for wind instruments in works by Stravinsky, Varèse, Milhaud and Hindemith, the vigorous orchestral timbre of Honegger's *Pacific 231*, the hallucinational colours of *Wozzeck*, and the impenetrable textures of Charles Ives. All these pieces together went to determine the range of timbre of new music, a range that was to hold for the Second Period as well.

Not many new elements were added; there was an occasional new colour, such as the Ondes Martenot in works by Honegger, Jolivet and Messiaen. The piano and percussion retained the position they had captured, sometimes expanding to become a characteristic orchestral group together with the harp, celesta, xylophone, etc. This was the case in works by Bartók (*Music for Strings, Percussion and Celesta*, 1936), Messiaen (*Trois petites Liturgies*, 1944) and Dallapiccola (*Canti di Prigionia*, 1941), in the latter two combined with a choir. Smaller ensembles too maintained the same picture. Differentiated playing techniques (glissando, 'senza vibrato', sordino, flageolets, 'Flatterzungen', extreme ranges) had more scope here, but did not differ in principle from what had been introduced during the first period.

The causes of this relative tranquility were twofold. In the first place we have seen how closely innovations in musical language and tone colour went hand in hand, while the second period was characterised by consolidation of the attainments of the first period. A second reason, not to be underestimated, is to be found in the division that had come about between creative music and the concert hall. This cleft made interaction increasingly difficult; the performance machine at the disposal of the concert hall underwent no internal modernisation but continued to concentrate on an established period of the past. Composers were expected to adapt to the associated performance practice, instrumentation and playing technique. Here and there they could give a little tug on the rope that bound them, but they could not pull far, if they wished to have their works performed! All in all, this was a particularly unhealthy situation, in shrill contrast to the lively and topical sound spontaneously created by jazz.

8

It is a remarkable fact that precisely in the field of tone colour America produced several most refractory figures. Were American composers less bound to orchestral tradition? Like the early futurists in Italy, however, the artistic result was not always in proportion to the good intentions. George Antheil was only an average film composer, but he added his name to every history book by writing a *Ballet mécanique* for ten pianos and several mechanical instruments. Henry Cowell was more serious, and he devised the term *tone cluster* to denote playing the piano with the flat hand or even the entire lower arm, striking all chromatic notes within a certain area (see Example 67). John Cage likewise attempted to alter existing instrumental timbre with his 'prepared piano', fitting the strings with dampers of various materials (rubber, metal, wood, etc). This may not only influence tone colour but also pitch, and noise effects may be created, making the piano even more of a percussion instrument than it already was. The significance of Cage's experiments remained limited initially, but in the light of present-day concepts of musical material, his activities proved to be of more than incidental value. At any rate, in this field too, the piano appeared to be the pre-eminent 'working instrument', and many later electronic experiments were based on the tonal material of this instrument.

The Franco-American composer Edgard Varèse was by far the most important of these figures. Born in 1883, he thus belonged to the great generation of Schönberg, Stravinsky and Bartók. In contrast to these composers, however, Varèse occupied himself primarily with tone colour, to the extent that other aspects – harmony, melody and rhythm – were subservient and indeed reduced to their most elementary form. The liberation of sound was his ideal, i.e., the abolition of limitations imposed by our instruments and our music system too. What he would have liked most was for composers to design their own instruments, as architects choose their own materials. This required not only a thorough knowledge of the acoustical properties of sound material, but still more a feeling for concrete tone colour and its tangible reality, independent of harmonic or melodic associations. This explains Varèse's strange instrumental forces: his *Ionisation* (1931) calls for thirteen players, the instruments including percussion, rattles, bells, celesta, piano and sirens. But

the same primary sense of sound is also found in *Octandre* (1924), for more
traditional instruments:

EXAMPLE 65

The musical structure is very elementary, and in its blocklike form characteristic of Varèse: two elements A and B that alternate continuously. There is also
a melodic element, shared by the trumpet and E♭ clarinet, a motif of three
notes which is repeated continuously, reminiscent of the melodic style of
Stravinsky's *The Rite* (see chapter 6, section 2).

A and B also differ rhythmically, and this is reminiscent of Stravinsky's
variable ostinato technique (see chapter 2, section 7). But there is no constant
unit here, and an organic breathing is created that is slightly different each
time. The simultaneity is a simply constructed 12-note field with four nuclear
notes (Example 66, upper stave), to which three notes are added in A, and the
remaining five in B, including the melodic notes E♭ and D (lower stave).

This brings us to the Viennese composers: total chromaticism and
Klangfarbenmelodik. The indicated instruments show how the timbre changes
from A to B. But the great difference between Varèse, Stravinsky and the
Viennese School lay in the priority given to tone colour. Here, chromaticism
is an aspect of timbre and not vice versa. The low register (of A), the struc-

EXAMPLE 66

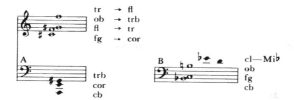

ture of the chords and the dynamic contrasts between A and B are all features that can be traced back in the first instance to just as many aspects of tone colour, Varèse's single fundamental preoccupation. This octet therefore sounds different from all works of the same type written before and since. The element of tone colour was reduced to an almost physical state of nature, a condition for which the composer later found a striking term: *organised sound.* It was the first half of this definition that kept the work of this composer within the realm of art, despite radical differences from all that we have thought about music until now.

9

Pierre Boulez too felt attracted to combinations of percussion and plucked instruments as mentioned above, including idiophones in particular. His treatment of tone colour was rich and characteristic, though it lacked the strictly functional significance already found in Webern; his lineage from Debussy and Messiaen probably helps to explain this. That his treatment of timbre could create unprecedented refinement is illustrated by a passage from the *Improvisations sur Mallarmé* (Example 67):

This entire page can be reduced to a ten-part chord (Example 68), the only exceptions being the first notes in the piano and celesta and E♭ in the harp (appoggiatura in bar 2). All other notes and even their register are determined by this one chord, including the voice. They are, as it were, different rhythmicised timbres of the same ten-part chord. We have already seen something similar in our analysis of Example 35 – a combination therefore of *Klangfarbenmelodik* and tone field. One could indeed speak of 'rhythmicised timbre'. The manner in which this is achieved is indicated by the instrumental scheme next to the chord. Nearly all individual notes are heard in various instrumental timbres.

EXAMPLE 67

EXAMPLE 68

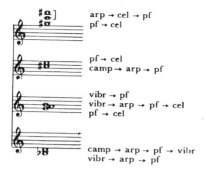

Besides the actual choice of instruments, their treatment is also particularly characteristic. The most important playing techniques on the pages quoted are given below.

Harp. In the entire piece there is not a single glissando; instead, short and dry notes are produced by 'près de la table' and 'étouffez' execution (the technique required by Stravinsky in all his works).

Vibraphone. The normal damping of the vibraphone is operated by the pedal, damping all notes simultaneously. Here Boulez uses the 'étouffez avec les mains' technique, enabling some notes to be damped at the bars while others sound on.

Piano. The vertical line at the opening octave indicates a tone cluster, mentioned in section 8 in relation to Cowell. Everything played above it (on the preceding page) continues to sound. The totality of this refined sound now undergoes very differentiated damping through the *gradual* release of the cluster ('relever très lentement la main du grave vers l'aigu').

Maracas and cymbal. Maracas are small, oval rattles producing coloured noise. Here Boulez uses the middle of three prescribed noise pitches (three pairs of maracas), mixed with the different noise of a large suspended cymbal.

Finally, the perfect blend of timbre in the first bar should be pointed out, with the chord played on bell, vibraphone and piano. The small notes may be played freely within the boundaries indicated by the arrows ⌐——⌐.

In the music of Boulez, tone colour too had an exuberance that was less fortunately adopted by many of his disciples. The strict but differentiated austerity of Webern was thus abandoned. Nevertheless, this was not a general tendency in the post-war period. In electronic music in particular, a highly functional treatment of tone colour was evident (Stockhausen's *Electronic Studies* and *Gesang der Jünglinge*). Electronic procedures confronted composers with quite a new aspect: the timbre itself could be 'composed' and was no longer dependent on *a priori* existing instruments. What remained were the late works of Stravinsky, bearing witness to an imposing ascesis. But perhaps this required the maturity of a master, behind whom was the labour of a lifetime of composition.

Exoticism and Folklore

'IT IS NOT SUFFICIENTLY REALISED THAT WESTERN MUSIC, AFTER ALL, IS BASED ON OLDER FORMS THAT ARE IDENTICAL WITH — OR, AT ANY RATE, COMPARABLE TO — THOSE FOUND TODAY OUTSIDE EUROPE AND "EUROPEAN" AMERICA.'

(Jaap Kunst)

I

A European goes to Japan to learn the art of archery. He desires to draw near to the spiritual world of the East and believes that this celebrated practice of archery is a good way to begin, since he is already somewhat skilled in handling pistols and weapons. However, the first thing demanded by his master is complete inadvertence. 'The true art', he exclaims, 'is purposeless and inadvertent. The more persistently you try to consciously aim the arrow in the right direction, the less you will succeed in approaching the essence of this art. You are obstructed by a will that is much too purposeful. That which you (yourself) do not do – or so you believe at least – does not happen either.'

This story, told by Ernesto Grassi,[1] offers us a glimpse of a different world, strange and for some perhaps absurd. For if we ponder on the words of this Eastern master, do we not encroach upon the fundament of our individualism? 'Come away from yourself, from your subjective moments, from your consciousness, from your ego, and return to the original being', is the translation of his answer. 'This self-oblivion conveys one to a condition from which mankind attains a new spiritual freedom, a state of originality and directness which stands – and now a more familiar sound – at the beginning of all creative labour.'

This book aims to avoid any semblance of philosophy. The story is merely an illustration of the chasm between two worlds, a chasm that no longer runs between East and West however, but across our own soil, cutting straight through our Western culture to cause fatal confusion. On the one hand are the offspring and advocates of (German) romantic subjectivism, for whom the subjective expression of the artist is in the foreground. His inner stride, his emotional tension, his moods and experiences make and determine the work of art. We see the type of composer who has his counterpart in the concert virtuoso: both are exponents of a personality cult carried to excess. On the other side of the cleft we see the artist as a person who, at the essential moment in the creative process, is ego-less, setting himself aside in order to surpass himself. He is not spectacular, and he usually works in utter servitude to a god, an ideal, or an employer.

Both concepts exist in our Western world, alongside one another and intermingled, in all sorts of gradations and with the emphasis on the first-mentioned. In the East the situation is the reverse. Nothing is more striking than to experience how an authentic Indian singer 'gets going'. He sits down in what we would consider a rather awkward position. But he is never out to exploit or exhibit the vocal apparatus! To the endless zooming of drone strings he concentrates on the *raga* that he is about to sing. He slowly explores the steps of the scale, and as he proceeds he becomes increasingly free of himself, until he is finally swept along upon the magical stream of sound. The music can begin. The moment of will is secondary: the artist surrenders himself to become a voluntary and excellently trained medium in the service of music. Striking in this context, finally, is that the concept of 'harmony' crops up again and again in Eastern reflections on art, where in the West we prefer to speak of the passion, the tension and emotion of art. This goes for both composers and performers. The few artists who consciously pursue the first ideal are therefore quickly branded as cold and insensitive. It is a deeply anchored misunderstanding left to us by the subjective-romantic view of the world.

The bowman transported us without transition into the world of the East, and the controversy thus evoked immediately went far beyond local differences between East and West. We are concerned here with basic concepts and tendencies. But the question arises: why exoticism? Can we learn anything from it, and if this is the case, is it necessary to do so?

First and foremost, let it be said that the question is entirely theoretical. Artists allow themselves to be influenced and stimulated without delving into such problems. But leaving this aside, the Western attitude to the East can be divided roughly into two groups. On the one hand is a group very much determined by fashion. From the chinoiserie of the *fin-de-siècle* to (Zen) Buddhist novelties of contemporary intellectuals, we are witness to a continuous but superficial contact with the East. Picturesque outward appearance usually forms a substitute for the artist's own personal concept. On the other hand is a group that does accept the East as an autonomous world of its own, but as a world that is too far removed from our intellectual and cultural life to be able to influence it. Moreover, we are strong and vigorous enough – it is said – to guarantee an evolution of our own.

The latter view is undeniably healthier and more realistic, but probably requires qualification. A basic fact of our time is the increasing and now unavoidable contact with every region of the world. This contact has long lost its narrow diplomatic and commercial character and expanded into a much more comprehensive amalgamation. We must bear in mind here that the process of acculturation (hybridisation), the fusion and adoption of elements from different cultures, may be counted among the most familiar phenomena of universal art history. Finally, it is not improbable that our own art reveals lines of evolution, free and from within, that in some respects approach certain Eastern concepts more closely than was ever possible within our former and closed cultural pattern.

2

In the above words 'the East' is a rather vague way of describing an abundance of non-Western cultures. And in most cases we cannot pinpoint possible influences, for it is usually more a question of general artistic (and aesthetic) concepts than of clearly defined technical resources. Yet from this point onwards it is useful to make a distinction between the art of highly developed Eastern cultures (the Arab, Indian and Chinese-Japanese worlds) and those of more or less primitive peoples. The latter art is of course highly variegated too, but 'primitivism' as a general term is used so often in contemporary Western art that further investigation is well worthwhile.

The most vivid example of this primitivism remains Stravinsky's *The Rite*. The newness of this score was to a considerable extent due to an extremely direct approach to the phenomenon of music. All listeners have undergone – beyond its modern refinement – the primal force of this work. It has usually been attributed to rhythm, but on further consideration this is only partially true. We must venture on, and in so doing investigate the melodic aspect in particular. The work proves to conceal many melodic features that – even considered strictly in terms of material – display striking similarity with the melodic world of primitive peoples. Let us look more closely at this aspect by examining a varied selection from the rich motivic material of *The Rite*.

EXAMPLE 69

The following characteristics may be observed (Example 69):

A number of motifs (A-F) moves entirely or principally around a nucleus of three notes (see Example 22); F-L have no upbeat and move downwards; B, D, E and L comprise no more than two or three notes (see also Example 25); the pendulous movement is conspicuous in A, B, D and L. Related to this, but considered more broadly, one is struck by the many repetitions of motifs (ostinato) and the additive rhythm of most fragments.

What does this have to do with primitive melody? The shape of primitive melody is pre-modal, i.e., it came into being without the influence of a note system. Musical consciousness was not yet aware of the octave as an interval, and still less of its subdivision. The only and exclusive material of such melody was the interval, which was usually not fixated: 3rds and 2nds could vary in size. At this stage absolute intervals were not important – they (probably) become so only with a consciousness of the octave and its subdivision. Perhaps we can imagine the melodic process as follows: primitive man sang and became absorbed by a particular note; interval by interval, with this note as his sole point of reference, he felt his way through the outer space of music. We can presume two possibilities:

1. Recitative, in which the unsteady intervals of speech were fixated, and in which the inflexion of words soon brought about the addition of several adjacent notes to a central note, or induced undulating movement between a small group of notes;

2. The 'call', issuing from a peak of tension and gradually falling into relaxation; this may have caused thetic descending motifs – a most elementary form of energy release.

Details and nuances are not relevant in the context of this book; of interest to us among these numerous possibilities is the fairly frequent occurrence of a certain melodic nucleus comprising a combination of the major 2nd and minor 3rd. The lowest point of the call was naturally rather unstable, but it is assumed that the interval of a 4th soon brought more stability, and was subdivided (by being filled in) into this relationship of 2nds and 3rds, and sometimes into a tetrachord. Two melodies follow (my own transcriptions):

EXAMPLE 70

Ethnomusicologists emphasise that such small melodic nuclei may on no account be viewed as 'incomplete' pentatonic or other scales. They are entirely autonomous melodic forms, though as a framework they may indeed occur in more elevated musical structures of later date. The burial song quoted forms an example in the bud: the nucleus B-A-F ♯ is already extended to a tetrachord by adding the subsidiary note G ♯.

From the various shapes of these primitive melodic nuclei we have chosen this particular one since it reminds us quite astonishingly of many of our children's songs. Moreover, this same nucleus is found at the basis of the melodic structure of Debussy's *La Mer*, and these same intervals (not fixated but fluctuating between major and minor) form the basic material of the first movement of Schönberg's *op. 11*! Three works, all written around the same time. Three works which each in their own way represent a different approach to musical material, and in their reaction to tonality revert not only to modal but even pre-modal concepts, at a moment when the fixated division of the octave in major and minor scales began to become a thing of the past, and melody became released once more from vertical ties.

The characteristics of Stravinsky's melodic style in particular, and to a certain extent that of Debussy too (see chapter 3, section 3), are surprisingly similar to those of primitive melody: note nuclei, undulating movement, extremely few notes, thetic descending motifs, and motif repetition. Stravinsky unawares applied several important features of primitive melody. Unawares, for although contemporary painters could indulge themselves in primitive images and masks, primitive music had not yet been heard in Europe. Only after World War II did leading gramophone companies overcome their traditional hesitation and devote attention to exotic as well as primitive music.

One also speaks of primitivism with regard to Carl Orff. Comparison with Stravinsky, however, is rather problematic. The latter remained first and foremost a composer. In other words, the ever new problems that he encountered were tackled and solved in an essentially musical manner. Orff's development drove him increasingly towards music drama in which music, text, dance and action were viewed as a single unity. As a result his music is not autonomous and does not aim to be such: the musical element is just one component. Orff's music consciously ignored the entire heritage of musical achievement left to us by the past.

The music of Orff is essentially monophonic: parallel movement and heterophony merely create a very elementary form of simultaneity. But this monophonic writing also rules out vertical-harmonic development. Ostinato structures and an additive juxtaposition of separate segments complete this picture and create a whole that is much more elementary than the music of Stravinsky. In chapter 2 we drew attention to Orff's rhythm, which despite the relationship to that of Stravinsky, is considerably simpler.

Strictly speaking, it is therefore not fair to isolate the music of Carl Orff from the dramatic entity and judge it on its purely musical merits. And I believe that precisely here a similarity is to be found with not only primitive but also more highly developed art forms. For there, too, music is entirely functional, without any pretention whatsoever to be 'beautiful' or even 'ugly'. Orff did not always go this far by any means. But he was more fond of the almost physical, imploring monotony of a protracted ostinato than of its musical-aesthetic organisation. The same contempt for musical organisation also enabled him to write the most crudely tonal pages, which came to stand in an entirely different light, however, by reason of their radical working relationship.

Whatever the case may be, through Carl Orff a completely new dimension was added to Western music. It was not so much the elementary musical material as the breaching of our aesthetic approach to music that evoked reminiscences of practices long past. Is it not striking that the author of these large-scale music dramas, such as *Antigone* and *Oedipus*, was also intensively occupied with music for children?

3

Observations on primitivism in *The Rite* may raise the objection that Stravinsky's source of inspiration was Russian folklore, so that he did indeed have examples of elementary melodic form. This is certainly true, but we cannot be sufficiently aware of the fact that there is a world of difference between primitive melody as described above and the average sort of folk music heard today around the world. One could almost compare this situation with the geological layers of the earth: though a primitive 'layer' may occur incidentally in folk music, musical consciousness has now gained so many 'layers' that direct resemblance is rare. Moreover, the structure of the average folk music of today is further developed than the cited motifs from *The Rite!* Naturally, Stravinsky also made eager use of Russian folklore as a source of inspiration, but this brings us to another chapter concerning the influence of national folk music. Despite related traits a single example from *The Rite* illustrates how this melodic style, tinted by folklore, is developed much further: there is a clear modal framework, and the melodic structure is also more developed.

EXAMPLE 71

MUSIC OF THE TWENTIETH CENTURY

Something similar is found in *The Firebird, Petrushka, The Wedding* (here, incidentally, the nucleus of major 2nd and minor 3rd again plays a major role!) and other works of the same years. We have even come to speak of a 'Russian' period. The influence of folklore is not limited to melodic aspects. In a work like *The Wedding* it is even the question, whether one can actually speak of influence. Is there not sooner mention of an inner relationship, a typically Russian trait in the dramatic concept of this work?

Roman Vlad comments: 'This disquiet in the face of the twofold mystery of life ending and life beginning is the most significant feature of *The Wedding*.'[2] For here we see a Russian wedding in which the celebration is a ritual, in which the participants are conscious in a typically Eastern manner of the secret bond that binds the events of our lives. For precisely the same reasons we Westerners may be surprised to hear a lament and a wedding song from the Middle East, which in terms of character can scarcely be distinguished from one another. *The Wedding*, more than the Russian ballets, is a work that betrays the real origins of Stravinsky.

Nonetheless it was precisely Stravinsky who – in a European context – provided the best example of assimilation. After 1920 his oeuvre, with a few exceptions, was no longer influenced by folklore. He not only absorbed essential features of (particularly) Latin culture, but was to remain once and for all one of its leading figures!

In the case of Bartók this was a different matter. Folklore was a spring from which he was to quench his thirst throughout his life. Another contrast with Stravinsky should be pointed out here: for the latter, folklore was just one aspect, one of the many that determined his life's work. He never made a true study of it, due to a lack of genuine interest, and some commentators claim that his Russian period should sooner be viewed as a process of compensation: a nostalgia for his fatherland, a transitional phase towards a definitive assimilation of the West.

For Bartók, on the other hand, folklore was always in his focus of interest. He even became one of the most prominent authorities in the field of ethnomusicology. Here the creative artist and the academic researcher were united in one person. The significance of his work has already been discussed in chapter 1, section 4. His attitude can be elucidated again with just one quotation: 'Kodály and I wish to achieve a synthesis between East and West. Through our race and the geographical position of our country – the most extreme point of the East and at the same time the bastion of the West – we are capable of pursuing this.'

This statement is radical and far-reaching. And in this respect Stravinsky and Bartók had something in common: in their confrontation with folk music, both penetrated to the very heart of the matter. The national-folkloric movements of the nineteenth century set the first step, but in this field too the actual breakthrough was brought about only in the twentieth century.

With regard to Bartók's so-called Bulgarian rhythms, a few words should be added to what has been said in chapter 2, section 6. In the years 1933-42 the ethnomusicologist Yury Arbatsky made an extensive study of the music of the Balkans, and in so doing came upon the practice of tupan playing in southern regions – on the borders of Bulgaria, Yugoslavia and Greece. The tupan is a large drum, beaten on two sides, and related in construction and use to Turkish-Arab instruments. As in the East, the tupan too has great differentiation of sound, and the instrument is used entirely independently, even in the customary combination with a shawm. It takes many years to master it, and the same subtle interaction occurs between strict rules and free improvisation as in Arab and Indian music making.

The particular value of Arbatsky's information lies in the fact that his study of tupan rhythm was not only theoretical but also practical – he learnt to play for three years with a master of the instrument. He distinguishes between two basic durations: ♩ and ♩. . This basic proportion is unknown in the West, but for a correct approach to this rhythm it is necessary to have complete grasp of the 1:1 1/2 proportion. In other works, when combining these two values ♩ + ♩. one must not think in terms of five quavers: ♫ + ♫♪ but of two unequal units. Correspondingly, the notation should not be 5/8 but (1+1 1/2)/4. All combinations are possible: our 3/4 time could therefore be: ♩♩♩, ♩♩♩, ♩♩♩., etc. In the latter cases the triple bar is therefore asymmetrical and the rhythm 'limps': aksak rhythm. Once this basic value has been mastered, however, a subdivision in quavers and semiquavers can be made.

How does all this relate to Bartók's Bulgarian rhythms? His notation is not always consistent: in the Bulgarian dances from the *Mikrokosmos* he even gives both notations. The third dance, for example, is written in 5/8 time, while his tempo indication is ♩ ♩. = 80 (Example 72). The Scherzo from the *Fifth String Quartet* (see Example 4) has something similar, but Bartók's time signature is (4+2+3)/8 instead of 9/8. The notation of the fourth movement of his *Music* has been discussed in relation to Example 8 in chapter 2.

EXAMPLE 72

On the basis of Arbatsky's investigations a correct approach to performance would seem to be the following: the Bulgarian rhythm quoted in Example 72 is essentially bipartite: ♩+♩. The time unit 80 is clapped per bar and subsequently subdivided into two *equal* values. The final step is to convert this symmetrical division into an asymmetrical one: the second beat becomes a little longer and the first somewhat shorter, while the total remains M.M. 80. Instead of a rather tiresome additive sum of quavers, the buoyant, dancelike charm of this asymmetrical rhythm is created.

We have delved somewhat deeper into several technical aspects of the music of both Stravinsky and Bartók that are related to our subject, in order to emphasise once more that there is a close relationship between the consciousness from which the composer works and the resources that he employs. Naturally, this is primarily a question of mental assimilation, but both composers demonstrate that precisely then striking 'technical' similarities may arise, despite mingling with quite different stylistic resources. Only when the composer's approach is superficial do folkloristic elements seem picturesque, a hardly significant varnish, as is the case with most music in this category. The only exception is Manuel de Falla. Unfortunately, his most convincing work in this respect, *El Retablo de Maese Pedro* (1922), is little known. But it is only here that the hard and hot soil of Spain really bore fruit. The last traces of French-picturesque colours had disappeared. The composer became more ascetic and direct, while sparing colours and psalmodic-liturgical lines unambiguously evoked the spirit of ancient Castile. There is perhaps no other work that so clearly reveals the bond between man and soil.

4

The first traces of Negro music in Europe – leaving aside Dvořák, Debussy and Ravel – take us to the period around 1920. Stravinsky: *The Soldier's Tale* (1918), *Ragtime* (1918), *Piano Rag-Music* (1919); Hindemith: *Suite* (1922), *Kammermusik* (1921); Milhaud: *La Création du Monde* (1923), *Negro ballet*; Krenek: jazz opera *Johnny spielt auf* (1926); Weill: *Dreigroschenoper* (1928).

La Création du Monde (see Example 12) stands out particularly in this series. The heterogeneous tonal palette and free polyphony, the syncopated rhythm, and the melodic writing with its typical blue notes[3] lend this work an unprecedented freshness and spontaneity. This same blue-note melodic style ossified later in the domain of 'symphonic' jazz, becoming a stereotype formula from which only Gershwin's melodic invention escaped.

For a moment it looked as though jazz was thus destined to play an important role in Western art music. But this did not occur: with the exception of one or two stray pieces – Stravinsky's *Ebony Concerto* (1945) – everyone went their own way. The South American sounds eagerly absorbed by Milhaud around 1920 fared likewise.

The wave of jazz that swept across Europe after World War I was not without cause: the reaction to romanticism and the expansive drive of many young expressionists found unexpected support in the new music from America. It can be seen as a stimulus, rather than an influence, through a parallel stream. The fresh and carefree linearity of the early New Orleans style was an extraordinary fulfilment of the European desire for free counterpoint and a lucid, heterogenous tonal palette; the spontaneous joy of jazz performance was precisely what was sought as a reaction to overloaded romanticism. Finally, the rhythm of jazz – according to Karl Wörner a four-stroke engine with syncopation – had the elementary effect likewise pursued in new art music. Jazz, itself a blended product of two cultures, with quite a different background and attitude, proved to run briefly parallel with the ideals of European art music of the same period! We can conclude from this, above all things, that something amounting to the 'spirit of a time' exists, which can be expressed in all places and in the most different ways. In this context Berendt[4] remarked that later developments in jazz likewise displayed parallel tendencies, be it somewhat overdue, through far-reaching austerity (from Cool Jazz onwards) and the decay of tonal elements such as closed melodic structures, harmonic cadence functions, etc. Was this a question of European influence? It is hardly possible to say. Modern jazz indeed attempted to integrate elements of European music, but it is revealing that the results as such were insignificant. In this context a 5/4 bar in Brubeck may be something special, but in Bartók's works of thirty years earlier, it was familiar and common. To say nothing of the monstrosity of 'symphonic jazz'.

These unsuccessful attempts from both sides may give cause for astonishment. For there were many similarities in the resources employed. But a fusion was unsuccessful, despite the fact that it was achieved between the two such different forefathers of jazz. The main reason for this can probably be found in improvisation. This most characteristic feature of jazz influences the nature and structure of the music down to the last details: quality of sound, swing, elementary form, all are related to it. And this is the very thing that was missing up until this point from European art music: here it was not the momentary experience of time of the individual player which was essential, but an edifice rising above the moment, fixated and tending towards absolute validity. Moreover, as Dave Brubeck once remarked, jazz is characterised by 'the freedom of the individual, without losing the feeling of togetherness'.

The aesthetic around 1920 gave occasion to a brief flirtation, but the two partners were apparently not fitted for marriage. Meanwhile, time did not stand still. The present pursuance by the performer of greater freedom and a more essential contribution to the work of art, if ever achieved, will increase the chances of a conciliation. Whatever the case may be, the secret longing for one another's qualities lives on.

5

Let us return to our original antithesis between East and West, but now on a more elevated level, since we will now involve all expressions of Eastern art music in our comparison. However different these may be, they all have something in common, namely music making based on melic-rhythmic material, in which the vertical moment plays a secondary role. This does indeed exist: in East Europe, Africa, South and East Asia and the Far East, simultaneity is known in various guises. But the step towards a primarily vertical oral phenomenon, taken by the West, has never occurred. Precisely through the absence of a highly developed simultaneity, the melodic and rhythmic element has flourished unprecedentedly in the East. Closely related is the concept of *modality*, although known to us, its essence escapes us. For modality in Eastern art music is inseparable from a certain ethos. Music making takes the form of melodic patterns, possessing their own character through a certain constellation of notes, and representing an ethic, emotional or other value. These patterns – called *raga* in India, *patet* on Java and *maqam* in Arab countries – though based on a particular series of notes, are characterised just as much by technical elements including individual melodic curves, important notes, adequate ornamentation and sung parts. All of this together embodies the (recognisable) individuality of a raga, for instance.

By fixating these elements, beyond which the musician may not go, a closed entity is created which may often seem monotonous to us Westerners. Upon closer listening, great rhythmic and melodic differentiation proves possible within this framework, a differentiation brought about and driven by improvisation. One of the problems of serial music, namely the correct proportion between fixated musical elements and the freedom of the player, is resolved in the East in an ideal manner. There *melody steered by the player* occurs, which by reason of its almost physical directness and autonomy is unknown in Western music. But this freedom never becomes anarchy. The modal ethic is more than a subjective truth.

This was known among the ancient Greeks too: only in this perspective can we understand the astonishing statements that may give us an impression of the power attributed by the Greeks to their modes.

After the Hellenic era, the West adopted this age-old and typically Eastern modal concept. And once again we are faced with a stupendous process of acculturation. In the Middle Ages the inheritance of the Greeks, Byzantines and Arabs was slowly but surely transformed into a typically Western cultural heritage. In so doing, ancient elements were lost, while new ones emerged from the crucible. What was lost was the modal ethic, and a fundamental misunderstanding quickly arose: the whole range of defined modal-ethic properties became increasingly schematised until only the abstracted scales of earlier melodic patterns remained. The concept of 'mode' therefore became identified with 'note series', which is what we learn to this very day. A further reduction process – and perhaps a typically rationalistic Western one – is seen in the conversion of the medieval modes into our major and minor scales. Thereafter, equal temperament eliminated the last modal remnants by evening out the original subtle differences between the intervals.

How is modal music interpreted in the contemporary West? The first signs of renewed interest on a larger scale are found in the nineteenth century, when composers harked back to the Middle Ages or to modal remnants in folk music. Naturally, in both cases it was not possible to revive genuine modality, and indeed this was not the aim. What interested most composers was the picturesque, somewhat archaic or exotic tint with which their essentially tonal music could be enriched with new expressive means. Not until the extraordinarily sharp intuitive capacity of Debussy was a radical approach first made possible. At the beginning of this chapter the suprapersonal, timeless character of Eastern music was mentioned. We are now able to elucidate this in the light of the modal ethic. In the raga and related manifestations, that which the music is to express is already largely determined by *a priori* fixated musical elements. The *raga* 'does' it, and the player merely mediates: his task is to convey, as it were, the immanent musical message as purely as possible. The subjective element is entirely secondary. This by no means excludes the individuality of the player! Confusion of the terms individuality and subjectivity has often led Debussy to be considered as a romantic. In fact, he – the hyperindividualist – was the first non-romantic by reason of his horror of the German-romantic cult of subjective expression. It is therefore understandable that the gamelan enchanted him. At that point, however, and in technical terms, it was almost out of the question that it would be incorporated in his work. Javanese music, for example, has its own laws, which could not have been known to Debussy. But a 'translation' into the musical elements at Debussy's disposal is conceivable. Thus, a resemblance can be seen between the Javanese slendro-djawar scale and the whole-tone scale. Globally speaking, both have equal degrees and comprise five and six equal intervals, respectively:

EXAMPLE 74

The slendro scale, however, does feature subtle differences of interval, while Europeans rather tend to interpret slendro as a more familiar pentatonic series. It can be assumed that Debussy was also subject to this oral deception. The whole-tone series also cropped up elsewhere in those days as the outcome of strong chromatic alteration in late-romantic chord structure. Since Debussy was also indebted to this, a comparison with slendro seems on the whole to go a little too far (see, for instance, the *String Quartet* of 1893). Nonetheless, later whole-tone passages can be found that escape late-romantic technique, as again in *Voiles* (see Example 7). With a little ingenuity such passages can of course be explained in terms of functions, though only by adopting a literal approach. In fact, the very absence of harmonic functionalism is the reason why we no longer experience the chords as being 'altered': the sound has become autonomous. Here we penetrate to the very heart of the matter. The decay of the classical rules of harmony was rather general at the time. It could be said that functional harmony outgrew its own strength in the late romantic period. Debussy's endeavour therefore corresponded to this situation. But the music of Richard Strauss, for example, can still be explained in functional terms. And a little later the young Schönberg was to exert all his strength to replace the dynamic-constructive principles of the classical tradition by other equivalent ones. Among his contemporaries Debussy was without any doubt the only composer who managed to escape this. It was only he who desired but one function from a chord: that it should 'give pleasure'. Gone was the chord as a psychological means of expression, as a factor in harmonic tension. Gone too were charged architectures and strict development techniques. This is what Debussy desired, and this is what he indeed achieved in certain works. What a revelation gamelan music must have been! The rarified etherealness of the *Nocturnes* (*Nuages!*) had not been heard before in Europe. Debussy must have had one essential characteristic of this music in mind at all times, a characteristic which Jaap Kunst so strikingly typified as: 'she does not evolve, she is'.[5]

The pursuit of transparent, timeless music places Debussy in a position of his own. Eastern music could teach him a great deal. He was unaware of the fact that such music possesses laws of its own, but this was not of importance to him either. On the contrary. Precisely because of 'the other', the unknown, he was able to yield entirely to the marvel of freely flourishing sound. It is not improbable that this susceptibility drove him further than any of his contemporaries. 'I prefer a few notes from the flute of an Egyptian shepherd; he is part of the landscape, and hears harmonies that do not occur in your theory books.'[6] In purely technical terms this implied the cessation of chord functions, the elimination of leading-note tension, and the avoidance of genetic form elements. But on the positive side it also implied the use of other types of melody, the application of pentatonism and hexatonism (independently rather than as tonal-diatonic or chromatic derivatives – see chapter 7, section 1 on the whole-tone scale), and the chord as an autonomous phenomenon. And as to form, it implied a return to the elementary, which was to become decisive for most modern composers.

6

Since Debussy the 'neutralisation' of the chord (also strongly evident in *Voiles*) has become a common phenomenon. The tone field (chapter 4, section 4) is an expression of this, and total chromaticism also tends towards the same.

Another possibility is to establish a new modality constituted by the West. In the latter case, involving Olivier Messiaen, we are concerned with a direct influence from the East. Although tendencies towards total chromaticism are typically Western, they approach general Eastern concepts more closely than would ever have been possible in our closed cultural pattern of the past, as was mentioned in section 1. Let us consider both aspects – modality and total chromaticism – from this viewpoint.

Olivier Messiaen's fascination with modality was a much more real Eastern influence than rhythm. In chapter 4 a survey of his modes and their structure was given. Despite equal temperament and other limiting factors he was able to create a modal characteristic, due to the typically closed structure of his modes (similar constellations of notes that continually return). Each harmonic change is subject to this 'material closeness', giving rise to a truly static harmony: the choice and sequence of chords – within the framework of a mode and viewed strictly harmonically – are entirely unimportant. A remarkable effect parallel to total chromaticism also arises: the horizontal and vertical aspects of music become equal. This is the same equality that gives rise to Eastern heterophony. It can all be experienced by trying to improvise in one of Messiaen's modes. But again that mysterious balancing force is manifest that keeps the musical components in equilibrium. Precisely through this harmonic fixation, forces are released for melody and rhythm. On this subject, too, enough has been said in the relevant chapters. Melody and particularly rhythm are highly developed in Messiaen's music. With regard to rhythm the composer himself pointed out two main sources: India and the Ars Nova.

Although the Indian origin of many of Messiaen's rhythms cannot be denied, we should nevertheless take it with a grain of salt. Firstly, the composer took his information from an Indian manuscript compiled many centuries ago and no longer reflecting present-day practice. Moreover, the rhythmic patterns from it that are still in use are not always characteristically Indian, but are known on a much wider scale. Here is an example: the rhythm *viyaya* ♩♩♩. (of which Messiaen is very fond because of its symmetrical form) is also known in Turkey, Greece and the Balkans. It is a familiar rhythmic mode which, if we include its variants, will be found in many other places too. *Viyaya* means conquest. Other poetic names are: *vasanta* ♩♩♩♩. (spring), *gajalîla* ♫♩♩♩ (the game of the elephant), and *simhavikrâma* ♩♩♪♩.♩♩. (the strength of the lion). Without establishing any particular association with these titles, the composer indeed created a rhythmic technique not typical of the West by giving life and shape to abstract rhythmic formulas. He spoke of *personnages rythmiques*, while his contemporaries, so engrossed in the material, spoke of rhythmic cells or motifs. Viewed very generally, the (religious) symbolism in Messiaen's music was not strange to Europe. In the baroque and gothic periods we find echoes of this concept that go back to very early times.

Let us consider total chromaticism in the same light. Our example is from

Structures by Boulez, which is discussed at length in chapter 8, section 3. Example 98 gives the beginning of this work, presented schematically:

FIGURE 4

The horizontal lines indicate the number of series used in each segment. In the five segments shown here, 2, 4, 3, 1 and 6 successive series forms are therefore employed simultaneously. There are thus 24, 48, 36, 12 and 72 notes, respectively, in each segment. These notes are further arranged in equal numbers and distributed across all the registers. Each segment lasts eight to ten seconds. It is clear that there can no longer be any question here of harmonic-dynamic development, as a glance at the score will confirm. There is a statistical density of chromaticism per segment, but within the boundaries of *each* segment an indifference occurs with regard to simultaneity. Via a completely different path we thus encounter the same process of neutralisation created by the use of strictly closed modal series à la Messiaen. The sequence of notes, *viewed in terms of simultaneity*, is unimportant. Forces are released for other musical elements: in this sound environment they can be developed unrestrictedly, free of any vertical function. Clearly, the latter three sentences go for most Eastern art music, too. We are concerned here, *mutatis mutandis*, with a parallel development in the West. In terms of rhythm, the succession of segments is vaguely reminiscent of the Indian tala system. Each segment lasts for 78 demisemiquavers (the sum of all note values in the duration series), and they are constantly rearranged. The Indian tala system likewise consists of a sometimes large number of constant units, which may be 'filled in' differently in each period. But the comparison stops here. In Boulez the beginning of each segment is a *point of departure*, from which the rhythmic series unfold. In India the same point is a *goal* towards which the player works, and from which he jumps to the next one. Here, age-long training and well-balanced improvisation lend Indian rhythm unmistakable superiority.

7

Then there is the question of timbre. Among the exotic collection of instruments, we may be especially struck by the often highly developed arsenal of percussion. In particular, the range of nuance in the drum section and the functional relation of these nuances to the rhythmic structure of the music are matters that every contemporary composer has to deal with. We have come a long way from kettledrum beats every eight bars.

Another fascinating sound from the East is the gamelan, and the idiophone group in general. Naturally, Western developments in recent centuries have concentrated on the perfection of those instruments that enable direct transmission of expressive intentions. Vibrato on the strings, for example, has for many become an indispensable means of expression. 'Senza vibrato' is viewed as an exceptional and impersonal coloration. But the so-called 'expressive' tone of singers, wind players and pianists also has an illustrious history. For many players music making has become synonymous with the conveyance of personal expression.

The sound of the gamelan has a quite different character, entirely in keeping with Eastern aesthetic concepts. And although this cannot be literally employed, combinations of Western instruments offer many possibilities in this direction. The sound of *The Wedding*, for instance, has often been compared with the gamelan: four pianos, kettledrums, xylophone, bells, drums, cymbals, triangle and crotals. The instrumentation of this work occupied Stravinsky for a long time. It is perhaps enlightening that in one of the preliminary stages the scoring also included a pianola and a harmonium (both driven electrically), and two gypsy dulcimers. This interest in certain mechanical instruments corresponded to the reaction against romantic subjectivity.

The number of works with exotically tinted timbres thereafter gradually increased, particularly after World War II; relatively speaking, however, it remained small, and this was partly due to difficulties of performance. Messiaen's *Turangalîla-symphonie* (1948) is an example. Beside the usual wind and strings the following instruments contribute to the sound as a whole: glockenspiel, celesta, vibraphone, piano, Ondes Martenot, triangle, three temple blocks, wood block, Turkish cymbals, suspended cymbals, a pair of cymbals, Chinese cymbals, tam-tam, tambourine, maracas, tambourin de Provence, small drum, large drum and eight bells. Messiaen's pupil Boulez also made his fascination for such exotic sounds quite clear (*Marteau sans Maître, Improvisations sur Mallarmé*). Naturally, he employed them quite autonomously, free of any exotic-pictorial effect.

This chapter concludes with several remarks made by the Japanese composer Hidekazu Yoshida. Recent global developments have not left Japan unaffected. The assimilative capacity of Japanese artists is astonishing and indeed goes so far that one may wonder whether it is not at the expense of their indigenous culture. Yoshida firmly denied this, and it is difficult for outsiders to judge. But it is interesting to see how Yoshida's remarks run surprisingly parallel with the line of thought sketched above, according to which exotic influences felt in the West were viewed mainly as a general reaction to German-romantic subjectivism. After remarking that the present generation of Japanese composers has a particular affinity with Debussy, Yoshida writes: 'Moreover, Debussy's rather static harmony appeals to Japanese feeling much more than the strongly expressive dynamics of German classicism and romanticism.'[7] Further on, he underlines what has been said several times above: 'To

reveal and express outer impressions or emotions lies far from Japanese art...
This is the reason why young Japanese dodecaphonists prefer Webern to
Schönberg or Berg. Of course, I know that Webern's music cannot simply be
described as abstract. But in comparison with Schönberg and Berg, it sounds
much more restrained. And so we Japanese felt Webern's music to be primarily particularly cool, concise and precise, which is why it enchanted and
attracted us.'

It is food for thought that many years ago the musicologist Paul Collaer
already compared Webern's music to Japanese art... Could it be that music,
despite all local differences, can claim to be a universal language of humanity?

CHAPTER SEVEN

From Free Atonality to 12-Note Music

Most innovations discussed in the preceding chapters stemmed from composers outside the Viennese School. The division thus arising in this book between (extended) tonal and atonal music is not a matter of principle. There are two reasons for discussing atonality separately. On the one hand, the movement presented a fairly closed entity, and its line of development in the first half of the twentieth century is clearer to follow than that of any other trend. On the other hand, and here lies the main reason, the innovations of atonality were not only more radical but also more comprehensive. In the light of more recent developments, the question even arises whether this development did not offer the greatest opportunity for a future synthesis of all innovations of the first half of the twentieth century. Whatever the case may be, this tendency was evident, and the fact that many composers consequently hovered on the edge of a (musical) abyss is a side effect that can only disturb those who are too cautious.

I

THE DEVELOPMENT TOWARDS FREE ATONALITY. The disintegration of the sense of tonality, and the corresponding dispersal into elements, brought the following aspects to the fore:

1. Musical elements that were once secondary, subordinated to tonal form categories of a higher order, became autonomous;

2. The lack of tonal coherence called for the pursuit of a unity that could bind the dissociated musical language in another manner;

3. New concepts of form arose, partly due to the replacement of diatonic principles of structure by chromatic ones.

1. *Autonomy.* The manner in which rhythm became autonomous has already been sufficiently discussed. Released from its metrical context, it developed into the floating rhythm and autonomous rhythmic structures of Stravinsky and Messiaen.

In the Viennese School, however, the emphasis lay on pitch structure. With regard to melody and harmony, the disintegration of the classical diatonic scale created a whole new range of problems. That Vienna formed the stage for this was largely thanks to expressionism, which viewed chromaticism in particular as a powerful means of expansion. For Schönberg, Webern and

Berg chromaticism was primarily a question of expression. A new world of sound was created, the laws of which were only intuitively applied. Schönberg explored these innovations in his *Harmonielehre*.[1] 'In the sequence of chords there is obviously a tendency to avoid notes from the previous chord.' This brought chromatic expansion with it, expressed in Schönberg in the incidental use of chords of 4ths, 'for when accumulated they contain all twelve notes'.

The consequence of this was important: harmony lost its function as a (cohesive) element of form. It was no longer causal and functional, and neither was it the coincidental resultant of linear part-writing. On the contrary, it was carefully weighed on the merits of its expressive potential in particular. The first definitive manifestation of this was in Schönberg's *Three Piano Pieces op. 11* (1909). There was a striking parallel with Debussy, who – from quite a different aesthetic approach – demanded the same of his chords: not functional, but purely expressive. But this was achieved by Debussy with existing chords, a fact that only went to make this phenomenon even more remarkable. For if even a concrete dominant-7th chord could be stripped of its function, this implied that the laws of nature upon which classical harmony were said to be based were decidedly unstable.

Melody too became freer of the tonal context, moving increasingly towards motivic procedures. The motivic element became autonomous: motivic units became related to one another rather than to a higher tonal organisation as had previously been the case.

The melodic element disintegrated even further, however, down to the *interval*. The resulting emancipation of the interval had many consequences which must be briefly discussed. The first clear signs were found once more in Debussy, where *the function of the interval itself* began to play a role. In chapter 4, section 8 and chapter 3, section 3 the interval was discussed as a colour contrast, an instability factor, and as 'protoplasm' – a sort of material kinship with the capacity to bind together the most divergent melodies. The intervals preferred by Stravinsky also come to mind, as well as the leaping intervals of the Viennese composers, and their preference for chromatic relationships, etc.

This increasing sensitivity with regard to the interval also gave rise to the phenomenon of *athematicism*. This was already referred to in section 3 of chapter 3, where a comparison was drawn with classical thematicism.[2] The term 'athematicism' can now be further defined as the *non-fixation* of melody in a recognisable thematic form that may thus acquire a thematic function. In other words, the melodic curves of a work change incessantly, and not one of them becomes a basis for thematic development. The thematic element lost its primary significance and became an 'outcome'. An outcome of what? Of interval structure. The analysis of *op. 11* (Example 77) reveals a typical case of athematicism in the first bars. Traditional thematicism is also evident, however, as in the varied repetition of the opening theme in bars 9-11.

Athematicism was much more agile, more elastic than classical themati-cism, which was bound to metrical and harmonic forces. Erwin Stein described the difference as follows: 'Melody is mostly formed, not as before, by melodic variation of rhythmic motifs, but by rhythmic variation of melod-ic motifs.'[3] And behold, via a detour we have returned to early polyphony. For the melodic masters *par excellence*, in the fifteenth and sixteenth centuries, also considered allegiance to the intervals to be more essential than adherence to certain rhythms.

2. *Pursuit of Unity.* The creation of free, atonal harmony, however, and an equally free and elastic athematicism were not without problems. The broad background to all innovation in those years – the disintegration of the sense of tonality – also implied the disintegration of thorough tonal coherence.

Obvious attempts to solve this problem were the application of classical form schemes in atonality (*Pierrot lunaire*, *Wozzeck*), and the dependence of form on text (in the same works, and in *Erwartung* and the many songs by Webern). Many smaller forms were also employed: 'I once explained my pref-erence for small forms as a reaction to my predecessors. Now it is clear that this was a restriction, since it did not prove possible to construct large works without laws and articulation forms.' (Schönberg).

A strong motivic-contrapuntal technique also offered solace. Nevertheless, various aspects of atonal linearity are incomparable with early polyphony, for the following reasons:

a. The emancipation of sound mentioned above was primarily a process of consciousness – one could not simply throw overboard several centuries of development and refinement in this field;

b. The same was true of the new techniques of development, in which not only strictly linear but also homophonic means of variation were employed. Traditional polyphony was hardly aware of the variation as such, as a *change* in the musical material; the latter was employed throughout the voice texture, and in combination with inversion, retrograde, etc., this was usually suffi-cient. The homophonic style, on the other hand, emphasised the actual trans-formation of the musical material through division, expansion, etc.;

c. As to the structural regulation of simultaneity, a new aspect now came to the fore: the unifying principle became responsible for not only the hori-zontal but also the vertical unfolding. Examples will be discussed later in the chapter;

d. The pursuit of unity resulted in a procedure in which everything was reduced to a single point of departure. This gave rise to a very sophisticated variation technique. Variation became essential to further atonal development and was to extend to other musical elements in addition to pitch.

One of the most important resources in the creation of a new unity was to be found in the interval itself. We have already seen how not only the divergent themes of *La Mer* (chapter 3, section 3) but also many melodic shapes in *The Rite* (and Schönberg's *op. 11* discussed below) were bound by the preponderant use of the same intervals. In this context we spoke of a sort of interval protoplasm. This unity of interval, found intuitively in the period, anticipated something that was to grow after 1950 under a new name: material structure.

3. *New Concepts of Form.* In the classical-tonal tradition the organisation of form was strongly causal. Chords, phrases and form elements succeeded one another logically, and tonal form had a closed unity. This consistency, this causality was to disappear. In the music of Debussy – it was always he who took the first steps! – harmonic functionalism already disintegrated. One could put it as follows: no resolution, but a (free) succession of chords. This went for all musical components: *generative form* was to make way for *chain structure*, the free juxtaposition of components. This developed more fully after 1950. Chain structure, incidentally, had an honourable ancestry: almost all musical forms that the world has ever produced belong to this category.

Chain structure would seem to contradict the pursuit of a unifying principal, mentioned under (2). A basic motif in Beethoven represents great musical energy that is subsequently developed by means of variation. The form is *generative*. At the other extreme, in the form of Debussy or Webern for instance, the procedure is ostensibly the same. Yet here there is no mention of generative development. The kinship is one of common interval material; there is no causality, but rather an additive structure of analogous musical components. Free form, clearly gaining ground in Debussy, corresponded to non-functional harmony, floating rhythm, melody without thematic function, etc. All form components merged into a single concept, once referred to by Debussy as 'rhythmicised time'. Inherent to this was a certain equality of the various components (equality in terms of form-function): rather than the musical language being fixated in several primary form categories, such as melody and harmony, a highly mobile, fluctuating form arose. Hence the constant changes of tempo, dynamics, timbre, rhythm, tone density and melody (athematicism!), and the erosion of traditional contrasts between homophony and polyphony. Naturally, all this occurred almost unconsciously, and to differing degrees. Both tendencies are found in Schönberg in particular, whereas later he was to opt increasingly for the classical generative form type. In fact, Schönberg projected his entire origin in the world of Beethoven and Brahms. Webern, on the other hand, was to place increasing emphasis on his affinity with early Dutch polyphony. In Schönberg's hands variation meant development and expansion; in Webern's hands it was *another aspect of the same matter*.

   We must therefore try to avoid a schematic approach to the subject. While *op. 11* displays both tendencies, the *Six Little Piano Pieces op. 19* (Example 45) are almost Webernian in their exclusion of any classical development. The period of free atonality was a time of transition; this meant that most tendencies were reflected in one and the same composer, in one and the same work.

The aforementioned ran exactly parallel with another process: the replacement of diatonic structural principles by chromatic ones. This was not undertaken intentionally – it was simply that chromaticism implied other laws. This can be clarified by comparison with sculpture, in which the close interaction between material structure and design is strongly visible, and in which the artist may not ignore this material structure with impunity, for wood reacts otherwise to bronze or concrete. Chromaticism worked differently from diatonicism; we can even go as far as to say that chromaticism undermined the laws of diatonicism. Naturally, we are referring to the fully realised chromaticism of atonality, in which chromaticism was not a mere colouring of the diatonic scale. We are faced here for the first time by the real consequence of equal temperament: we have at our disposal twelve autonomous notes in the octave, which only await an adequate notation system with twelve independent symbols. This chromatic octave is entirely symmetrical and can be divided into equal parts in various ways:

a. Twelve equal minor 2nds (atonality).

b. Six equal major 2nds (Debussy). NB: parallels between Debussy and the Viennese School have already been pointed out. Debussy preferred to avoid genuine chromaticism. Yet his division of the octave into six parts (the whole-tone series) produced the same result! For apart from symmetry, the main features of the whole-tone series are the absence of leading notes, and 4ths and 5ths, the basic intervals of tonal diatonicism.

c. Four equal minor 3rds. This includes the chord of the diminished 7th, renowned for its tonal ambiguity; but it was also the framework of Messiaen's frequently employed second mode (see chapter 4, section 3).

d. Three equal major 3rds. The augmented triad, likewise often employed in late romantic music for the same reason as the chord of the diminished 7th.

e. Two equal parts, producing the tritone, the chromatic half-octave. The tritone relationship played a major role from the beginning, particularly in Bartók, whose modulations frequently oscillate at the distance of a tritone. Vertically speaking it had already cropped up in *Petrushka* in the form of two combined triads separated by a tritone. See also chapter 4, section 3 (2) and section 8 (5).

Thus, the gravity of the major and minor scale was opposed to the symmetry of chromaticism. In tonality all notes relate to a single fundamental, while in atonality they relate to one another. Two elements were therefore absent in atonality: the gravitational force of the fundamental (˘), and the traditional causal relationship, cadence function, etc. (›). Not until this non-hierarchical total chromaticism arose, therefore, was an interchange possible between above and below, before and behind. The directed passage of time in tonality became a spatial juxtaposition in atonality.

Atonal chromaticism, born of the pursuit of new expressive resources, lent form to new structural principles arising from the symmetrical nature of chromaticism:

a: We are now able to understand Schönberg's theory of musical space. Its principle is that horizontal and vertical elements are identical in musical space, being merely different aspects of the same phenomenon. A horizontal motif of several notes can be compressed to a single chord: it remains the same musical object – only the shape is different. The traditional distinction between melody and harmony therefore disappeared. This also explains the preference for classical polyphonic variants such as inversion and retrograde: these too, being *mirror forms*, are *identical* to the original material. Example 75 elucidates this:

EXAMPLE 75

The pre-eminently chromatic 'Bach' motif P (prime form) is mirrored horizontally in I (inversion). In R it is mirrored vertically from back to front (retrograde). IR is a combination of the two (inversion of retrograde). In S it is compressed into a simultaneity. In this case, moreover, P is identical to IR, and I to R.

b: *Chromatic completion.* A high degree of chromatic balance can be obtained by filling in chromatic fields.[4] This chromatic completion is even found in the extended tonality of Bartók's *Fifth String Quartet*, in which the 11-note theme is completed by a held B♭ (Example 76).

EXAMPLE 76

Other examples include Bartók's *Sixth String Quartet* (Example 29), the fugue subject in the *Music* (Example 54), the second theme from his *Violin Concerto*, and many passages in the *Fourth String Quartet*. Such completion is a logical aftereffect of chromatic symmetry. In a negative light it can also be deployed to counter tonal tendencies. But this hardly seems essential, which is why examples by Bartók are deliberately quoted here. This last remark brings us to the third point.

c: The use of *tone fields*, familiar from Debussy. It is striking that Anton Webern, the very composer who explored chromaticism furthest of all, employed many tone fields (see Example 78). Yet here again there is no mention of distinctly preferential notes! Tonal gravity, however, is absent. The tone field (see chapter 4, section 4) provides a new structural resource to replace traditional tonal devices. Certain notes do dominate, but they are neutralised, stripped of any gravitational force, as Debussy had already done with much more traditional chords. Later (see Example 91) Webern developed these tone fields into complete symmetrical blocks in which the real structure of chromaticism – symmetry – came very clearly to the surface.

There is a widespread misunderstanding that in atonality each note must be treated equally in terms of frequency and value. Brief reflection is enough to reveal the absurdity of this. Such a situation could only be attained by the continuous and comprehensive use of all twelve notes, above and after one other. If that was the case, wouldn't it be more fun to play with a *real* box of bricks?

2

To illustrate the above matters, two pieces from the early period of free atonality will now be analysed: one of the *Three Piano Pieces op. 11* by Schönberg (1909), and one of the *Five Pieces for String Quartet op. 5* by Webern (1909).

EXAMPLE 77

Bars 1-11 of Example 77 (Schönberg, *op. 11*) represent a small A-B-A form. The horizontally unfolding motif in A (the first three bars) has a traditional appearance. There are two characteristic aspects: the interval structure (only 3rds and 2nds) and the chromatic 6-note field (creating considerable chromaticism within a short period). The 3rd and 2nd (major or minor) prove to function as interval material. The chord in bar 3 is similarly formed (as one sees by reading the lowest note B♭ an octave higher). The middle section B is built on the same basis: the soprano has a 3rd, the alto two 2nds, while the tenor has both intervals. It is a typical example of athematicism: a horizontal, vertical and diagonal unfolding of certain intervals, and all this with a free application of rhythm! This is well illustrated by the shifting voices in the next two segments of B. Bar 13 introduces a different rhythmic version of the same intervals F-D-C♯ and A-F♯-F. Athematicism is not constant here: the repeated section A (bars 9-11) is a traditional thematic variant. Comparison of the two reveals that while the athematic variation has a far greater span, it is much more difficult to recognise. A highly differentiated musical ear is required to perceive this cohesion.

A closer look at the chromaticism in this fragment reveals an increasing density. The first three bars A form a 9-note field, as do the first two segments of B; the third adds D♭ to create a 10-note field. The repeat of A (bars 9-11) also forms a 10-note field, while bar 12, finally, presents a field of eleven notes. Although total chromaticism is not yet consciously pursued, there is clearly an extremely refined, intuitive use of chromatic possibilities. It is remarkable, for instance, that while the first 11 bars contain very dense chromaticism, the note E♭ is avoided. This note is introduced as a bass in bar 12, turning all the foregoing into a sort of 'chromatic upbeat'! The other important note in bar 12, the high C♯, is not heard in the preceding three bars. The entire passage is a good example of chromatic completion, not applied mechanically but in an extremely supple manner: it does not fit together quite well enough to assume a conscious technique. Thus, the doubling of the note F in bar 2 would be inconceivable in later, classical dodecaphony.

Finally, the atonal use of large leaps should be pointed out, though still a very modest feature in this work. It occurs in bar 12 in a line descending across more than four octaves, although it really amounts to a succession of descending chromatic 2nds (B♭-A-G♯-G-F♯) filling in one of the two basic intervals, the 3rd.

The *Three Piano Pieces op. 11* are considered to be the first atonal compositions. Beside many and surprising new elements there are also traditional traits, while the spirit of the work, like the pianistic style, is entirely in keeping with late romanticism.

MUSIC OF THE TWENTIETH CENTURY

EXAMPLE 78

The *Five Pieces for String Quartet op. 5* by Webern are among the finest and most approachable expressions of the composer's first atonal period. The fourth piece (Example 78) can be divided into four sections:

1. The first two bars present an exposition of the material. Everything is extremely concentrated, and we need a musical magnifying glass to see the details! The first and second violins have three chords in A-B-A form. F is a common note, and the highest line E-F♯-E is related to it chromatically, while the two other voices undulate between B and C. The creation of chromatic relationships was one of the most striking features of the young Webern. It is therefore quite natural that the highest note E is countered by an E♭ in the cello part. The vertical structure of the chords is also based on a chromatic relationship, occurring in both chords between the (vertically read) notes B and C, and F and E. The viola motif E-F♯ is a free imitation of the high notes in the first violin. Finally, chromatic fields occur in the form of a chromatically filled minor 3rd (E♭-E-F-F♯) and a minor 2nd (B-C). From bar 3 the remaining notes are introduced; placed in succession they form a filled minor 3rd (G-G♯-A-B♭) and a minor 2nd (C♯-D). Further on, both intervals are to play a specific role.

2. Bars 3-6 present another aspect of I. In the first and second violins and cello a successive horizontal version of the three chords in I is chromatically related (⎯):

EXAMPLE 79

It is now clearer that interval diminution occurs: the 5th, tritone and perfect 4th, respectively. This is to have its repercussions in the closing formula of II, the group of semiquavers in bar 6:

EXAMPLE 80

Separated by a major 2nd, interval augmentation occurs from major 3rd through perfect 4th to diminished 5th. Moreover, the first four notes C-E-F♯-B are those of the first violin in bars 1-2. This closing formula naturally begins on C, chromatically related to the preceding C♯ in the cello. This also goes for the analogous closing formula of section III in bar 10, which begins on F against the flageolet E in the cello. But there is more to be discovered in section II. In bar 3 a repeat of the motif E-F♯ in the viola commences against F in the first violin. The following C in the first violin is chromatically related to C♯ in the cello and B in the second violin (bar 4). The chord G-C♯-F♯-C at the beginning of bar 4 is strongly related to the preceding one. If one moves the lowest note to the top, or the top note to the bottom, the same interval augmentation is obtained. Thereafter, the conclusion of II commences: in the viola F♯-G-F♯, the undulating movement from I; in the first violin and cello a melodic extension of the second violin motif in bar 4, with the parts shifted in relation to one another.

3. Bars 7-9 present an extremely static tone field. Here, pedal point and ostinato are the trusty resources while, unusually for Webern, chromatic ramifications are *absent*. The first violin B is even related by an octave to the second violin. All this creates clear contrast, reinforced by the fact that the chromaticism changes into a Debussy-like *overtone scale*: when read vertically this tone field indeed comprises many of the overtones of the note E:

EXAMPLE 81

The little violin motif above is again in A-B-A form, with B as a short deviation from the field of harmonics:

EXAMPLE 82

4. The last three bars contain a free and shifted repeat of earlier elements from I and II. We recall the chromatic field mentioned under I, consisting of a chromatically filled minor 3rd and a minor 2nd. Though the role of the minor 2nd has meanwhile become clear, note the line B-C-B (bars 1 and 2) via F♯-G-F♯ (bar 5) to D-C♯ (bar 6). The minor 3rd has a similar structural line. In the opening two bars E♭-F♯ demarcate the compass. In bar 6 the minor 3rd (G-B♭) crops up again in the conclusion of fragment II. This line is now prolonged via B-G♯ (bars 7 and 8), C-E♭ (bars 8 and 10) to E♭-F♯ (bar 13), the 3rd with which the piece also commenced. The tone field in this little piece therefore provides a clear form contrast in respect to the other sections. Other conspicuous features are the strongly chromatic ramifications which, as it were, crystallise from note to note, and the enormous reduction of material. Unlike Bartók and sometimes Stravinsky,

Webern's chromaticism is not thickset, but is characterised by relaxed and wide textures. For a further discussion of this movement, see the rhythmic analysis (chapter 2, section 5).

3

The name of Debussy has cropped up frequently in the foregoing pages. Let us now summarise the salient similarities so far found between the musical structure of his own works on the one hand and those employing free atonality on the other:

1. Autonomy of simultaneity and increasing differentiation of other musical elements (fluctuating tempo, timbre, dynamics, etc.)
2. Release from the classical causal context
3. Analogous structure of total chromaticism and the whole-tone scale
4. Influence of the interval
5. Tone field
6. Floating rhythm

Naturally, one should avoid generalisation. We are primarily concerned here with Debussy and Webern, and as far as the former is concerned, with only a small part of an oeuvre which was written much earlier. Moreover, both composers shared a resolute aversion to any sort of pathos. Let us compare Schönberg and Webern.

Schönberg (1874-1951), the elder of the two and the teacher, underwent a gradual development from late-romantic floating tonality to atonality. His late-romantic period (up to 1908) included *Verklärte Nacht* (1899), a 'symphonic poem' for chamber music ensemble (string sextet). This work by the 25-year-old composer was highly romantic in its expression, like the poem by Richard Dehmel upon which it was based. The harmonic style was daring, but did not venture beyond the boundaries established at the time by Mahler and Strauss. Conspicuous, however, is the strongly developed motivic-contrapuntal treatment that was to become so characteristic of Schönberg's further development. Via the *Gurrelieder* (1901), *Pelléas und Mélisande* (1903) and the *Chamber Symphony* (1906), he came to the last work of this period, the *Second String Quartet op. 10* with soprano (1907-08). It has the same heavily charged romanticism, the same motivic density; the simultaneity, however, is much further developed, and in the final movement in particular it reaches the boundaries of tonality.

Expressivity was the main cause of increasing chromaticism. The transition from tonality to atonality was only an outcome of this. Schönberg's early years of free atonality were characterised by a remarkable productivity. 1909: *Three Piano Pieces op. 11*, *Five Orchestral Pieces op. 16*, *Erwartung op. 17*; 1911: *Six Little Piano Pieces op. 19*, *Herzgewächse op. 20*; 1912: *Pierrot lunaire op. 21*. Here free atonality was spontaneously and volcanically explored. No compositions were completed in the years 1914-23; instead, Schönberg reflected on the new situation, and this was to find expression in the 12-note technique. Thus, *bound atonality* made its entry in 1923.

The most important characteristic of this historic course of development was a subjectivism taken to the very limits, coupled to a desire to convert it into objective forms. If we add to this Schönberg's most complex musical imagination and his inclination towards the absolute and the uncompromising, then we can see why it was precisely he who drew the consequences from late romanticism. A late romantic and a vigilant renewer: the division arising from this was not felt deeply until the stimulating forces of expressionism had been extinguished.

Webern's life (1883-1945) knew no such division, unless it was that of a great composer who was misunderstood throughout his life. Until the very end he was not aware of the full extent of this cleft. 'I believe that people will be astounded!' he wrote passionately in 1944 about his string orchestra transcription of *op. 5*. But nobody was astounded! And this was hardly to be expected at a time when official musical life was becoming increasingly superficial. Poignantly symbolic of these years is the fact that a contemporary music festival in Vienna not only failed to perform Webern's music, but that the composer was too poor to buy a ticket and was allowed to listen at the door.[5] His life's end, like that of Bartók, formed the greatest indictment against the official contemporary music world. His modesty and reserve bring another great fellow countryman to mind: Anton Bruckner. Both composers worked towards a world of their own, the full scale of which even they themselves were not aware.

Although Webern learnt much from Schönberg, he went his own way. Even his expressionism was chaste and austere, as the *Five Movements op. 5 for string quartet* (1909) reveal. Right and left are the words 'soft', 'fading', 'very calm': rather than being driven by impetuosity, the composer's new tonal world was the opening of a lifelong inner monologue. The next instrumental work, the *Six Pieces for orchestra op. 6* of 1910 (see Example 58), was a relapse; it is much less differentiated than *op. 5*, with a somewhat forced and facile pathos. Webern was apparently susceptible to the outward influences of his time. But he recovered quickly, and in 1913 and 1914 he wrote three instrumental works, *op. 9, 10* and *11*, of which the *Six Bagatelles op. 9*, for example, leave an impression of concentrated and highly refined atonality. Webern approached a 'punctual' style here, and motifs that were still comparatively long for his style in *op. 5* were now split up almost to the interval. Comparison with a work like Schönberg's *Pierrot lunaire* from the same period is most enlightening, in that it illustrates how the two composers drifted apart. But in both cases a surprising turn of events was in store. Schönberg maintained silence until 1923, while Webern turned to song, composing a considerable number from *op. 12* to *op. 19* (1915-26). With the exception of *op. 12* these songs all require large instrumental forces: timbre was an important vehicle for the expressionist Webern. But at the same time we see that remarkable process of consolidation manifest among all great composers of the time, and revealed in Webern through an increasingly contrapuntal style. A well-known example is *op. 16*, the *Five Canons on Latin Texts* (1924). Whether the use of texts in Webern's music was related to the pursuit of formal unity remains uncertain. Whatever the case may be, on the whole his songs are no longer than the instrumental pieces. Perhaps there was a reaction here to the preceding 'punctual' phase, for the melodic line in the vocal part (particularly in *op. 12*) is of unusual length and tightness for Webern. Forty years later a similar reaction was evident among young composers against the punctual style of about 1952.

We have described Webern's music as an 'inner monologue'. This was his greatness and at the same time his limitation. Of historical significance is the fact that he drifted away from Schönberg and thus from the world of late romanticism and expressionism. In its place a new classicism slowly emerged, in the sense that expression became not an aim but a result of form. Traditional subjectivism veered around in a new identity between form and content. By stripping atonality of its expressionist principle, it was able to develop from a local, central European affair into a worldwide renewal, which stirred not only the young generation of 1950 but also an ageing master like Stravinsky.[6]

Webern's music is absolutely individual. He does not overwhelm, neither shock, nor make matters easy for the listener. It is entirely up to the latter to penetrate this closed world. The restriction lies especially in the strongly emphasised asceticism and purity of the composer. This characteristic was later to lead to the steep heights of the *String Quartet op. 28* (1938), the most reduced, naked music ever written. At the same time Schönberg slowly but surely slid back to a form of tonality, while Alban Berg wrote his last work, the *Violin Concerto* (1935), which in terms of both technique and spirit was entirely in the tradition of late romanticism.[7]

4

BOUND ATONALITY. In chapter 1 the second half of the first period was typified as displaying a strong tendency towards reduction and consolidation of accomplished innovation. This was indeed an almost general characteristic, and one of its manifestations was a renewed interest in counterpoint, as is witnessed by Hindemith, Stravinsky and Bartók. In the case of Bartók it took the form of strongly chromatic counterpoint (especially in the *Fourth String Quartet*, 1928) applied in a most individual manner that sometimes closely approached the Viennese School. Essentially, however, Bartók's music too remained tonal. Of the Viennese School it was Webern in particular who introduced an increasingly contrapuntal density in his series of songs. This brought him to follow certain procedures also customary in 12-note technique, but what is essential is that, with or without this 12-note technique, through the use of counterpoint he reached the stage of *bound atonality*.

Characteristic of this gradual process was that sound lost significance purely as a means of expression and became increasingly determined by structure. In other words: the expressionist tonal world attained around 1910 was not altered, but slowly and surely objectified. A pianist playing the end of the *Piano Variations op. 27*, one of Webern's most severe works of 1936, may therefore catch an echo of the free, expressionist period of 1909 (*op. 5*, beginning of the last movement). And so the adoption of 12-note technique in 1924 brought no change in his compositional style.

Schönberg's last work before he fell silent was *op. 22: Four Orchestral Songs* dating from 1913-16. The *Five Piano Pieces op. 23* were written in 1920-1923 and deserve our attention in view of the fact that one of the movements employed 12-note technique for the first time. Although the technique of the other movements may perhaps be considered a preliminary to this, it is particularly interesting because it reveals a remarkable parallel with Webern's preoccupation in the same period, namely counterpoint. The technique is serial, in other words the musical material is based on a series, though not yet of 12 notes. The beginning of the third movement of *op. 23* is as follows; the linear development of the series is given below for comparison:

EXAMPLE 83

Naturally, this again is a form of bound atonality. Although the series comprises only five notes, in terms of total chromaticism the simultaneity in this movement is no different from much 12-note music. Nonetheless, Schönberg was to introduce the 12-note series; it was to remain the standard for all classical dodecaphony until about 1950.

The opening bars of the first 12-note work (the fifth movement of *op. 23*) follow; historically speaking, if not artistically too, they were of the greatest historical significance:

EXAMPLE 84

At the beginning of this chapter, we have seen that chromaticism as a material evoked new and individual laws. Though composers understood them intuitively, especially Webern once more, this was not enough. For if we compare the material of classical tonality, the diatonic major and minor scale, with the autonomous chromatic series, the latter proves to be at a strong disadvantage:

EXAMPLE 85

Major scale
    different intervals
    a single tone centre to which all notes are related
    differentiated hierarchy: distinction in significance of the notes
    triadic structure
    leading-note function

Chromatic series
    all intervals equal
    no tone centre, all-round symmetry
    no hierarchy, but grey, levelled equality
    no specific vertical structures
    no leading-note function: twelve autonomous chromatic notes

Conclusion: the diatonic material is *formed.* A composer using the major and minor scales *well,* must almost automatically write tonal music – a close interaction is present. Atonal, chromatic material is *formless* (see also section 1). Symmetry and non-hierarchy steer the composer towards atonality; however, this chromatic material requires greater structuralisation.

    The 12-note series brought about the desired structuralisation once and for all. The idea is simple: if the notes of a chromatic series cannot differ in *significance*, they must differ in *place.* Traditional functions of the notes are replaced by their interval relationships: they are involved with one another. The composer fixates the twelve chromatic notes in a certain order that is binding throughout the composition. Formlessness is turned into a concrete sequence of pitches and intervals. Chromaticism thus gains form, and the 12-note series becomes *material structure*. Put somewhat schematically: where a tonal composer can begin directly, basing his work on well-structured material, the atonal composer must first form his material, his series. He can create a different series for each composition, adapted to his specific ideas and desires. Naturally, in practice this distinction does not usually exist. Webern wrote: 'Our – Schönberg's, Berg's and my own – series usually arose because an idea became related to the whole intuitively conceived work, which then underwent careful consideration – exactly as one can follow the genesis of Beethoven's themes in the sketchbooks.'[8] These 'considerations' were: the preference for certain intervals, for certain correspondences within the series, such as symmetry, analogy, groups of three or four notes, etc. This also implies that the 12-note series is in principle not a melody or theme! For the latter are form categories of a higher order, while we are concerned here with a very early preliminary forming of the material. The two may coincide, of course, just as a traditional theme sometimes amounts to part or all of a diatonic scale, for instance.

Another consequence is that the 12-note series may indeed ensure unity in a composition, in that a certain coherence may be experienced. Of essential importance, however, is the manner in which the composer goes on to handle the series; in other words: coherence must be realised on a higher, musical level, rather than remaining only a question of material. Misunderstanding on this point has proved fatal to many a composer.

The series in itself, however, is not sufficient. Decisive for the music is its unfolding. It is therefore hardly possible to speak of *the* 12-note technique, since the variations are unlimited. But several general points may be mentioned. In the first place the series is employed in four forms: P = prime form, I = inversion, R = retrograde, IR = inversion and retrograde. These are called *mirror forms* because they mirror the basic series horizontally or vertically without affecting its basic shape. They are identical.

EXAMPLE 86

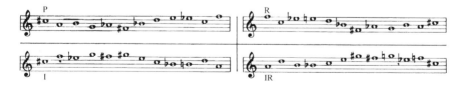

The reader should refer to what has been said in section 1 on musical space. According to this concept, the horizontal and vertical are identical, and the notes of a series can therefore be arranged both in succession and simultaneously. In the same line of thought, a series can be divided into groups of three or four notes, for example, that lead an almost autonomous life as small cells. In this context the description of athematicism in section 1 is of importance. Other options include transposition, octave displacement, rotation, interpolation... Discussion of all these phenomena would amount to an analysis of the individual style of various 12-note composers. There were hardly any generally valid laws, and what was required is an unlimited imagination. For, as has been said before, the reduction of the entire musical discourse to a single point of departure gave rise to a richly developed art of variation. Variation techniques grew unprecedentedly as continuous innovation became an aesthetic principle in itself. Literal repetition was quite rare, except in a few later works by Webern.

Faithfulness to the original intervals and pitches (see section 1) implied that variation was primarily a *rhythmic art*. And once more we encounter curious similarities. Indian raga players do precisely the same when they create variations on their melodic-modal formulas, while our distant ancestors gave rhythm to their cantus firmus, sometimes in short, broken fragments, and sometimes in endlessly slow threads winding through a polyphonic texture.

The 12-note technique was nothing other than the crystallisation of compositional practices and concepts that were intuitively manifest in the preceding period of free atonality. This transition is therefore imperceptible in the oeuvre of the Viennese composers. The technique was like a new tool in the hands of the same players. Of interest is the view of Herbert Eimert,[9] who believed that the first notions of dodecaphony had been in the air for a long time, and were formulated by three other figures independent of Schönberg: Hauer (from 1908), Golyshev (from 1914) and Eimert himself (1923).

5

The following analyses help us to discuss several of the possibilities and to elaborate on the differences between Schönberg and Webern which have already been mentioned.

Let us first examine the theme from the *Variations for Orchestra op. 31* (1928), Schönberg's first orchestral work to employ 12-note technique. The primitive organisation of his firstling *op. 23* (see Example 84) had been overcome, and the work is a magnificent sample sheet of Schönberg's mastership and versatility, for almost every variation reveals quite a different facet. From the extremes of variation 7, with its light and almost pointillist touch, to the actual theme, which is discussed here as a characteristic example of the composer's bond with tradition.

MUSIC OF THE TWENTIETH CENTURY

EXAMPLE 87

EXAMPLE 87 (CONTINUED)

12-note structure. The series P (for the entire work) and the extremely frequent form I10^{10} (Example 88). The second half of P1 has the same notes as the first half of I10 but in a different sequence, a common feature in Schönberg. Thus, it is possible to employ P1 and I10 simultaneously and in parallel motion without causing note doubling.

EXAMPLE 88

The series continuation is as follows:
    theme: P1   IR8   R3   I10
    chords: I10   R3   IR8   P1   with subsidiary voice P4 (cellos).
The two parts therefore move in opposite directions.[11]

Musical structure. The theme in the cellos, with its ascending line and lyrical character, is in four sections. These coincide with the forms of the series employed (which is not always the case by any means). In the score it is indicated by H (*Hauptstimme* = main voice).

All the characteristics of a solid and traditional structure are present: metrical organisation, small leaps, normal *Sekundgang*, moments of rest at the end of each phrase, and classical motif structure. Each phrase contains three variants of the rhythmic motif A.

    A: ♪♩.♪♩ (the final note may be extended)
    A1: ♪♩.♪♩ (thus with the addition of ♪)
    A2: 𝄾 ♩.♪♩ (thus with the subtraction of ♪)

A1 and A2 also occur in diminution, indicated by small letters. The sequence of rhythmic motifs corresponds with the forms of the series (prime direction or in reverse; Schönberg does not employ rhythmic inversion).

Theme phrase 1:	A	a1	A2	›
Theme phrase 2:	A2	A1	A	‹
Theme phrase 3:	a2	a1	A	‹
Theme phrase 4:	A	A1	A2	›

Each motif of the theme has the same number of notes as the simultaneous chord. The arrangement of the forms of the series produces another correspondence: all chords are the *vertical and inverted* projections of the motifs. In musical terms this implies a precise reflection of melodic intervals in the accompaniment, something already found, though employed intuitively, in the early songs of Webern.

The words 'melody' and 'accompaniment' have been used instinctively. For despite strict structure in rhythmic-harmonic and melodic terms, and despite strict interaction between theme and chords, the essential truth of this example is that Schönberg achieved a result that only deviates in terms of harmony from the classical-romantic tradition.[12]

The above example was a paragon of strict logic. Let us now examine the somewhat freer treatment in the *Piano Piece op. 33a* of 1932 (Example 89):

12-note structure. Once again two forms, P1 and I6 are employed, with the same correspondence: the second half of P1 has the same notes as the first half of I6, in a different order (Example 90). The series is divided into groups of three, four and six notes; in our fragment we see three groups of four, named A, B and C for P1, and A1, B1 and C1 for I6. The 5th plays a prominent role: P1 and I6 are related by a 5th; moreover, the series includes three 5ths.

EXAMPLE 89

EXAMPLE 90

The series continuation (in groups):

bars 1-2:   A B C, C₁ B₁ A₁

bars 3-5: $\dfrac{\text{C₁ B₁ A₁}}{\text{C B A}}$

bars 6-7:   A B C, C₁ B₁ A₁

bars 8-9: $\dfrac{\text{A A B C}}{\text{A₁ A₁ B₁ C₁}}$

Musical structure. The preference for 5ths and the division into groups provide two important means of contrast. At various points in the work, accumulations of 5ths create contrast in the generally more complex simultaneity. In Example 89 there is a first and very modest instance of this in bar 5. The effect of contrast is even stronger by means of the division into groups. Group B is distinguished from A and C by a more blended character, enabling direct recognition and characterisation of the vertical sound (the same goes for

EXAMPLE 91

EXAMPLE 92

Webern's series in *op. 30*, see Example 94). The division into groups also enables a more flexible use of the series. The first two bars present an exposition of the two fundamental forms: this is the material that is later to be of influence, among other things through the ascending and descending curves. In bar 3 a motivic development begins, and it is conspicuous that the four-note motifs gradually dissolve into other groups.

The rhythmic density of bars 8 and 9 leads to a variant repetition of bars 1 and 2. The A group occurs twice in bar 8, rhythmically different, and bar 9 demonstrates how group B provides contrast in the simultaneity. An important means of articulation with regard to the form is the time span within which a series (i.e. the complete 12-note field) occurs. This does not always coincide with rhythmic density: bar 1, rhythmically calm, contains a 12-note field, while bar 8 includes no more than eight chromatic notes.

Webern's *Piano Variations op. 27* dates from 1936. It is a work of extreme severity and austerity, most characteristic of this period (Example 91).

12-note structure. The principal forms are given in Example 92. Both halves of the series fill a chromatic 4th. The note B is a pivot, being the end of P1 and I3 and the beginning of R8 and IR8; thus, the corresponding tritone in the middle, which is to play a prominent role.

The series continuation is given schematically in Figure 5:

FIGURE 5:

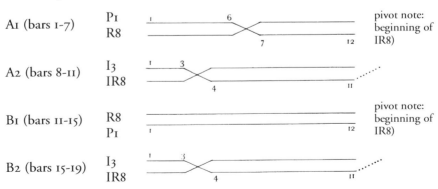

Each segment combines two forms that are each other's retrograde. It is a different version of Schönberg's aim to combine the forms such that their simultaneous employment does not give rise to doubled notes.

Musical structure. The fragment reveals a four-segment structure, determined by the above distribution of forms. Each segment therefore has a mirror structure and thus forms a closed unit. A further similarity is the constant occurrence of small groups. The vertical pitch structure, finally, is often determined by a chord consisting of the 4th and the tritone. This is a result of the chosen combination of the two forms.

The mirrored segments are never entirely symmetrical. Rhythmically speaking, the second half of A1 is not a mirror but a repetition with interchanged voices. In A2 the second half is diminuendo. B1 also has a dynamic difference in addition to contrasts of register and interval (the minor 9th becomes a major 7th). B2 provides dynamic contrast and a difference in density.

The differentiated asymmetry thus created is greatest in the second half (B1 and B2) and goes to dissipate an exaggeratedly schematic mirror image. This brings us to the differences between the four segments, which are also perceptible on another level, namely in dynamics and chromatic density. The same chromatic material – 24 notes – occurs continuously in an ever-changing time span. This is also particularly evident in the small groups, which can be more or less pressed together both horizontally and vertically. A1 presents a calm and even distribution. A2 is strongly tightened. B1 is less so, but has on the other hand striking contrasts in its mirrored halves. B2 begins with considerable density but loosens up later. The ritenuto brings the transition to the next form section.

Thus, the symmetry inherent in chromaticism is revealed here in the musical form. The interaction between material and form is greater than was the case in Schönberg. There is therefore no longer a trace of traditional thematicism; instead, quite different types of form contrast emerge. Rather than being abstract, however, they are perceptible musical quantities, but of a different and often more subtle order. The mirrored blocks stem from traditional tonal fields and lend structure to the greater form. Note repetitions and correspondences originate in the chromatic fields; they are, however, completely free from tonal gravitational forces. Rather, spatially juxtaposed blocks each represent a different aspect of the same material. The vertical pitch structure within these blocks is fixated both horizontally and vertically.

The final example by Webern is taken from his *Variations for orchestra op. 30*, dating from 1940 (Example 93). At first glance it appears to be a freer composition; upon further investigation, however, it is a score of particular significance.

An analysis of only the 12-note technique is not adequate here. In Schönberg's *op. 31* we have already seen how he endeavoured to give structure to the rhythmic element. Webern was to enlarge upon this. It is necessary to

EXAMPLE 93

		A			B			C			D		
series forms	P		P2 a		b		c	R1 c	b	a	P1 a	b	c
	H	P1 a	b	c	R1 c	b	a	R12 c	b	a	P2 a	b	c
rhythm	H	a	b	c	(R) c	b1	(R) a	c	b1	a	(R) a	b1	(R) c
duration	H	7 ♪	3 ♪	3½ ♪	3½ ♪	5 ♪	7 ♪	3½ ♪	3 ♪	7 ♪	7 ♪	5 ♪	3½ ♪
position	P		lh		l		l	l	l	lh	l	h	l
	H	l	h	l	h	l	h	l	h	l	h	l	h
instrumentation	P		vla		vlc		arp, cb	trb, tb	crd	arp, vla	fi—ote	ob	fi—ote
	H	cb	ob	trb	vl	cl—b	vl	vlc	fl, ob, cl	tb	vl	cl—b	vl
dynamic	P		f (fp)		f		p, ppp	f	sf	p, pp (>)	sff	p > pp	pp >
	H	p < > pp	f >	f < >	f	sf > p	p > pp	f	f <	p >	f < ff (<)	sfp > pp	pp < pp
density		1	2	1	2	1	2	2	1½	2	1½	2	1½
tempo	♪ = 160 / ♪ = 112						rit.			rit.			molto rit.

approach the work equally schematically and to gather all musical aspects in a single diagram.

These eight different aspects will be examined one by one in the *Hauptstimme* (H).

EXAMPLE 94

Series forms. The series itself (Example 94) is a classic example of extreme reduction. It is symmetrical: P1 = IR12 and R12 = I12. Only two different forms are therefore possible (leaving aside transpositions), referred to below as P and R. The reduction goes further: there are three related four-note groups, (a) and (c) have two minor 2nds and a minor 3rd, (b) has two minor 3rds and a 2nd. The entire series thus consists of two intervals and has the greatest possible unity of series form, interval, motif and chords.[13] Identical four-note groups also arise between the fourth and seventh, and the sixth and ninth notes! The series continuation employs P1 and P2, R1 and R12. P1 and P12 are identical (the same pitches), as are P2 and R1. As far as the *Hauptstimme* is concerned, a crosswise relation is therefore created between A and C, B and D (even the register position remains the same).

Rhythm. Here again there are three cells: (a), (b) and (c). They remain coupled to the similarly named pitch cells. Even the internal structure of the three cells reveals the same mirror image: (c) is (in diminution) R of (a), (b) is likewise mirrored in itself. The subsidiary voice always enters later.

Duration. The duration of the three groups demonstrates that (a) and (c) remain constant, while (b) lasts for three and five quavers alternately. This is a rationalised form of Stravinsky's variable ostinato (see chapter 2, section 7).

Position. The register change occurs very regularly from high to low. Coupled to this is a structuralisation of the instrumentation.

Instrumentation. Here again the correspondence between A and C on the one hand and B and D on the other is evident: the former with low strings, high woodwind and low brass, the latter with high strings, low woodwind and high brass.

Dynamics. There are two main grades, *f* and *p*; instead of the all-too utopian post-1950 differentiation, therefore, we see a much more effective means in the form of transition dynamics. Webern was probably conscious of the problem of dynamics, since he also took care to give the subsidiary voice (P) the same loudness as the *Hauptstimme*.

Density. Here again we find regularity, and correspondence between A and C on the one hand, B and D on the other. The numbers indicate (1) one four-note group; (2) two simultaneous four-note groups; (1 1/2) two simultaneous four-note groups, one of which is in the form of a brief vertical sound.

As in *op. 27* the high degree of symmetry is dissipated *vertically* by the combination with the subsidiary voice, which is not symmetrical,[14] and *horizontally* by the tempo.

Tempo. There are two tempos in the relation of approximately 4:3, which continually interrupt the symmetry. The fermatas too contribute to this, while the ritenutos, on the other hand, run parallel to the main division of the musical discourse.

From the above we can draw the following conclusions:

1. The work reveals a pronounced *autonomy* of many musical elements, which thus gain structural functions. This is the essential similarity with Webern's successors. How this comes about, with or without series, is secondary.

2. There is a constant interaction of symmetrical and non-symmetrical elements, which we also encountered on quite a different level in Stravinsky's rhythm.

3. Pitch correspondences of the sort discussed in relation to *op. 27* are also found; they form one of the most remarkable charms of Webern's music. Notes of the same name are heard at the same pitch; the high and low B♭ at the end of C is an exception. Further remarks on this fragment are to be found in chapter 3, section 8.

Only now can we understand the full scope of Webern's remark: 'Everything that occurs in the piece is based on the two ideas contained in the first and second bars (double bass and oboe).'[15] Elsewhere, however, he wrote: 'Fundamentally, my overture is an adagio form, but the recapitulation of the main theme appears in the form of a development, so this element is therefore present too.' And when he quotes overtures by Beethoven and Brahms in this respect, we are inclined to rub our eyes. Did this remarkably modest man indeed fail to realise what a new world he had created?

CHAPTER 8

From 12-Note Music to…

I

The step from Webern to the post-war period seems indeed to be but a small one. Let us first summarise the achievements of Webern.

The causality and gravitational pull of tonality became things of the past. The concept of 'musical space' was introduced by Debussy (*le temps ritmisé*), Stravinsky and Schönberg, and the former two in particular departed also from development form. But it was not until Webern that the new concepts of form discussed in the previous chapter (section 1) evolved.

Two processes were evident which may seem contradictory at first sight. In the first place there was a tendency towards differentiation. In the expressionist period this had been expressed primarily in strong chromaticism, motivic fragmentation and subtle playing techniques. Differentiation was later pursued more consciously and extended to other elements, even including tempo. But at the same time there was a tendency towards reduction. This stemmed from Webern's sense of balance and comprehensibility (*Fasslichkeit*), and perhaps from a mystical trait which came to the fore at a later stage, a trait not unfamiliar to figures such as Schönberg and Hauer.

In Webern's early work the principle of constant variation was still prevalent. In *op. 21*, however, he already employed literal repetition, and thereafter the symmetrical blocks discussed previously. Although subtle shifting may occur in such mirrored structures, contrast is reduced to a minimum by reason of the fact that the primary factor is ultimately pitch. All this still gave the composer a broad margin between repetition and contrast. The influence of reduction is also felt in the series, which is mirrored in itself, limited to just a few intervals, or divided into analogous cells.

Through the pursuit of differentiation, elements that had once been secondary became autonomous. However, in Webern these remained functional, continuing to lend structure to a form that is primarily a matter of pitch organisation. The so-called punctual music of a later period was to abandon this bond too, subjecting various musical elements to coequal, serial organisation.

The pursuit of reduction brought about an attitude towards the series that was immanently present but not yet clearly manifest. The series lost its last 'thematic' character and became a *regulating factor*, creating quantitative distinctions and measurable proportions. A greater and more conscious difference was made between the series as a preliminary moulding of the material, and the unfolding of this material in the musical form. In the years 1950-55 young composers were to do all that was within their power to abolish this division by upholding the fundamental unity between what was referred to as material determination (*Materialbestimmung*) and material composition (*Materialkomposition*).

This last point takes us on beyond Webern, whose achievements in the course of a lifetime were inherited by other composers. It is hardly surprising that the first so-called serial compositions seem almost primitive in comparison with those of Webern. In this respect a work such as Messiaen's *Mode de Valeurs et d'Intensités* is comparable to Schönberg's *op. 23*, the first 12-note piece. But this was not to be for long, and Webern's influence was to fade with the increasing command of the new material. A new phase was heralded.

2

Messiaen's *Mode de Valeurs et d'Intensités* was published in 1949; it was the first example of music in which four musical elements are determined in a series: pitch, duration, dynamics and touch (it is written for piano). The work is not based on four different series, therefore, but on a single series of pitches, each with its own fixated duration, loudness and touch. The composer called this a mode:

EXAMPLE 95

The mode comprises 36 notes distributed across 3 registers, 24 durations, 12 touches and 7 dynamic degrees. Durations increase evenly from 1 ♪ to 12 ♪ in the highest register, from 1 ♪ to 12 ♪ in the middle one, and from 1 ♪ to 12 ♪ in the lowest range. Example 96 illustrates how the three staves correspond with the three registers of the mode, and the manner in which the modal fixation pursued by Messiaen is created. The first note E♭ ''', for example, is played *ppp* and legato, and this remains valid for every E♭ ''' in the entire piece. The same goes for the other notes too. But the *succession* of notes, on the other hand, which was binding in dodecaphony, is free. Certain formulas may arise, however, as is the case with the first three notes of the middle stave.

EXAMPLE 96

Critical listening to this work reveals that the result is not by any means as differentiated as the technique would lead one to suppose. The reason lies primarily in the durations chosen. While there is far too much diversity of duration (from 1 ♪ to 48 ♪), it is smoothed out again by mutual relationships. Nobody can distinguish between durations of 11 ♪ and 12 ♪. Theoretically this should be possible between 1 ♪ and 2 ♪, since this is a proportion of 1:2, but within the whole these values are so fast that considerable inaccuracy will occur. Moreover, Messiaen introduced a kind of gravitational pull by lengthening the notes from high to low. The result is that the listener really only distinguishes between two general averages: high and fast, low and very slow.

This composition technique therefore lends existence to the note itself, not in a relationship to other notes, but as an individual and autonomous quality shaped by four components. The simultaneity, even more than in Webern's mirror structures, is entirely static – which is hardly surprising in view of Messiaen's familiar preference for modality. There are 36 tone objects, beyond which nothing is possible, but within which these independent tone objects move like stars in a mysterious universe. Music gained a new dimension, and this is what brought young composers around 1950 to listen in fascination – only later was criticism to follow.

3

One of those young composers was Pierre Boulez, a pupil of Messiaen and Leibowitz. The latter confronted him with 12-note music, which was to be of decisive significance for his further development. However, classical 12-note technique as taught by Leibowitz quickly became too academic for him, and he moved towards a freer manner of writing based on short melodic and rhythmic cells. An example from this period is the *Second Piano Sonata* of 1948. A rhythmic analysis is given in Example 20; below is a short consideration of the pitch structure of this work.

The first two bars present a 12-note series, divided into three cells A, B and B1 (Example 97). The mutual coherence of these cells reminds one of Webern:

Cell A: a 5th is followed by the smaller interval of a 4th.

Cell B: after the 5th comes the larger interval of the minor 6th.

Cell B1: the vertical inversion of B.

EXAMPLE 97

The entire segment (Example 20, bars 1-10) is built up of groups of three, four or six notes from the series, plus the inversion (commencing in bar 3), which is no longer complete. The free interplay of the cells has become more important than the development of the series. Interval characteristics also play a role once more. The main intervals in this segment can be represented as two, four or five units with inversions, in which the unit is the minor 2nd. In the ensuing segment (not given here) we see a slowly increasing ascendancy of interval number one, the minor 2nd, which is already present in cell A (D-D♯ and A-G♯). Thereafter, a third segment follows (likewise not given here)

which is the IR of the first. Thus, despite the impetuosity of Boulez's first works, there is a tendency towards strict form which was to predominate in the later works *Polyphonie* and *Structures* (livre I).

Structures (1952) for two pianos has already been mentioned in chapter 6, section 6. Here again the first movement is based on several segments, the first of which is given in Example 98.

In each segment a number of forms of the series occur one above the other: two, four, three, one and six, respectively, etc. They begin and end together, since note duration is also determined serially. Each pitch series is thus coupled to one and the same duration series, with a total of 1+2+...+12 $\flat$ =78 $\flat$, but each time in a different succession. Both series are derived from Messiaen's *Mode de Valeurs et d'Intensités* (see Example 95); the pitch series is the same (the upper twelve in Messiaen). The duration series employs the same type: a series of values between 1 $\flat$ and 12 $\flat$. A glance at the example reveals that pitch and duration change with each note, while loudness and touch remain the same. But they too are organised serially, though they change only with each segment. The first segment has two series forms: PI (Piano I) and II (Piano II). The upper duration series (expressed in $\flat$) is: 12, 11, 9, 10, 3, 6, 7, 1, 2, 8, 4, 5; the lower series is: 5, 8, 6, 4, 3, 9, 2, 1, 7, 11, 10, 12.

The question arises how Boulez arrived at this succession and what criteria determine its continuation. The answer is provided by Györgi Ligeti.[1] It can be summarised in a few sentences.

All material is subject to the given pitch series. Boulez numbers these from 1 to 12 (Example 99) and subsequently creates a transposition beginning on note 2 while retaining the numbering of the first series (Example 100). Then he commences a transposition on note 3, etc., thus creating a group of number series which he organises as a sort of chessboard. The same procedure produces a second chessboard based on II. The reader inclined to reconstruct these two chessboards will notice that the above mentioned duration series in Piano I occurs in the bottom row of the second chessboard, while that of Piano II is in the bottom row of the first chessboard (both read from back to front). Now the picture becomes clear: all sequences of the four parameters that are to be organised can be deduced from this chessboard. They can be 'read' horizontally, vertically or diagonally. *How* this actually occurs is unimportant; we must occupy ourselves with the question *why* the composer chose this procedure.

The intention is clear. The relationships in the given pitch series literally form the all-embracing criterion. The chessboards are slightly clumsy but convenient representations of these relationships. Thus, Boulez aims to give the four parameters a high degree of organisation, and to obtain unity by relating these parameters to the same mutual relationships. The similarity

EXAMPLE 98

EXAMPLE 99

EXAMPLE 100

MUSIC OF THE TWENTIETH CENTURY

with Messiaen is only superficial. For Boulez disrupts the fixation of the *Mode de Valeurs et d'Intensités* by choosing different series continuations for each parameter or, in other words, by reading the chessboard in another direction each time. In the best case the result is a wealth of differentiation never previously attained, particularly in terms of rhythm.

Unfortunately, there are drawbacks too. Firstly, a fundamental question arises: can such divergent musical elements be reduced to one and the same numerical organisation? Does this not give rise to an abstract unity that takes no account of the individual structure of each of the musical elements? The numerical relationships upon which the work is based do not arise from the structure of the material. If Boulez had numbered his pitch series quite differently – for example C as 1, D♭ as 2, D as 3, etc., which would have been more logical, the result (a different chessboard and other notes) would have been the same, in the sense that this type of organisation is in fact not a musical organisation. At least one could then have derived a certain pleasure from the relationships of the details. But now these too usually escape us because of the extreme differentiation: nobody discerns even the simple structure of the basic series P if it is constantly intersected by its inversion.

The various series segments which succeed one another are also only perceptible under favourable circumstances (through dynamic contrast, for instance), to say nothing of duration proportions. Too much differentiation gives rise to uniformity. This organised differentiation is in sharp contrast to the simplistic block forms of the series segments. The problem of form has become acute. Messiaen's *Mode de Valeurs et d'Intensités* stood at the beginning of the so-called punctual style. The single note, as an autonomous tone object released from its relationship with other notes, gained concrete existence through the modal fixation given to it by Messiaen. The note became a discernible characteristic quantity. In Boulez, each note with its four components is the resultant of constant series intersections. The whole is actually much more elastic, but the note as an autonomous tone object is under pressure. Although there is a semblance of punctuality, it is the result of the complicated and indiscernible nature of the whole, through which the music acquires a static character.

4

It is important to summarise the main features of this transitory period of punctual music.

1. Various parameters (provisionally only four: pitch, duration, dynamics and timbre) were ordered by means of series. It was the beginning of serial music proper, as distinct from earlier 12-note music in which only pitch was organised through a series. The series acquired an increasingly regulative function. Composers adopted a statistical approach, thinking in terms of mutually related quantities. Mirror structures and transpositions made way

for a system of permutations, enabling far more variants in a rational manner. On the other hand there was an attempt to compensate the dissociation of the elements through an equally rational bond: the reduction of all proportions to a single basic series.

2. In determining and developing both series and permutation systems, composers overestimated the interaction between the differentiated detail and the greater form. We have already seen the considerable discrepancy between both quantities in Boulez, where the greater form is hardly perceptible. There was insufficient understanding of the fact that it was indeed the elaboration of the form that required the greatest compositional intervention. This lesson, given by Webern, was learnt only later.

3. The more differentiation, the more coequality; the more determination at the outset, the less calculable the result. This paradoxical situation was again only understood later. It has two consequences:

a. The composer loses his grip on the musical structure. Nobody can foresee the resultant that will emerge at a given time from the permutational process. The composer is still able to intervene freely, but this begins to resemble the navigation of a rudderless ship.

b. It has already been pointed out that the constant intersection customary in this 'parameter polyphony' creates an indistinct situation. The resulting pitches and durations are quite different to those of the individual series, and large leaps go to weaken interval characteristics. We have already seen that free atonality, on the other hand, went to increase interval sensibility (see chapter 7, section 1). The statistical approach to note material in punctual music led rather to desensitisation of not only the interval but all musical components. A kind of 'Brownian movement' arose that could just as well have come about in a completely disorganised manner. It revealed more than ever how little musical ordering could be achieved by rational organisation alone.

4. Perhaps we can consider the punctual phase of music as an enormous, rationally guided expansion of what Webern in particular viewed as a possibility for the future. Composers thrust ahead into completely new areas. In the intoxication of discovery (hardly to be excluded by rationalism!), mistakes were as understandable as they were inevitable. Within a few years this technique outlived itself. Of greater importance was a phenomenon that ran parallel, for this expansion resulted in excess and prolixity, diametrically opposed to Webernian concepts of comprehensibility and reduction.

5

Boulez's attitude later became slightly less rigid. The *Improvisations sur Mallarmé* in particular are considerably more lucid than his earlier, overcomplicated style, revealing the individual poetry of his music (reminiscent of Debussy) much more clearly. But let us now turn to the three-years-younger

Stockhausen. This composer had all the qualities to become the pacesetter of new developments: a sharp and analytic mind, a penchant for the absolute, great inventive power, and a sensitivity to the pure tonal material similar to that of Varèse. Most innovations of the past ten years have originated in Stockhausen's oeuvre. From his earliest works, around 1950, there was a growing tendency to reduce the entire musical organisation to his concept of time structure (to be discussed later). His primary concern was to ensure the mutual cohesion of all musical elements through this time structure, and at the same time to achieve the same inner cohesion between material and form.

Though this involved serial technique, it was not entirely workable. Typical of Stockhausen, indeed, is his early motivation for the use of electronic resources, which he applied from about 1952. Until that time, timbre in serial organisation was a thorn in his flesh. For the timbre of instruments can be only superficially influenced: it is really determined by the construction of the instrument, over which the composer has no power. For Stockhausen there was but one consequence: prefabricated resources were to make way for personally composed timbre starting from the sine wave. He desired to return to the very heart of the matter; but being no dogmatist, a few years later (1955) he composed his *Gesang der Jünglinge*, a first and grandiose synthesis of purely electronic and vocal tone resources. Since then he has found new points of departure for composing instrumental music again. The year 1956 was decisive for further development in this direction, and in this year he also formulated his thoughts on the time structure of music.[2] With reference to the punctual phase described in the previous section (section 4), we will attempt to present the essentials of his theses.

6

The main objection to punctual music was indeed the coequality resulting from a surplus of detail differentiation. The first step towards escaping this was the introduction of a kind of *series hierarchy*. Instead of constantly reeling off complete series simultaneously or in juxtaposition, it proved useful to deploy them in different functions.

If, for example, one had a basic series of 12, 11, 9, 10, 3, 6, 7, 1, 2, 8, 4, 5 (Boulez's *Structures*), it could be subdivided into smaller groups by applying another series (for instance 1, 2, 8, 4, etc., which would result in 12 / 11, 9 / 10, 3, 6, 7, 1, 2, 8, 4, etc.). These little groups in turn could be used serially to create a higher ordering. The further development of such serial organisation is not of importance here. Naturally, the basic principle remains the pursuit of unity in the proportions of all elements.

A much more important aspect is the choice of the proportions themselves within the series. From Messiaen onwards our duration series were based on the addition of the smallest unit (1 ♪ to 12 ♪). Stockhausen calls this a *subharmonic sequence*, for if we convert the durations ♪♪♪ etc., into much shorter durations of pitch frequencies, we obtain for instance 1/2000 second, 1/1000 second, 1/666 second In terms of (periodic) pitches this produces by approximation:

EXAMPLE 101

The problems arising in the employment of this subharmonic series have already been mentioned in the discussion of Messiaen and Boulez. There is, however, a *harmonic sequence* too, if one assumes the division of a larger unit:

EXAMPLE 102

$$\circ = \downarrow + \downarrow = \overset{3}{\overbrace{\downarrow + \downarrow + \downarrow}} = \downarrow + \downarrow + \downarrow + \downarrow = \overset{5}{\overbrace{\downarrow + \downarrow + \downarrow + \downarrow + \downarrow}} \text{ etc.}$$

So-called irrational values arise, which are never evaluated individually, but always in relation to the undivided unit. The same applies, as regards pitch, to the overtone spectrum. Stockhausen employs the term *harmonic phase spectrum*, which is really nothing other than a conversion into durations of the pitch relations in a harmonic overtone spectrum:

EXAMPLE 103

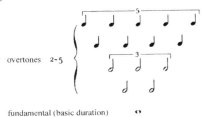

The overtones (partially) determine the timbre, and their conversion into the harmonic phase spectrum therefore amounts to *sound rhythm*. What we have really done is to convert the overtone spectrum with its microrelationships into note duration (=macro)relationships by means of a huge time-magnifier. Here we approach an essential point in Stockhausen's argument, i.e., the correspondence between macro- and microrelationships, which can be elucidated as follows: if we hear certain pulses at a decreasing distance from one another (a rebounding marble, for example), the perception of *duration* changes at a certain moment into a perception of *pitch*. This moment occurs at about 16 units per second; it is represented graphically in Figure 6:

MUSIC OF THE TWENTIETH CENTURY

FIGURE 6

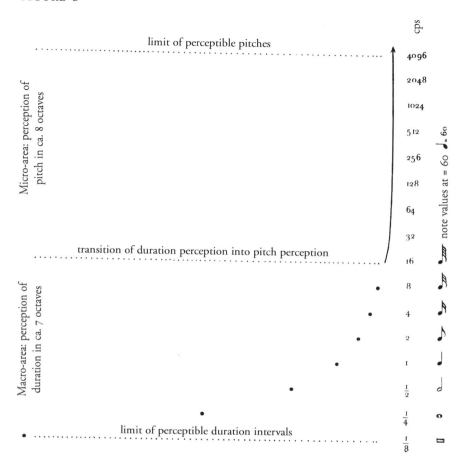

The vertical axis gives the octaves: the duration-octaves in the macro-area change into pitch-octaves in the micro-area. Why not continue – according to Stockhausen – the tempered 12-fold division of pitch octaves in duration octaves too. Though this cannot be written down in traditional notation, metronome marks produce the following logarithmic table between for instance ♩ and ♪ (♩ = 60): ♩ = MM 60, 63.6, 67.4, 71.4, 75.6, 80.1, 84.9, 89.9, 95.2, 100.9, 106.9, 113.3.

The next octave therefore begins with ♩ = 120, but now we can 'transpose' by taking the same numbers from the first octave ♩ = 60, etc.) and adopting ♪ as the unit. If we apply this to the following series (from *Gruppen für drei Orchester*) we obtain:

EXAMPLE 104

M.M. ♩ = (rounded off)	76	60	80	67	64	71	101	90	95	113	85	107

basic duration unit

proportions

2 :	10	12 :	7	5 :	9	7 :	2	3 :	5	10 :	4
4 :	3	6 :	13	8 :	11	13 :	6	9 :	12		

Here we have a number of basic durations, indicated in metronome marks and corresponding with the pitch proportions within the series, reaching as far as the octave positions (basic duration units). These basic durations are too small to be of practical use. Stockhausen therefore introduced the term *basic duration group*. He says: if for instance the proportion between the first and second basic duration is 2:10, this means that 10 of the first basic durations are equal to 2 of the second:

EXAMPLE 105

The proportion between the second and third basic duration is 4:3, so that 3 of the second basic duration are equal to 4 of the third:

EXAMPLE 106

These four basic duration groups therefore indicate the proportion between the first three notes of the series: 10: 2
3:4. The second member has a different proportion to the preceding and following ones (as does the third member in relation to 2 and 4, etc.). Stockhausen expresses this by overlapping the second basic duration group with the third (Example 107). This overlapping thus produces a rest (if the next proportion is expressed in a larger number), or otherwise a temporary vertical accumulation of various basic duration groups.

EXAMPLE 107

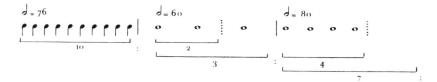

In Example 103 (the harmonic phase spectrum) we saw how each basic duration has its own 'overtone spectrum' in terms of durations. Stockhausen applied this too, not for each individual basic duration, but for a whole basic duration group – a group spectrum, therefore. Such a spectrum is viewed as one large complex with a certain characteristic, which can be serially determined as to density, dynamics, timbre, etc. By means of ties and rests, the danger of exaggerated periodicity inherent in such spectrums can be avoided. Time can be structured in the macro-area from harmonic spectrums to 'time noise', just as timbre ranges from harmonic to noise spectrums.

The above is particularly well illustrated in the composer's *Gruppen für drei Orchester*. The score is so large that there is little point in trying to fit a page into this book. We would refer the reader to the Universal edition.

7

Although the above summary of Stockhausen's article may suffer from conciseness, a lengthier discussion has been avoided since this book is intended either for readers who are able to consult the original text (despite its difficulty), or for those who have a teacher at hand. For apart from a technical introduction to the *Gruppen für drei Orchester*, our main concern here is with the background to these ideas, which are typical of Stockhausen and therefore of many of today's serial composers. Although various objections could be made to the reasoning as such, this is not of great importance at this moment. It should be pointed out once more that in the past too, art is known to have arisen from mistaken premises. We are concerned with the stimulating interaction between the thought and action of the composer. The creative process is more complicated than we are able to fathom.

Let us now examine this against the background of an ancient European tendency, inherited from the Greeks, a tendency towards unity down to the very deepest layers, and expressed in numerical relationships. European history has witnessed numerous analogous endeavours, and it is hardly surprising that this concept has cropped up again among serial composers of today. Schönberg already expressed the fundamental unity between the horizontal and the vertical. His successors went further in search of the bond between the various parameters, between the material and musical form, between the micro- and macrostructures. Is this analytical reasoning, this constant pursuit of control over the material, ultimately a form of undifferentiated reasoning? Would it not be better to take as our point of departure the abundance of phenomena, our sensory and aural-psychological reactions, which appear time and again to breach the above postulate?[3]

Whatever the case may be, from our distant forefathers, who transformed an inconceivable wealth of Eastern song into neatly trimmed Gregorian chant and proceeded to reduce the ancient modes to two diatonic scales (see chapter 6, section 5), we have now arrived at a single chromatic series that, through lack of further reduction possibilities, tries to impose its relationships onto the very furthest boundaries of musical material.

Each impoverishment, however, enabled a new development to take place: this is the amazing thing about European music. Viewed in this light, Stockhausen's endeavour formed a positive answer to the disintegration of an old style.

8

In section 4 we discussed various tendencies that began to emerge during and after the phase of punctual music. Around 1956 these became much clearer and enabled composers to draw certain conclusions.

1. The statistical approach to music came to the foreground. The primary consideration became the ordering of higher categories of form rather than the organisation of detail. This was already indicated by use of the term 'group' to refer to what is really the smallest unit, characterised by the detailed effect of pitch, duration, timbre, etc.; within the group, however, a certain freedom was possible without encroaching on the characteristic of the group. This freedom was also evident in an easier use of interval proportions than was ever conceivable in classical dodecaphony. It was no longer a question of 'this and this' or 'so and so many' notes, but of a certain degree of density. Density, register, direction of movement, degree of periodicity and many other concepts emerged as aspects of music that could be ordered serially. Attention to elements of detail made way for a more global determination, and thus for the concept of *form*.

2. In this process the series became increasingly neutral, functioning more and more as a regulatory factor. Proportions became decisive: a 3rd from a pitch series is a 5/4 proportion that can be manifest in any other musical element. In so far as pitch series were still employed, they likewise had a neutral character and were naturally no longer bound to the twelve notes. The series in *Gruppen* still had twelve notes, and indeed a pronounced shape of its own, presumably to attain large proportional contrasts in the macrofield. The *Klavierstücke I-IV* however, dating from 1954, retained only the rudiments of the 12-note series. In the second and third pieces, respectively, they are as follows:

MUSIC OF THE TWENTIETH CENTURY

EXAMPLE 108

Nono's *Il Canto sospeso* (1956) was based on the *all-interval* series shown in
Example 109. Something similiar occurred in Messiaen's *Livre d'Orgue* (see
Example 16).

EXAMPLE 109

3. The outstanding scholar Györgi Ligeti, who has already been mentioned,
introduced the concept of *interval permeability*. In section 4 we have already
observed how the interval, and indeed other musical elements too, lost its
own existence by being taken up in higher, statistically determinable quantities.[4] This desensitisation evoked new problems and new possibilities. The
music became manifest in layers, no longer characterised by the detail but by
a global 'material state' (rough, granular, smooth, etc.). Such layers could be
combined, and exact synchronisation was obviously no longer relevant.
Indeed, exactness acquired a certain margin: synchronism was not essential,
but rather the spatial distribution of 'material states'. Something of the sort
had already been achieved by Messiaen, among others, with his modality, in
which a certain indifferentiation likewise arose in terms of sequence of notes
and intervals. In serial music composers went further: different tempos were
combinable, and the new concept of *field magnitude* emerged, heralding
another important phase in new music that is usually described as *aleatory
composition*.

9

This did not appear out of thin air. Directly after the rigorously punctual style
of the *Structures,* Boulez reacted with his *Marteau sans Maître*, completed in
1954, in which the tempo in particular fluctuates through the many changes,
directions such as 'tempo et nuances très instables', etc. The work breathes a
freedom and suppleness that reminds one immediately of Debussy. The many
short notes, separate or clustered, and the irrational values create a sort of
written-out rubato (see Example 35). This differentiation, which was also
manifest, though somewhat differently, in Stockhausen's work of the same
period, moved the latter to express the following thoughts (freely cited): 'An
inaccuracy factor arises in performance. The areas within which this factor is

manifest are time fields, and their dimensions are field magnitudes. In the past too this margin existed in performance, but was coincidental. Now we wish to capture these inaccuracies functionally. A series of field magnitudes, rather than a traditional series of fixated durations, can now be determinant.'

This meant the abandonment of our quantitative system of fixed-value notation and the creation of a way of indicating the boundaries within which indeterminacy may occur, something that could be done in many ways. In Example 67 Boulez used the sign ⌐——⌐ to indicate the boundaries within which a number of short notes may be freely placed. Stockhausen developed a different method to indicate *action duration*, based on the principle that *note duration* is no longer counted, but determined during performance by means of a particular action prescribed by the composer. Thus, the time between two notes, for instance, may depend on that required by the player to move his hand, on the degree of complexity of a given touch or pedal movement, or on breathing considerations, etc. Once again, such physiological reactions had always existed; but Stockhausen wished to incorporate them functionally in his music.[5] Although it sounds paradoxical, all this revealed a desire to control musical elements that cannot be accurately committed to paper. It is clear, therefore, that it was not a question of the absolute values of these elements, but of their mutual relationships.

The rapidity of these innovations was remarkable. While the correspondence between macro- and micro-areas discussed in the previous sections was still hardly formulated, new territory was being explored. And each discovery required years of elaboration! Perhaps it was this hurried course of events that caused problems in Stockhausen's first composition in this field. Let us take a closer look at the *Klavierstück XI* of 1957.

Nineteen groups are written down on a large piece of paper, all of very different length and without any suggestion of sequence; some are illustrated in Example 110. According to the composer each group is in itself the result of serial ordering, based on different series to organise field magnitude proportions. We must take his word for it, since we have arrived at a situation in which serial manipulation can no longer be reconstructed without the help of the composer. Some groups include the familiar notes in small print that are to be played 'as fast as possible'. Action duration is taken into account, for the composer says that 'difficult chords and large leaps with one hand obviously require more time than simple chords and smaller intervals'. Although the notes in normal print have the customary quantitive notation of duration, an unexpected element is to play a role. Stockhausen prescribes the following: the performer is to glance unintentionally at the page and play the first group that catches his eye, in the tempo, dynamics and touch of his choice. The latter, however, are classified by the composer beforehand: there are six tempos, for instance, ranging from tempo 1, very fast, to tempo 6, very slow. Subsequently, the player's eye is caught unintentionally (without any attempt to connect particular groups) by another group which he now plays in accordance with directions given at the end of the previous group. Each group can be connected to any of the other eighteen, and all nineteen groups can therefore be performed in the prescribed degrees of tempo, dynamics and touch. The characteristics of all groups are therefore variable within the chosen boundaries. The field magnitude of a following group is determined by indications at the end of the preceding one.

A performance does not necessarily include all the groups. If a group is repeated, indications are given for small modifications in the second rendering, usually in the form of somewhat elementary octave transpositions. If a group occurs for a third time, it also brings one of the possible realisations of the whole piece to an end. The work is an example of open form, without direction or termination. The groups are spatially juxtaposed and can be combined in countless ways. In the many commentaries on this composition two aspects have been neglected or confused.

1. The *action duration* – a decidedly positive element. Instead of 'counting' with a margin of inaccuracy, a spontaneous reaction arises, a realisation of the time structure at the moment of the action itself. Such music can therefore no longer be approached from the score, since the time structure is now determined by the *perception time* of the performer himself, which is inseparable from physical reactions and abilities. Such freedom is therefore ostensible. Nothing is added to an existing structure (unlike jazz or basso continuo technique); on the contrary, the player remains entirely bound to the composer's directions, but he becomes involved right down to his physical reactions. Notice that this action duration takes place within the boundaries of each group. The mutual bond between the groups is quite a different matter; it is created by means of what one could call:

2. the *spontaneous decision*. The player is required to glance 'unintentionally' and to link the very first group that catches his eye with the preceding one. The word 'chance' crops up here and is indeed to stay with us, whether relevant or not. But it is not a question of chance, for the performer may choose from no more than the 18 options determined by the composer. All possibilities are already enclosed in the concept. At best there is mention of an unconsidered decision at the last moment – freedom, indeed, but a freedom without sense. The actual time experience of the action duration is absent, as is the considered decision of the composition process. It is a freedom that is only possible thanks to another concept of form, that of the open form without causality. These new concepts of form have already been discussed at several points, especially in relation to the theory of musical space. In this light Stockhausen's *Klavierstück XI* is hardly new, but merely a confirmation of a concept of form already found in Debussy.

Stockhausen's step was to transfer choice from the composer to the performer; instead of a single notated version, many realisations of a piece become feasible.

EXAMPLE 110

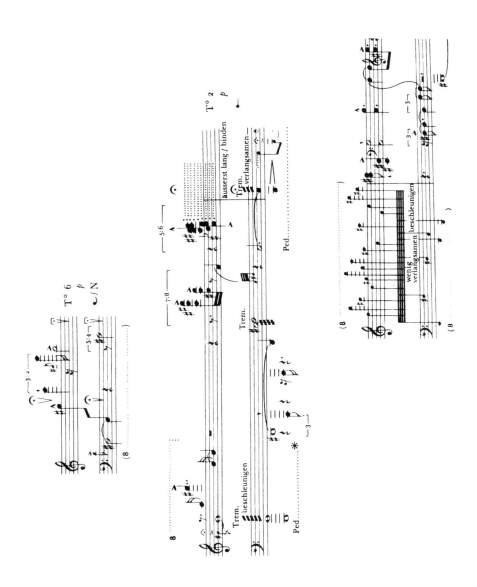

MUSIC OF THE TWENTIETH CENTURY

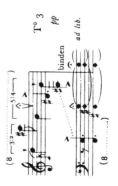

Boulez was the first to recognise the real problem of the *Klavierstück XI*. In the same period, but independently of Stockhausen, he worked on his *Third Piano Sonata*; at the same time he was confronted by the work of Mallarmé, whose literary preoccupations ran remarkably parallel despite the great disparity in time. In Boulez, too, the player gains a more important role, but this does nothing – the composer believes – to change the problem of form. He felt the necessity to develop a new form that adapts to the material available to the serial composer, which was constantly becoming more elastic. But form to Boulez was something more than the mosaics of Stockhausen's music, which were really nothing other than constantly changing combinations from millions of options. If the performer was free to choose, then his choice should preferably be made after some consideration, and with only a very limited number of possibilities that were precisely determined by the composer.

An example is the overall structure of the *Sonata* (comprising five movements in the first concept): Antiphonie, Trope, Constellation, Strophe, Séquence. The sequence of the movements is free, providing that Constellation is always in the middle. The internal structure reflects the same approach. One of the movements, Trope, has four components: two so-called *structures complexes* (Parenthèse, Commentaire) and two *structures simples* (Glose, Texte). In the 'complex structures' the performer is again free to include or omit certain additional variants (given between brackets).

The sequence of these components is indicated in an ingenious manner. The unnumbered pages of the score are in a ring binder, and the player may begin where he wishes. The sequence is therefore directed – we usually read from front to back – but not predetermined (Boulez speaks of a *forme circulaire*). There are normally four options, therefore, depending on the starting point:

P,   C,   G,   T
C,   G,   T,   P
G,   T,   P,   C
T,   P,   C,   G

But since the Commentaire section is included twice, four other possibilities become available, depending on where this section is placed (it may only be performed once); this can be represented as in Figure 7. Altogether eight different sequences are therefore available; compared to the millions in Stockhausen, this illustrates just how much more control the composer has retained over the final outcome.

The Trope from Boulez's *Third Piano Sonata* provided only a first and simple answer to the new problems of form. Although the composer already established new structural concepts, the territory as such was as yet hardly explored. This is particularly evident if we bear in mind that the free sequence

FIGURE 7

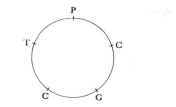

of sections, which caused the most sensation in the beginning, was merely one aspect of the complex concept of form that awaited exploitation.

However the case may be, through these preoccupations, form acquired unprecedented autonomy, despite the astonishing authority granted (for the time being) to the performer. This is already observed in the work of Mallarmé, who concentrated far more on the structure of language than on its significance, or, in other words, attempted to convert this significance into a symbolism of absolute value. Form had a life of its own, bringing the artist to an attitude of anonymity, since the intrusion of purely personal incidents was undesirable.[6] Those with some knowledge of Asian culture will hardly be surprised by this. But in Europe relationships are different, and particularly for those less gifted than Boulez it is fitting to recall the words of Paul Valéry, a confidant of Mallarmé. Concerning the latter's ambitions he spoke later (in his *Lettre sur Mallarmé*) of 'diviniser la chose écrite' (divining that which is written). But, he went on, 'ce n'est point l'œuvre faite et ses apparences ou ses effets dans le monde qui peuvent nous accomplir et nous édifier, mais *seulement la manière dont nous l'avons faite*' (it is not the finished work and its appearances, or its effects on the world, which can fulfill and edify us, but only the manner in which we have accomplished it).

10

The concept of aleatory music has now broadened considerably, and we must certainly mention one other composer under this heading.

We have already examined two aspects: action duration and the spontaneous decision in Stockhausen, and intervention possibilities in Boulez. In the latter the performer is like a driver who may choose from a limited number of roads, while the road map itself remains the domain of the town planner. Boulez described Stockhausen's solution as chance, while Stockhausen used the term *gelenkter Zufall* (guided chance); but as we have seen, in reality the element of chance was less present than one might imagine. All this only made the problem of form most acute, and the composer who was to draw particularly radical conclusions was the American John Cage. Cage came to Europe in 1958 – I remember a momentous concert at the World Exhibition in Brussels – and was quick to cause the necessary stir. From his point of view our controversy between tonality and atonality was long out-dated. He believed that modern serialists kept far too much to traditional paths, exposing themselves to a constant risk of academicism.

A number of similarities, however, can also be found. Like Boulez, Cage's music reveals a pursuit of objectivity, or rather anonymity, which helps the sound to 'come to itself'. But his conclusions were much more radical. Instead of trying to bind the notes, his school attempted to soak off their adhesive, formed as it was by centuries of convention. If one hangs on to the notes, if one has 'musical' ideas, one cannot allow the notes to be themselves. And 'being themselves' means that there is no superimposed expression. (Many modern composers would go along with him up to this point, and the much older Varèse, with his 'liberation of the sound', was even a precursor.) And it also means that there is no man-made organisation. Thus, Cage reached a conclusion diametrically opposed to our early serialists: not com-plete determination, but rather complete *indetermination* was essential. (One of the most shocking experiences of recent times is to discover that both points of departure lead to the same degree of indetermination.) In order to achieve this indetermination, Cage used to make particular use of chance actions such as the tossing of coins, etc. Other means may also be employed, such as the oracle of the staves from the ancient Chinese book *I-Ching* (which illustrates the influence of Zen Buddhism on this composer), or mathemati-cal methods.

More recently, however, the accent has shifted towards the unforeseeable-ness of the performance itself, involving the actual performers. It is remark-able how completely different paths form striking parallels with modern European composers! Fifty years earlier Charles Ives, following quite a differ-ent line of thought, created the same sort of music as that of the young Schönberg and Stravinsky. Despite the shift towards live performance, a score was naturally still required as an instruction for the players. But the score must not be viewed as a ready-made, notated form. And this is where Cage differs: the composition is not an autonomous object, but a performance process. Obviously, this process has its boundaries – determined by the action of the players and by a number of characteristics – but essentially the music has no precedence above either note or noise. While it does have its own exis-tence, it remains 'transparent' in relation to its surroundings. Its boundaries become diffuse, and counting is not required, for we exist 'in time'. Stopwatches rather than bars serve to indicate when an occurrence of sound must take place within this time. Christian Wolff, a composer from the Cage group, replaced Stockhausen's eye ('unintentional glancing') with the ear: cer-tain occurrences of sound, caused by the one player, evoke reactions from the other (*Duo for Pianists II*). The outcome is determined by the performers themselves; finally, musical form may be conceived as 'the length of the pro-gramme'.[7]

Cage is among those Westerners who have listened to the Japanese bowman in chapter 6. Just how far his interpretation is correct, we will leave to the experts.[8] Is this still music? Surely we see an influence on contemporary music that cannot be underestimated. Can everybody do the same? But not everybody does, is Cage's reply. Strong differences of opinion emerge. It is impossible to imagine the fascinating whirlpool of new developments without Cage. Whether the music comes from inside or outside, we cannot escape it.

'One day when the windows were open, Christian Wolff played one of his pieces at the piano. Sounds of traffic, boat horns, were heard not only during the silences in the music but, being louder, were more easily heard than the piano sounds themselves. Afterwards, someone asked Christian Wolff to play the piece again with the windows closed. Christian Wolff said he'd be glad to, but that it wasn't really necessary, since the sounds of the environment were in no sense an interruption of those of the music.'[9]

II

The above discussion helps us to clarify the concept of aleatory music. It is a generic term for all aspects of music that are not predetermined. The relationship between determined and undetermined elements plays a role in all types of music. The undetermined element brings unforeseeableness with it, and can occur both in performance and during the process of composition.

Unforeseeableness can be manifest in differing degrees. In the performance of a classical composition, for example, the degree to which the fixated notation can be deviated from is limited. Performance of a piece by John Cage, on the other hand, can involve a high degree of unforeseeableness. But even here general patterns of expectation can be formulated.

Finally, with regard to developments in the music of the period 1950-60, the following aspects are of importance:

1. In Cage's work the element of chance – to use this dubious word once more – was a means to obtain indetermination and to escape from the human grasp of the music. Young European composers, on the other hand, were concerned with gaining even stricter control of the musical material: even this indeterminable area of free choice was consciously incorporated in the process of composition.

2. Bearing in mind changing concepts of musical form, we can say that part of what once belonged to the individual and 'unique' work of art is now ascribed to the material employed by the performers. There is a certain inclination to make matters absolute, which corresponds logically to the excessive attention given to musical material that we have observed from 1950 onwards.

3. Expansionism, moreover, is not foreign to serial technique, in the sense that there is an inclination to exploit all the possibilities of the chosen material. The limited means of dodecaphony of the past have been extended to

become an all-embracing permutation procedure; it soon became apparent, however, that this again was not sufficient to harness the wealth of resources that had been rallied. A written serial score realises only a few of the countless possibilities, and the free choice of the performer can at least compensate this to a certain extent. The element of chance becomes a wider margin in the realisation of the (unforeseeable) permutation process. Far from coincidental is the attendant departure from the unique, once-and-for-all determined work of art. A remarkable dichotomy seems to arise between the realised condition of a single work of art and the 'possibly realisable' that is potentially present in the same. Here creative expansionism collides with ultimate boundaries.

4. The element of chance can serve to fill another gap. With all due respect for their sometimes brilliant ideas, one can nonetheless consider that both Stockhausen and Boulez have maintained an only too simple notion of the role of what they call 'surprise' in the musical process. The former wrote: 'The degree of information is therefore at its highest when at any point in a musical discourse the moment of surprise is at its strongest: the music constantly has "something to say".' (Just before this he specifies: 'Surprise only occurs when the unexpected happens.')[10] Boulez shares this opinion: '... for any music that is a masterpiece is a music that allows the capacity to surprise at any moment.'[11]

This is not the place to contradict these ideas, but it is clear that from this point of view too, the involvement of the spontaneous decision of the performer is most welcome: the 'surprise' within the boundaries of a work may increase, and the same goes for each subsequent performance.

5. Increasing differentiation posed considerable problems with regard to traditional notation, which was not at all equal to its task. By involving the performer, this difficulty was eased on the one hand, while on the other new symbols had to be introduced to indicate players' actions. It was inevitable that this issue also had to be tackled once more, as is described in section 14.

12

In the reaction against abstractions, serial music lost more and more influence after 1960. Boulez has remained a bastion of serial academicism, but Stockhausen has changed enormously. He is no longer the great renewer, but continues to react with great flexibility to any external stimulus that he encounters. He is long past the stage of solving problems of form and technique. From *Carré* (1960) and *Originale* (1961) onwards his work comprises ever more heterogeneous elements including happenings, pop, quotations, indeterminate sound production (contact microphones), etc.

The use of contact microphones has now become very widespread, and this opens up a new direction in the application of electronic resources. In days past, electronic music was accurately recorded on tape in a studio. Many considered this an advantage: the composer exercised maximum control, while the inconstancies of live performance were eliminated. But this strict view could not be maintained, and in a next step (discussed in section 9) aleatory techniques were introduced, at first very cautiously among Europeans but after 1960 much more freely. Improvisation groups even appeared on stage working with electronic apparatus. The principle is simple: microphones attached to 'instruments' (that may or may not be recognisable as such) pick up vibrations that are normally neither audible nor usable and feed them to loudspeakers via amplifiers and possibly modulators. A new and hitherto unknown world of sound is brought to life. Unexpected surprises may occur too, and with them an immediate response from the performer. This was a typical feature of the post-1960 period.

Once again it was Cage who led the way with such experiments. More important, however, was his awareness of the situation. For in his first experiments with chance phenomena he discovered that he was still attempting to drag 'successful' results out of chance actions. Realising later on that this attitude was equivocal, he came to accept the induced results of chance. The result was no longer important, but rather the attitude of open-mindedness. Thus, he came to distinguish between chance actions and indetermination. In the first case the composer employs chance as a means, but to a limited degree such that he remains within a self-determined global circle. Indetermination, on the contrary, exceeds this circle: the result is in every respect indefinite; such music crops up out of time, undefined and incidental, only to disappear once more without a trace. 'All things are interrelated,' Cage said, 'and taken up in the stream of time. Any (human) pursuit of a stated "aim" is a simplification, and a departure from reality.' The lessons of Cage were developed further by an American 'second generation' around 1960. And once again the aesthetic consequences of the concept of indetermination were applied more radically than in Europe. In the work of La Monte Young, Terry Riley, Robert Ashley and the Fluxus Movement, almost all existing values and concepts relating to music were turned well and truly upside down.

La Monte Young (1935) worked with long chains of chords that developed systematically. His material is economical, and naturally comprises all that is 'sound', including that produced by nature, machines, and electronic resources. Performances may last a week or more and incorporate other elements such as light, movement and theatre. His contemporary Terry Riley followed the same course. His music consists of long chains of repeated motifs, usually in elementary diatonic note patterns. Tape loops and feedback systems provide the characteristic tone colours; electronic and instrumental resources merge. These and other Americans shared a broad interest in widely different idioms including jazz, pop and non-Western music.

Chance action – indetermination: many composers throughout the world now work within these borders. Only few are conscious of the background so brilliantly evoked by Cage in his writings.[12] What is clear, however, is that serial concepts are disappearing; there is a growing reaction to their abstractions and a tendency towards greater directness in music making. This is also expressed in the instrumental works of Berio, Ligeti, Kagel and others: music that is tailor-made for certain specialists, musicians who are required to make a creative contribution of their own rather than only faithfully reproduce a more or less authoritarian score. Such music renounces serial, abstractly determined sound differentiation in favour of a more direct form of expression. Not only the actual notes, but sighs, scratches, shouts and moans become part of music making. The instrument literally becomes an extension of the human body.

Similar tendencies are found in music theatre. This rather vague term embodies so much variety that a comprehensive definition can hardly be given. In general, it can be viewed as a reaction to traditional theatrical and operatic forms, which have caused the nineteenth century to live on, leaving current issues to the realm of film. The 'raree show' idea has also been abandoned, since divisions between audience and stage, between different participating disciplines, required abolition. Various directions emerged, from the political engagement of Nono (*Intolleranza*, 1960) to the more light-hearted or autonomous approach of Kagel (*Sur Scène*, 1960) and Ligeti (*Aventures*, 1962). Nono connected with traditional opera, while Ligeti created a 'composition with scenic, verbal and musical means'. Unlike the traditional *Gesamtkunstwerk* there is a tendency to grant the incorporated elements a life of their own, independent of one another and only joined by a common period of time. Once again, vocal and instrumental techniques are extended to such a degree that the two flow together.

All such innovations amount to repeated attempts to break through existing boundaries! From the beginning of the twentieth century, the failure of instrument making to keep pace with musical developments made itself increasingly felt. Factories were usually highly industrialised, geared to the mass production of traditional instruments and leaving no room for altruistic research in an artistic sense. Today's composer must still make do with instruments developed hundreds of years ago: thus the continual expansion of playing techniques towards the boundaries of human endeavour; thus the contact microphones; and thus the ongoing specialisation of the few players devoted exclusively to new music.

13

In the meantime another new type of constructivism emerged in the work of the Greek composer Iannis Xenakis. 'Faire de la musique signifie exprimer l'intelligence humaine par des moyens sonores' (music making is the expression of human intelligence by means of sound), where intelligence is to be understood in the broadest sense of the word, embracing all human faculties involved in music making. Classical Greece is revived in the composer's ideas

– the pursuit of truth and beauty are merely two different aspects of the same human endeavour; boundaries between art and science become vague. The composer must draw on all knowledge offered by contemporary learning in order to gain command – in a spiritual sense too – of his material. Mathematics, philosophy, information sciences, cybernetics and computer technology: Xenakis demands much of himself and others. He is one of the most visionary artists of our time.

Of the new composition procedures that he has introduced, let us discuss one: the stochastic method (the calculation of probability). Unlike serial technique, which essentially aims to join one determined element to another, stochastic processes commence with the organisation of the whole. For Xenakis assumed that the laws that must determine the many elements of detail in a composition are of a statistical nature. The strict determinism of serial technique was now replaced by stochastic methods, used to study and formulate the laws of large numbers, of rare phenomena, of aleatory process-es, in short of all matters that are in principle indeterminate, escaping strict causality. This applies not only to music, but equally to many natural phe-nomena such as the ticking of rain drops, the chirping of thousands of crick-ets or the applause of a large crowd. Chance, though it may not become defined, can to a large extent at least be regulated and applied within the framework of a composition by means of stochastic laws: 'le désordre con-trôlé'. We have come a long way from the simplistic heads-or-tails games of many post-serialists, and far from Cage's views on indetermination.

The laws of probability[13] enable the composer to control the genesis and development of musical phenomena, such as the continuous or discontinu-ous transformation of large numbers of pitches, durations, densities, registers, speeds, etc. In reality, all this implies a definitive victory over linear thought, which had always survived in serial technique. The note, now freed from the series too, becomes more than ever an autonomous sound object, a small component of the large-scale macroscopic processes initiated by Xenakis.[14]

Initiated in the double sense of the word! For historically speaking too, Xenakis was the first composer to work so consistently with huge blocks of sound. *Metastasis* dates from 1954, and *Pithoprakta* ('Action through proba-bility') from 1956. The tone fields of Ligeti, the new Polish composers and countless others since, all date from about 1960 onwards.

14

Classical notation moved increasingly towards exact representation in sym-bols of the pitch and duration of notes. A certain spatial element was involved in so far as 'high' and 'low' in the music roughly corresponded with the nota-tion:

EXAMPLE III

Although symbols of *pitch* were well suited to tonal music, from the period of free atonality onwards the problem arose that this notation was tailored to diatonic intervals, and that chromaticism, which had become independent, still had to rely on accidentals.

A rather abstract notation had developed for the *duration* of notes. In the above example, for instance, the four semiquavers together occupy as much space on paper as the much longer dotted minim. For other musical elements we have made do with additions in the form of dynamic signs, playing directions, tempo indications, etc.

These are the very elements, however, that have become increasingly important in the past one hundred and fifty years. From the moment when Beethoven made durations absolute by introducing metronome markings, it was not long before scores contained a great variety of directions, pretending increasingly to record the sound concept of the composer as exactly as possible. This development led among other things to the abolition of the notation of 'fingerings' for transposing instruments and the introduction of absolute pitches (scores in C).

Two problems were therefore presented:

1. Increasing independence of the elements of music found no adequate expression in the notation system.

2. Increasing differentiation could not be accommodated in the notation either: a division arose between what was notated and what could be performed. One of the consequences of this has already been mentioned in section 9.

In electronic music it had already been discovered that no notation system was capable of representing the sound adequately. Most electronic scores are therefore working scores, containing a description of *how* the sound should be produced rather than *what* it is to sound like. And with the advent of aleatory music (in the broad sense of the word, as it has been discussed), it became possible to employ such 'action scores' for instrumental music too. The production of sound was indicated by means of graphic signs; the optical image represented, as it were, the path or paths to be followed by the player in order to realise the musical intention. This rapidly led to an autonomy of the graphic image, which came to be considered quite separately from the sound.[15] Let us limit ourselves here to those scores that still aim to represent music, and discuss several of the possibilities.

Example 112 shows a figure used by Luciano Berio, one of the greatest composers of the new generation, in his *Tempi concertati*. It means that the player may begin where he wishes, reading from left to right or vice versa; the figure may be repeated, and must be played as fast as possible. The arrow is a proportional sign indicating that the final note of the figure should be sustained until the end.

EXAMPLE 112

In *Liaisons* by Roman Haubenstock-Ramati, proportional notation applies to three elements: pitch, duration and loudness (Example 113). The horizontal line represents the middle of the note range and therefore amounts to a further expansion of the notation system. The composer indicates that the player must read from left to right.

EXAMPLE 113

In Stockhausen's *Zyklus* for percussion, the spatially enlarged score can also be turned upside down. The piece employs the ring binder with unnumbered pages found elsewhere since Boulez's *Third Piano Sonata*. Each composer begins his score with a page full of instructions.

It would be premature to draw final conclusions concerning the development of a new notation. A single example will suffice from the score of the above-mentioned *Liaisons* by Roman Haubenstock-Ramati, for vibraphone, or vibraphone and marimba (Example 114). The score may be read either horizontally or vertically (in both directions), but in principle one may not depart from a chosen direction except at the arrows. The complete piece is therefore the sum of the spatially represented areas, which in themselves are largely determined by the interpretation of the performer(s).

The following provisional conclusions may be drawn:

1. New manners of notation have arisen from new musical concepts. A mutual interaction may be expected, in contrast to classical notation, which through its obsolete system has exercised a most inhibiting influence on many composers. Moreover, the function of notation has changed, the accent coming to lie more and more on the actual performance in which the players are

EXAMPLE 114

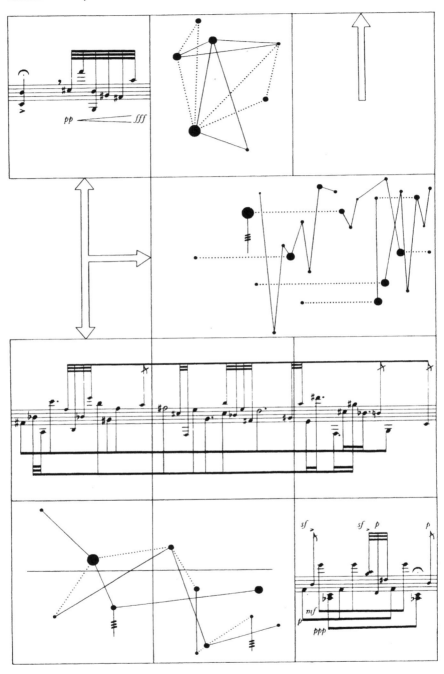

directly involved. The less the notation pretends to, the freer the music is able to develop.[16]

2. Neither old nor new notation enables us to assess new music by reading it. The first is unable to represent the increasing differentiation and autonomy of the musical elements, while the second has been adapted to action and the performance itself. At best the notation offers overall information on external aspects of the music. Let us wait until this becomes clear to the many and industrious jury members who supply us with festival programmes every year by reading that which is unreadable for days on end.

Only a few of the more extreme tendencies in new music have been mentioned above. But like all that has been said, this short exploration too is only intended to give the reader an impression of the paths along which this music may be approached. And since the main intention was to be informative, emphasis has been laid on innovative aspects, in so far as they can be rationally described. While historical, technical or stylistic aspects can be specified, the artistic value can never be captured in words. In some of the works mentioned or described, this value can be felt intuitively; others, on the contrary, seem mouldy as soon as one has seen through the outer innovation. But they are all characteristic of a trend, an attitude belonging to this period, which already seems to be making way for another one, bringing newer and freer insight. Comprehensiveness does not need to be our aim – today less than ever. Mobility has become characteristic, and the word itself is indicative of different but analogous tendencies in music and literature, sculpture and urban development. How can it be otherwise at a time when the possibility of bringing planets out of their orbits is under consideration!

Musical developments take place rapidly. For some composers creative work assumes the appearance of scientific invention. Imagination, stimulated in and by rational thought, may produce fascinating results. Rational thought has never been foreign to musicians, despite all romanticised ideas. In the past, however, results were almost directly manageable and perceptible. This is no longer the case. Rationally guided, early polyphony differs from modern serial structures as do the methods of Galileo or Newton from the modern calculation of a fourth dimension. Here again a division has occurred. Our working activity is in danger of becoming autonomous, separated from a directly perceivable horizon. The modern sorcerer's apprentice knows no boundaries; but he is still inhibited, and a large number of existing ensembles and instruments have no place in his imagination. Equal temperament is stubbornly maintained; all attempts in a different direction run into as yet insurmountable practical problems. The anachronisms of an age-old notation system have been mentioned above... Not without reason has the 'compositional crisis' become a stereotype phenomenon for many contemporaries.

Is there another path? Are those who compose in a traditional manner, in all possible gradations, really as lacking in imagination as is sometimes suggested? One often cannot avoid answering in the affirmative when one hears the results. But the same is true of the numerous epigones and parasites who swarm around the great innovators of today.

Many minds, both conservative and innovative, are gripped by a fatal sectarianism. 'Old' and 'new' have become terms of valuation, and neither camp takes the trouble to investigate the other world. The traditional composer understands nothing of the staggering flights which a modernist may make. The latter, in turn, does not realise that deep wisdom may be concealed in music aiming to be simple, well-balanced and self-restrained. Our somewhat clamorous musical life, controlled by publicity, does what remains to make life difficult for those who are genuinely interested: they look upon a distorted image. Only their successors in the year 2000 may again benefit from a panoramic perspective. And things will look quite different by then. But however the final relationships may come to be, one characteristic of our time will always remain conspicuous: the unprecedented abundance of phenomena. The contemporary Western world bears witness to a vitality that is diametrically opposed to the culture pessimism all too easily professed by all too many.

Hilversum 1961-62, 1969, 1976.

CHAPTER 9

From the Sixties to the Present Day

Contemporary Musical Life in the Light of Five Characteristic Features

It is hardly sufficient to discuss the newest developments in music exclusively in terms of their manifestation in the music world at large. Much of what is happening today reaches the public concert circuit only occasionally, if at all. Naturally, the same applies to the media and the music press in so far as they, in turn, form a reflection of events in the concert world. I have therefore drawn on a second source in order to obtain a wider view of the contemporary scene. Every year since 1960 I have enjoyed the privilege of seeing tens and sometimes hundreds of new scores and, as a composition teacher, jury member and workshop director, coming into contact with similar numbers of young composers from all over the world. And although this again forms a limited and subjective picture, the combination of information from both sources has at any rate given rise to a different interpretation, to a hierarchy of values which does not always correspond with generally accepted opinion.

A first consequence of my view is that I prefer not to take the customary year 1968 as starting point for a discussion of the most recent period of contemporary music. If there is a turning point at all, I would place it somewhat earlier, in the course of the 1960s. For the innovations of the preceding period took place largely in the fifties, and the first signs of change became visible quickly afterwards. The newest period in music therefore spans some thirty years and reveals an exceptionally complex and multicoloured picture. I have attempted to distill five characteristics which I believe to be of importance to both the present situation and its further development.

1. The geographical distribution of musical activity

An increasing amount of contemporary music is written in other parts of the world. What began in Japan now extends to Korea, China, Taiwan, Indonesia, the Philippines and other Asiatic lands, as well as hitherto almost unknown African and South American countries. Any future musicologist making a study of the second half of the twentieth century will therefore have to take into account a broad and diffuse distribution of creative activity across the entire world, rather than the mere transfer of musical centres (previously mainly limited to Europe and the USA).

Such countries, it is sometimes said, have made a late start and need to do some 'catching up'. Does this imply that their composers must undergo the same evolution as we have experienced, and conform to our norms? Or may we expect them to go their own way and defend other values? The latter would seem a good deal healthier. Music is not an international language, however often and unhesitatingly this is claimed. Any musical idiom is the result of a long cultural tradition. Where international conformity occurs at so many levels, it is for the artist to do justice to the variegated wealth of our multicultural society.

This struggle is undertaken with varying success by many non-Western composers. Most remain in the shadow, through lack of resources or unfavourable local conditions. Some have achieved a certain recognition: Yuasa, Takemitsu and Ichyanagi (Japan), Chou Wen Chung and Tan Dun (China), Isan Yun (Korea), Slamet Sjukur (Indonesia), Jose Maceda (the Philippines), Essayed (Morocco) and others. For most of them the Western model has been the decisive factor. It would be incorrect, however, to estimate their significance entirely in these terms.

The participation of so many non-Western composers has undoubtedly contributed to the most striking phenomenon of the 1970s: the massive return to tonal or modal, or at any rate diatonic, composition. The significance of this cannot always be estimated. Where an atonal period has not occurred one cannot speak of a return. On the other hand, one may have expected east European composers, after the collapse of the Iron Curtain, to plunge into the once forbidden atonal avant-garde style, but this reaction has not followed. Reversion to a diatonic style may of course result from a certain conservatism, or a submission to consumptive expectations. But this is not enough to account for the phenomenon. Despite the brilliant results of historical atonality, one wonders whether this was not a typically central European product, based too closely on the Western tempered tuning. Viewed within the present perspective, atonality would appear to be a finishing point rather than a starting point.

EXPANSION AND STABILISATION. Even where the influence of the atonal avant-garde style of the preceding period is still felt, one can no longer speak of radical innovation. The greater part of contemporary music production leans on the accomplishments of the fifties, including serial, statistical and aleatory techniques, spatial performance, electronic resources, new notation symbols and suchlike. In this sense our period is comparable to that of 1920-1945, when innovations from the beginning of the century were subject to expansion and stabilisation. The new post-1960 generations have not produced the type of 'forerunner' who attracts crowds of composers. The names of senior figures such as Boulez, Stockhausen, Cage, Ligeti and Berio therefore still dominate the official picture. Boulez exercises great influence on Cartesian France, Ligeti leaves his mark on north European composers, while the phenomenon of Cage is still evident in many mature and immature endeavours to achieve the 'liberation of sound'.

All this is not to say that no characteristic developments have occurred in the most recent period. I would mention the most important ones here:

New playing techniques – The passion for detail among serial composers of the fifties has instigated the further exploitation of new playing techniques. If each note in a serial score is the resultant of predetermined pitches, durations and dynamics, therefore differing from each preceding note, this requires the utmost concentration on the part of the performers. But the latter hardly wait passively! From the very beginning performing artists have set their mark on new music: the flautist Severino Gazzelloni, singer Cathy Berberian, pianist David Tudor, percussionist Christoph Caskel, trombonist Vinko Globokar and the Dutch bass clarinettist Harry Sparnaay. Through the stimulation provided by such players a large number of new scores have seen the light of day, scores that have become more and more demanding on the performer. Today these accomplishments would seem to have become common property: much new music presupposes as a matter of course notation methods and performance techniques that would have been inconceivable fifty years ago. Naturally, this influences the musical idiom which, generally speaking, tends towards greater sound differentiation.

The pursuit of more complex structures – The process of increasing differentiation is encouraged by another simultaneous development among a number of composers: the pursuit of more and more complex musical structures. In Europe in particular there is a true fascination with complicated and highly developed techniques, a tendency already evident in the early works of Stockhausen, Boulez and Xenakis. In the seventies and eighties it has led to the work of figures such as Brian Ferneyhough, who has reached and sometimes exceeded the boundaries of what is playable and perceptible.

Minimalism – In our period such extreme attitudes have brought sharper definition to contrary tendencies. Extreme complexity has its antithesis in minimalism, a predominantly American movement which become popular in the seventies in particular. A different but equally characteristic contrast is that between composers occupied with abstract categories of thought, formalisation processes, computer research and such, and colleagues at the other extreme who pursue a most simple type of music and aesthetic, from the American Philip Glass to recent works by the Polish composer Henryk Gorecki.

Electronic music – A characteristic of our time that may not be neglected is the further development of electronic music. As we know, the first elementary electronic studios were set up around 1950. A major step in technical terms was the introduction of voltage control in the mid-sixties. The advent of the computer shortly afterwards was a great occurrence, although the first results in the field of music were hardly spectacular. I recall a speaker at a symposium in California in 1977 who chalked a board full with numbers and tables, but in the end only produced one or two meagre sounds resembling a bassoon. Technology moves faster than music. In my opinion composers have dwelt too long on tone synthesis, the pursuit of new timbres. In the past ten or fifteen years in particular there seems to have been more interest in the potential contribution of the computer with regard to our structural concepts of music. This is a much more interesting field, but a great deal of time and energy is still required to master the associated technical problems.

Enrichment of acoustic instruments – Electronic resources are also employed to extend and enrich existing acoustic instruments. In early days, around 1960 I believe, contact microphones and suchlike were employed during live concerts to transform traditional instruments. This certainly produced interesting results, but only after about 1985 was methodical research undertaken in this field. An example is the activity of the Media Laboratory of the Massachusetts Institute of Technology in Boston, where some 200 researchers work on new communication machines. On the musical side the composer and cellist Tod Machover is involved there in what he calls *hyperinstruments*. Existing instruments are linked to microcomputers via newly developed interfaces. Every movement of the player, the speed and pressure of the bow, the angle between hand and bow etc., are tracked by sensors and reproduced in an enlarged or transformed mode. Here technology functions as a sort of magnifying glass to bring out the tiniest subtleties of human expression. How this will be reflected in composition of the future we cannot foresee, but it is quite clear that by then we will be miles removed from today's synthesizers and their prefabricated sounds.

It is understandable that such developments occur mainly in affluent countries. Considerable funding is required for this research: the Media Laboratory is sponsored by Apple and Yamaha among others.

The Dutch situation – Before I round off this panoramic overview a few words should be said about the situation in the Netherlands. In comparison with most other countries the picture is positive: we have a favourable climate for new music, a reasonably effective infrastructure, government support, institutions, ensembles etc. This has contributed to the prosperity of Dutch music, bringing to fruition the forebodes of the first half of the century. But we should entertain no illusions, for we remain a small country. Our cultural export is minimal, while as of old we have the perhaps somewhat provincial tendency to import all sorts of things from abroad. Naturally, this also has its advantages, and in Amsterdam one can hear more international music than in most other cosmopolitan cities. Judging from my experience in the past forty years, however, most imported new music is not superior, and is indeed sometimes inferior to that of the ten best composers whom our country boasts.

The whole span of Dutch music production fits well within the main contours of the European tradition: expressionism, constructivism, neo-classicism, neo-romanticism. One development, however, forms an exception and perhaps displays typically Dutch traits. It would be incorrect to give it a name in view of the diversity of composers involved: from Louis Andriessen, Guus Janssen, Paul Termos, Willem Breuker, Gilius van Bergeijk and Chiel Meyering to, more recently, Rob Zuidam. As everywhere, this development has not brought technical innovation to the musical language: composers continue to draw from the arsenal of resources available from 1950 and before. But common to all is a certain aversion to the conformism, abstraction and ponderousness of much contemporary music. Influences are therefore most divergent and include many American elements: jazz, pop and minimal music. The American forerunners were John Cage, Robert Ashley and La Monte Young, with emphasis on live performance, happenings, music theatre and suchlike. Correspondences, however, are psychological rather than stylistic. The general idea is to let some fresh air into a sometimes rather mouldy and academic modernism.

But from fresh air one can catch cold. A surplus of inventiveness and frivolous novelties may sometimes be at the expense of genuine engagement and visionary imagination.

To summarise, the music composed in the most recent period is characterised by broad geographical distribution, extension of innovations of the preceding period, and a rich range of trends. Concepts based on a single-track, straight-line evolution from central Europe belong once and for all to the past.

2. Interaction between different cultures

One of the most important aspects of the recent period is the interaction of different cultures on a planetary scale. This development too naturally has a long history, but in the sixties a decisive step was taken thanks to music technology. The availability of recordings made it possible for the first time to become acquainted on a large scale with the most divergent music cultures, thus opening up a domain hitherto only familiar to a handful of specialists. In the development of creative talent the very first musical impressions are of great significance. How differently may a composer develop if in his most impressionable years he experiences not only the shock of Beethoven or Berlioz, but also of Guillaume de Machaut, Indian classical music or Japanese biwa playing. Nevertheless, a breakthrough did not occur in this period, and the significance of this phenomenon, in Europe at least, was strongly underestimated. A dominating Eurocentric undercurrent was and remains active. While the entire world opened up, young composers continued even after 1960 to debate the pros and cons of atonality, Stravinsky and the like. And in the seventies mature composers such as Henze, Berio and Kagel still found it necessary to paraphrase Wagner, Mahler and Beethoven. And neo-romanticism, this typically late-European product, still rings on in the present work of the German composer Wolfgang Rihm.

There are other sounds as well, of course. Among the most talked-about composers of the older generation are Olivier Messiaen and Karl-Heinz Stockhausen. Though opinion differs on their work, one thing is certain, and that is that both have engaged in a confrontation with non-Western cultures that goes further than the customary musical tourism encountered in so much contemporary music.

Only from about 1980 has a further breakthrough occurred in the music of the youngest generations. This took place earlier in America and, to a greater degree, among composers from other parts of the world who became involved in the confrontation between local cultures and dominating Western influence.

The interaction of cultures in contemporary music is the central theme of an international workshop in which I have been closely involved from its beginnings in 1977. In the first years it was still necessary to point out the importance and inevitability of this process, but more recently this seems to have become a matter of course among participants. Their musical and cultural horizons have broadened, gaining more and more genuine significance in the process of composition. In the present context I can mention only a few of the questions that they have addressed:

- The identity problem: to which group, to which culture, to which tradition do I belong? (An urgent question, particularly for a number of non-Western composers.)
- Even if I have been essentially affected by a different music culture, how can I translate it with contemporary resources?
- Are the different idioms compatible?
- What are the technical implications?
- To what extent must I investigate the background of the other culture?

In short, one becomes interested in quite different problems to those of preceding generations. In its most radical form this is a change of mentality. The concept of tradition gains new content: it is not a licence for conservatism, nor is it based on nationalist or ethnocentric sentiments. The entire cultural heritage of humanity is unprecedentedly rich and diverse. The most vital question that can be posed is whether this offers fertile soil for future musical developments. If we wish to address this, we will need to take account of significant counterforces. Growing multicultural awareness contrasts strongly with the centralised bureaucracy and technocracy of modern states, the cultural hegemony of a number of larger lands and the associated suction of national chauvinism, and, finally, a world economy that encourages conformity – via music commerce – rather than a pluricultural society.

3. Female composers

Before discussing one last major aspect of our time I would draw attention to two phenomena which, while perhaps less conspicuous, are important enough to be mentioned.

In the first place, the most recent period has witnessed an increasing number of female composers. I have no statistics and can only speak from my own personal experience. When I began teaching composition in 1961 I had only male students. At the end of my career, in the mid-eighties, it was usual to have at least a few female candidates for my composition class. At the workshop mentioned above, held this year in Amsterdam, eight female composers participated alongside ten males, all young people from very different countries. But among older generations too women's names crop up frequently, including the Dutch Tera de Marez Oyens, the Russian Sofia Gubaidulina (also known in Holland), Jacqueline Fontijn (working in Belgium), the French Betsy Jolas and the American Pauline Oliveros. Younger female composers making their way into the music world include Doina Rotaru from Romania, the Finnish Kaya Saariaho and the Australian-Chinese Lisa Lim.

I would hesitate to comment on the background to this phenomenon. These are certainly not incidental cases as in days past, and if this tendency continues the question will arise of its influence on future composition and musical thought. Whatever the case may be, my own experience is that women are no less capable than men in matters of composition technique: creative talent, musical intelligence, grasp of form and technical command.

4. Music outgrows the concert hall

I would like to illustrate a second tendency, felt under the surface but not to be neglected, with the later work of Morton Feldman. His music does not last the customary ten or twenty minutes: the *Second String Quartet* (1983) lasts six hours, and *For Philip Guston* takes four-and-a-half hours. The composer apparently assumes a different way of listening, not compatible with the measured enjoyment of the classical concert programme. In other words: music outgrows the concert hall. How we are to deal with this situation is not clear, and although radio and recordings go some way to help, their scope is limited.

In 1965 I worked for a year on a composition which was doomed in advance to be barred from the concert hall: *Spatial Music I.* Its organisation is so complex, due to the fact that the orchestra is completely split up by separating all the players, that it can only be realised adequately in a radio studio with all appropriate technical help. Indeed, it took no less than a week to record it.

A little later, and with other socio-cultural motives, music groups went out onto the streets. And here we have different principles, a different audience, and other acoustic conditions. All this must be of influence on the musical result; it is no music for the concert hall.

From 1963 the Philippine composer Jose Maceda made intensive use of indigenous instruments and musical forms, intending his work for performance in the open air and for an audience 'living in a modern tropical world', to use his own words. This culminated in 1974 in a work entitled *Ugnayan* (Interaction), involving twenty radio stations and the predetermined participation of inhabitants of the city of Manila and six Philippine provinces.

Finally, we have the vast production of electronic music, which is indeed heard in concert halls, but only because it has no authentic medium of its own.

The above symptoms have little to do with the demand for multifunctional concert halls, for we are not concerned here with alternative auditoriums but with 'music beyond the concert hall'. In the most recent period no feasible alternative has been found, and a solution would probably require profound changes in social structures and the function of music within them. Most composers therefore continue to produce pieces of ten, twenty or thirty minutes which fit nicely into traditional concert programmes.

5. Musical life under pressure

And so we come to the final but dominant characteristic of our period: the great economic and commercial pressure on the music world. As a rule, a healthy interaction may exist between musical life and material prosperity. The problem begins, however, when the activities and final products of that musical life are excessively determined by economic and commercial criteria. Today this phenomenon is felt almost everywhere, though of course it is most evident in the world of light music.

Mass production – Let us begin by observing that at the beginning of the twentieth century jazz was still undergoing an organic and natural development, before being discovered by the commercial world. The evolution of pop music, on the other hand, was closely bound up from the very beginning with the international music industry that arose at the same time. In our period pop music and all related genres have therefore acquired a gigantic share in the supply of music. A genuine mass production has emerged, conditioning the way many millions of people throughout the world listen. It is a sign of hope that artistically acceptable sounds are still heard from time to time, but most of it is polished in overcrowded recording studios to become a pure consumption product.

Economic interests are of the utmost importance here, as is illustrated by the fact that last year the gramophone industry (now mainly CDs and cassettes) had a turnover of thirty million dollars... Thirty years ago, in the days of The Beatles, music management was not yet entirely geared to this large scale, but today the production machine is a well-oiled affair. Five multinationals have a monopoly in this business: BMG, PolyGram, Warner, EMI and Sony. In recent years sales have also been undertaken by the larger supermarkets, where everything is viewed in terms of quick success and fast consumption.

Musical pollution – Background music forms an important by-product of the music industry. I consider this to be one of the most disastrous developments in the latest period. The never ceasing and hardly avoidable musical idiocy to which we are exposed today can only have a stupefying and blunting effect on the human mind. Music is nourishment for the human organism. Even before birth many millions of babies are already conditioned from day to day by the musical poverty that is poured out non-stop by a comparable number of loudspeakers. Here we find the musical counterpart of the increasing pollution seen in other areas of life.

Bureaucracy – In the world of classical music all this is more subtle, and the unsuspecting music addict may not notice it much. But here again we are confronted by signs of inflation, overproduction, classical 'top hits', a play-it-safe supply of music, the cultivation of top stars, and somewhat overheated publicity promoting 'world-famous' soloists and ensembles.

An additional problem is the top-heavy organisation structure of our music world. The complexity of modern society is reflected in a rather complicated network of persons and institutions without which the music world could no longer function. We have come a long way from the first, usually local and elementary organisation forms established by early nineteenth-century dignitaries to supply the bourgeoisie with orchestral concerts. Today matters revolve around managers, commercial directors, advisory committees, sponsors, trade unions, public bodies, impresarios etc. In this dense network we may still bump into the occasional music enthusiast who puts his time and energy into a good cause. But the present economic and organisational problems require – rightly – the participation of specialists in various fields – organisational, financial, legal etc., – resulting in a conflict of interests that does not always further an artistic vision.

It is clear that the role of this buffer group as an unavoidable link between musician and audience weighs heavily. For the management of the music world, new music is a particularly troublesome, economically uninteresting and marginal phenomenon. In many cases the widespread thirst for premieres witnessed today goes to conceal a lack of artistic conviction among programme makers. Just as one current event drives away the other in the news media, one premiere follows the other in the music world. A genuine and enduring interaction between composer and audience is no longer possible.

Consequences – In their urge to communicate, creative talents react to this situation, whether consciously or unconsciously. They have come to resemble speakers talking louder and louder in a noisy auditorium. If the success of a work depends on a single performance, there is a logical tendency to be spectacular and 'original', or to dramatise the musical discourse in an exaggerated manner. Much of today's so-called neo-expressionism has only its rhetoric in common with the authentic expressionism of the early twentieth century. Other composers seek refuge in political engagement, in compromise, or simply in the abandonment of their craft.

All this impedes genuine innovation. The majority of the composers known to me all over the world have little or no scope to develop, and therefore miss the necessary feedback from an audience. The naive belief that real talent will be discovered later may have been true in bygone days, but the mechanisms that control modern musical life rule this out almost completely.

Epilogue

The most important developments observed in the latest period are of an extramusical nature: the enormous geographical distribution of creative activity, the growing awareness of the fact that we live in a multicultural world with the associated signs of acculturation, and, finally, the strongly increased international economic and commercial pressure on musical life. All this gives rise to opposing forces which are difficult to control.

The modern composer can do little about all this. But it is precisely his marginal role as a creative artist in contemporary society that should enable him to consider matters from a distance and become aware of that which is essential. This could induce the perception that genuine innovation in music can no longer be based primarily on aesthetic and/or technical principles, but must be of a spiritual nature, in the broad sense of the word, as the only possible counterpart to our materialistically orientated society.

From: *Muziek in de 20e eeuw*, ed. J. Nuchelmans, 1995

Notes

INTRODUCTION

1   This does not mean that genuine artistic possibilities are lacking in this democratised pub-
    lic. On the contrary. They are constantly underestimated, however, by most programme
    compilers.

2   Igor Stravinsky, *Leben und Werk*, Mainz/Zürich 1957.

CHAPTER 1

1   For the works mentioned in this chapter see the lists on page 25, 26, 30 and 32-33.

2   The choice of works included has been made primarily on the grounds of historic, stylis-
    tic or technical significance. Although this often goes hand in hand with outstanding artis-
    tic value, this is not always the case.

3   The development of music in eastern Europe has not been considered, since the writer has
    insufficient material at his disposal.

4   Technical details concerning many of the works mentioned are discussed in the following
    chapters.

CHAPTER 2

1   Although the above observations sometimes deviate, as does the terminology, the essentials
    are based on the lucid distinction between time categories made by J. Daniskas in his
    Grondslagen ener analytische vormleer, Rotterdam 1948.

2   Apparently, Albert Verwey considerably moderated this statement at a later stage.

3   A. Honegger, *Je suis compositeur*, Paris 1951.

4   C. Sachs, *Rhythm and Tempo*, New York 1953.

CHAPTER 3

1   The *Sekundgang* was defined by Hindemith as the line that arises through the progression
    in 2nds of the main highest and/or lowest points in a melody. In our example the notes
    C ♯ (final note of bar 3) -B-A-G-F ♯ -E ♯ form a *Sekundgang* of lowest points.

2   In this modality one can really no longer distinguish between harmony and melody; both
    are determined by a common point of departure. In this respect we approach a similar
    principle in atonality (chapter 7, section 1).

CHAPTER 4

1   Debussy employed this regularly. See also Examples 21 (2nd and 3rd staves) and 54 (2nd
    stave).

2   The numbers indicate intervals, counted in minor 2nds.

3   P. Hindemith, *Unterweisung im Tonsatz*, Mainz 1937.

4   It is remarkable that the pure interval relationship too, between the minor and major 3rd,
    is smaller than our equal temperament would lead one to assume. For the tempered minor
    3rd is *smaller* than the pure minor 3rd, while the tempered major 3rd is *larger* than the pure

major 3rd. Equal temperament therefore 'exaggerates', as it were, the difference between minor and major.

CHAPTER 5

1   Igor Stravinsky, *Leben und Werk*, Mainz/Zürich 1957.
2   A. Schönberg, *Harmonielehre*, Vienna 1911.

CHAPTER 6

1   E. Grassi, *Kunst und Mythos*, Hamburg 1957.
2   R. Vlad, *Stravinsky*, London 1960.
3   The 3rd and 7th degrees of the scale may be both major and minor. Harmonically, this instability is experienced as 'colouring' of the 3rd and 7th. The origin, however, is melodic and may originate from the preference of many African Negroes for structures based on 3rds, adapted to the two main notes of the Western scale:
    Example 73

4   J.E. Berendt, 'Jazz und neue Musik', in *Prisma der gegenwärtigen Musik*, Hamburg 1959.
5   J. Kunst, 'The music of Java', in *Mededelingen Koninklijke Vereniging 'Koloniaal Instituut'*, Amsterdam 1937.
6   Debussy, *Monsieur Croche, antidilettante*, Paris 1921.
7   *Melos*, February 1962, Mainz.

CHAPTER 7

1   A. Schönberg, *Harmonielehre*, Vienna 1911.
2   Unfortunate terms such as 'athematicism' and 'atonality' have become too current to be avoided.
3   E. Stein, *Orpheus in New Guises*, London 1953.
4   This field does not necessarily comprise all twelve notes, but fills chromatically to the boundaries of a given ambitus.
5   All biographical notes on Webern are taken from: W. Kolneder, *Anton Webern*, Rodenkirchen 1961.
6   Characteristic is a statement by this anti-romantic composer concerning *Pierrot lunaire*: though he had no doubt as to its being a masterpiece, its aesthetic was entirely foreign to him.
7   In so far as this chapter is concerned with important contrasts within the Viennese School, a comparison of Schönberg and Webern is sufficient. Naturally, this implies no artistic judgement whatsoever with regard to the scarcely mentioned Alban Berg.
8   A. Webern, *Der Weg zur neuen Musik*, Vienna 1960.
9   H. Eimert, *Lehrbuch der Zwölftontechniek*, Wiesbaden 1952.
10 The numbers indicate the employed transposition, counted upwards from the first note of P1 (in this case B♭).
11 These four forms can be reduced to two basic ones: the pitches of P1 and R3 are identical, as are those of I10 and IR8.
12 Here we therefore differ from R. Leibowitz (*Introduction à la musique de douze sons*, Paris 1949), from whom the analysis of the series structure is taken. His considerations are decidedly brilliant and instructive, but unfortunately somewhat formalistic. Moreover, the rhythmic structure of the theme apparently escaped him.

13 The cells (a) and (c) contrast in vertical pitch structure with the generally milder (b). See also Examples 89 and 90.

14 Or rather, it is partially symmetrical: where the first half has rests, the second has chords.

15 A. Webern, *Der Weg zur neuen Musik*, Vienna 1960.

CHAPTER 8

1 *Die Reihe* 4, Vienna 1958.

2 *Die Reihe* 3, Vienna 1957.

3 Stockhausen's reasoning is in fact a curious example of obsolete quantitative thought that takes no account of modern phenomenological insight. His reasoning is correct as long as one assumes one-sided numerical relationships: both pitch- and duration-octaves can thus be expressed by the proportion 1:2. But in our *perception* there are essential differences between micro- and macrorelationships. The phenomenon of *octave identity* occurs in pitch but not in duration. In pitch intervals, on the other hand, we do not hear frequency proportions but rather linear additions. This is expressed in the traditional interval names of 2nd, 3rd, 4th, etc., while in atonal music too we hear the major 2nd as the sum of two minor ones, the minor 3rd as three, etc. In view of our perception, the first reaction of Messiaen and others was therefore understandable: the aural counting-up of pitch intervals was turned into a counting-up of duration intervals. But here again a profound difference of perception remains: we hear the difference between 10 and 11 minor 2nds (minor and major 7th) just as clearly as that between 1 and 2 (minor and major 2nd), while in note duration a completely different experience apparently occurred.

4 A recent orchestral work by Ligeti, *Atmosphères*, makes exclusive use of chromatically filled sound areas, thus definitively encroaching upon the individuality of the interval. Musical structure is now determined by measured units of other parameters such as density, timbre, register, dynamics. Here, where the role of pitch and interval is reduced to a minimum, one realises how fundamentally differently the musical ear reacts to other elements. The elements of music are not equivalent; each has its own level of action and requires its own structuring.

5 In quite a different and more abstract manner, something similar already occurred in Webern's *op. 27* (middle section of the first movement). Here the two hands also play a role in the mirror structure characteristic of the composition.

6 According to P. Boulez in an article in *Darmstädter Beiträge*, Mainz 1960.

7 See the article by C. Wolff in *Die Reihe* 7, Vienna 1960.

8 In Japan, too, Zen Buddhism has influenced art, including the celebrated Haiku literature. Despite all spiritual radicalism, however, form coherence remains a conspicuous phenomenon.

9 From a lecture by John Cage at the World Exhibition in Brussels in 1958.

10 'Struktur und Erlebniszeit' in *Die Reihe* 2, Vienna 1955.

11 Article by P. Boulez in *Darmstädter Beiträge*, Mainz 1960.

12 J. Cage, *Silence*, Middletown 1961; *A Year from Monday*, London 1968.

13 Several of these laws are known to us from physics (Gauss, Poisson, Maxwell-Boltzmann).

14 An analysis would naturally exceed the bounds of this book: just one minute from *Pithoprakta* would occupy many pages. It is perhaps of importance, however, to say that a thorough knowledge of Xenakis's methods is not required to undertake this. Although I differ with the composer here, I remain convinced that analysis of the score provides more insight into the music than knowledge of the production method. Those interested in the composition procedure as such should refer to the composer's writings, collected in two volumes: *Musiques formelles*, Paris 1963 and *Musique. Architecture*, Paris 1971.

15 Three tendencies can therefore be provisionally distinguished:
   a. *Result notation*, representing that which actually sounds. Beside traditional quantitative notation this includes the scores of Stockhausen and Boulez, in which field magnitudes are represented in one way or another.
   b. *Action notation*, primarily indicating what action has to be taken to obtain a certain result; the latter may be fixated to a greater or lesser degree.
   c. *Reaction notation*, concerned neither with the result nor the action, but with a synaesthetic reaction to an autonomous graphic image.
16 Forward-looking Hindu musicians have attempted to resist the introduction of classical Western notation as much as possible. They understand that its unmistakable advantages are outweighed by its paralysing effect on that which is fundamental to their own music: guided improvisation.

List of Examples

1. Stravinsky, *The Rite of Spring*
2. Hindemith, *Third Piano Sonata*
3. Pijper, *Piano Sonata*
4. Bartók, *Fifth String Quartet*
5. Jolivet, *Trois Temps*
6. Hauer, *Hölderlingesänge*
7. Debussy, *Voiles*
8 & 9. Bartók, *Music for Strings, Percussion and Celesta*
10 & 11. Stravinsky, *The Rite of Spring*
12. Milhaud, *La Création du Monde*
13. Stravinsky, *The Soldier's Tale*
14. Pijper, *Sonata for two Pianos*
15. Messiaen, *L'Ange aux Parfums*
16. Messiaen, *Livre d'Orgue*
17. Messiaen, *Cantéyodjayâ*
18. Blacher, *Second Piano Concerto*
19. Webern, *Concerto op. 24*
20. Boulez, *Second Piano Sonata*
21 & 22. Debussy, *La Mer*
23. Beethoven, *Piano Sonata op. 10 no. 1*
24. Debussy, *La Mer*
25. Stravinsky, *The Rite of Spring*
26. Stravinsky, *Violin Concerto*
27. Schönberg, *Pierrot lunaire*
28. Bartók, *Music for Strings, Percussion and Celesta*
29. Bartók, *Sixth String Quartet*
30. Hindemith, *Mathis der Maler*
31 & 32. Messiaen, *Les Corps glorieux*
33 & 34. Pijper, *Sonatina II* for Piano
35-37. Boulez, *Le Marteau sans Maître*
38. Debussy, *Le Jet d'Eau*
39. Debussy, *La Cathédrale engloutie*
40 & 41. Messiaen's *modes à transpositions limitées*
42. Bartók, *Third String Quartet*
43. Bartók, *Bagatelle 2*

44. Bartók, *Bagatelle 3*
45. Schönberg, *Six Little Piano Pieces op. 19*
46. Stravinsky, *The Rite of Spring*
47. Schönberg, *Five Piano Pieces op. 23*
48. Milhaud, *Saudades do Brazil*
49. Beethoven, *Third Symphony*
50. Stravinsky, *Mass*
51. Stravinsky, *Four Russian Peasant Songs*
52. Bartók, *Second String Quartet*
53. Hindemith, *Mathis der Maler*
54. Bartók, *Music for Strings, Percussion and Celesta*
55. Chord of the minor 7th in different versions
56 & 57. Gustav Mahler, *Das Lied von der Erde*
58 & 59. Webern, *Six Pieces op. 6* for orchestra
60-62. Schönberg, *Five Orchestral Pieces op. 16*
63. Stravinsky, *The Rite of Spring*
64. Bartók, *Fourth String Quartet*
65 & 66. Varèse, *Octandre*
67 & 68. Boulez, *Improvisations sur Mallarmé*
69. Stravinsky, *The Rite of Spring*
70. Primitive forms of melody
71. Stravinsky, *The Rite of Spring*
72. Bartók, *Mikrokosmos*
73. Melodic motifs from American Negro music
74. Javanese slendro scale and whole-tone scale
75. Basic forms of the BACH motif
76. Bartók, *Fifth String Quartet*
77. Schönberg, *Three Piano Pieces op. 11*
78-82. Webern, *Five Pieces for String Quartet op. 5*
83 & 84. Schönberg, *Five Piano Pieces op. 23*
85. Major and chromatic scales
86. Basic forms of 12-note series
87 & 88. Schönberg, *Variations for Orchestra op. 31*
89 & 90. Schönberg, *Piano Piece op. 33a*
91 & 92. Webern, *Piano Variations op. 27*
93 & 94. Webern, *Variations for orchestra, op. 30*
95 & 96. Messiaen, *Mode de Valeurs et d'Intensités*
97. Boulez, *Second Piano Sonata*
98-100. Boulez, *Structures*
101. Subharmonic sequence according to Stockhausen
102 & 103. Harmonic subdivision of a basic duration according to Stockhausen
104-107. Stockhausen, *Gruppen* for three orchestras

List of Abbreviations

Abbreviations used in the examples, in so far as they refer to instrumentation

arp	arpa, harp
C	coro, choir
camp	campane, bells
cb	contrabbasso, double bass
cel	celesta
cfg	contrafagotto, double bassoon
cl	clarinetto, clarinet .
cl-b	clarinetto di basso, bass clarinet
cor	corno, horn
cor-i	corno inglese, English horn
crd	(a) corda, bowed
csa-chi	cassa chiara, small drum
fg	fagotto, bassoon
fi	(a) fiato, wind-
fi-lgn	(strumenti a) fiato di legno, woodwind instruments
fi-ote	(strumenti a) fiato d'ottone, brass instruments
fl	flauto, flute
fl-a	flauto alto, alto flute
fl-ott	flauto ottavino, piccolo
gr-csa	gran cassa, bass drum
man	manuale, manual
mar	maracas
ob	oboe
ped	pedale, pedal
perc	percussione, percussion
pf	pianoforte, piano
pti	piatti, cymbals
sas	sassofono, saxophone
str	strumento, instrument
tb	tuba
timp	timpani
tmb	tamburo, tambourine
tr	tromba, trumpet

trb	trombone
vibr	vibrafono, vibraphone
vl	violino, violin
vla	viola
vlc	violoncello
Voc	voce, voice
Voc-T	voce di tenore, tenor

Acknowledgements

The following publishers kindly permitted me to reproduce examples from
their editions:

- Boosey & Hawkes, London (Bartók, *Sixth String Quartet*; Stravinsky, *The Rite*, *Mass*)
- Bote & Bock, Berlin (Blacher)
- J. & W. Chester, London (Stravinsky, *The Soldier's Tale*)
- Franco Colombo, Inc., New York (Varèse)
- Stichting Donemus, Amsterdam (Pijper, *Sonata for two Pianos*)
- Durand & Cie, Paris (Debussy; Messiaen, *Livre d'Orgue*, *Mode de Valeurs et d'Intensités*)
- Max Eschig, Paris (Milhaud)
- Wilhelm Hansen Musik-Forlag, Copenhagen (Schönberg, *Five Piano Pieces op. 23*)
- Heugel & Cie, Paris (Boulez, *Second Piano Sonata*)
- Alphonse Leduc, Paris (Messiaen, *Les Corps glorieux*, *L'Ange aux Parfums*)
- Oxford University Press, London (Pijper, *Piano Sonata, Sonatina II* for Piano)
- Edition Peters, Leipzig (Schönberg, *Five Orchestra Pieces op. 16*)
- B. Schott's Söhne, Mainz (Hindemith; Stravinsky, *Violin Concerto*)
- Universal Edition A.G., Vienna (Bartók, *Second*, *Third*, *Fourth* and *Fifth String Quartets*, *Music for Strings, Percussion and Celesta*; Boulez, *Improvisations sur Mallarmé*, *Le Marteau sans Maître*, *Structures*;
- Haubenstock-Ramati; Hauer; Mahler; Messiaen, *Cantéyodjayâ*; Schönberg, *Piano Pieces op. 11* and *op. 19*, *Pierrot lunaire*, *Variations for Orchestra op. 31*, *Piano Piece op. 33a*; Stockhausen; Webern).

About the Author

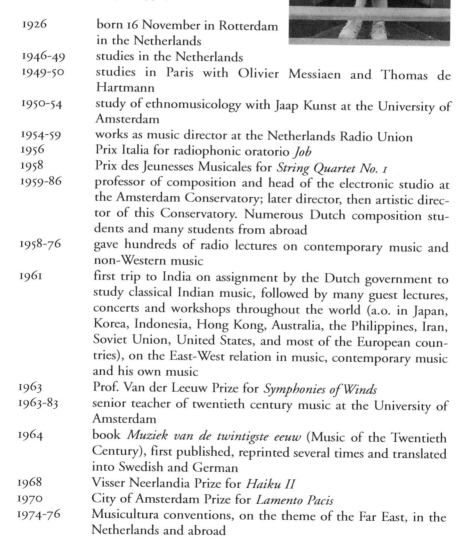

Ton de Leeuw (1926-1996)

1926	born 16 November in Rotterdam in the Netherlands
1946-49	studies in the Netherlands
1949-50	studies in Paris with Olivier Messiaen and Thomas de Hartmann
1950-54	study of ethnomusicology with Jaap Kunst at the University of Amsterdam
1954-59	works as music director at the Netherlands Radio Union
1956	Prix Italia for radiophonic oratorio *Job*
1958	Prix des Jeunesses Musicales for *String Quartet No. 1*
1959-86	professor of composition and head of the electronic studio at the Amsterdam Conservatory; later director, then artistic director of this Conservatory. Numerous Dutch composition students and many students from abroad
1958-76	gave hundreds of radio lectures on contemporary music and non-Western music
1961	first trip to India on assignment by the Dutch government to study classical Indian music, followed by many guest lectures, concerts and workshops throughout the world (a.o. in Japan, Korea, Indonesia, Hong Kong, Australia, the Philippines, Iran, Soviet Union, United States, and most of the European countries), on the East-West relation in music, contemporary music and his own music
1963	Prof. Van der Leeuw Prize for *Symphonies of Winds*
1963-83	senior teacher of twentieth century music at the University of Amsterdam
1964	book *Muziek van de twintigste eeuw* (Music of the Twentieth Century), first published, reprinted several times and translated into Swedish and German
1968	Visser Neerlandia Prize for *Haiku II*
1970	City of Amsterdam Prize for *Lamento Pacis*
1974-76	Musicultura conventions, on the theme of the Far East, in the Netherlands and abroad

1976-95	leading the annual International Composers' Workshop with Dimiter Christoff, alternately in the Netherlands and in Bulgaria
1981	guest professor at the University of California, Berkeley (Ernest Bloch's chair)
1982	Matthijs Vermeulen Prize for *Car nos vignes sont en fleur*
1983	Johan Wagenaar Prize for his entire oeuvre
1986-96	living in France as independent composer
1993	Edison Prize for Chamber Music CD (*Les adieux, Hommage à Henri, Trio*)
1996	dies 31 May in his city of residence Paris
1997	Matthijs Vermeulen Prize (posthumously) for *3 Shakespeare Songs*
2001	Edison Prize (posthumously) for CD 'Choral Works' (*Prière, A cette heure du jour, Cloudy Forms, Car nos vignes sont en fleur, Transparence*)

Index

Printed in Great Britain
by Amazon